This descriptive tale of the triumph of good over evil, by a talented, emotionally distant, young writer, is delightful. I await his next book.

Christine Overn, Academic Administrator

"Terry Fortuné is a writer with autism who hones his craft on a daily basis. I have seen him struggle with expressing his thoughts on paper only to triumph due to sheer determination to share his love of dragons. He has accomplished what few people have: a coming of age book where dragons and humans collide, and Shirai, the hero, becomes a survivor despite his limitations."

Diana M. Martin, MFA, Adjunct Professor,
Montgomery College, Rockville, MD

DRAGON DEFENDER

TERRY FORTUNÉ

iUniverse, Inc.
Bloomington

Dragon Defender

iUniverse books may be ordered through booksellers or by contacting:

iUniverse
1663 Liberty Drive
Bloomington, IN 47403
www.iuniverse.com
1-800-Authors (1-800-288-4677)

ISBN: 978-1-4502-8563-6 (sc)
ISBN: 978-1-4502-8564-3 (ebook)

Library of Congress Control Number: 2011900018

Printed in the United States of America

iUniverse rev. date: 3/18/2011

Dedicated to my grandparents who I hope will find happiness wherever they are.

Acknowledgements

I would like to acknowledge the following people for helping me get this book out into the world.

My father for putting up with my demands and being there for me, and my brother for tolerating and living with my idiosyncrasies.

My friend, Morgan Cherney, for the character illustrations he created.

For reading, rereading, editing, providing helpful suggestions, patience, and encouragement, I thank Chris and Diana.

I also thank my Great Aunt Fawzia, without whose support this book would likely not have seen the light of day.

For being my staunchest supporter, I especially want to thank my Mother, for her steadfast belief in me. Thanks Mom!

And most importantly, to the Dragons whose kinship helped inspire me with these wonderful fantasies, I say Thank you.

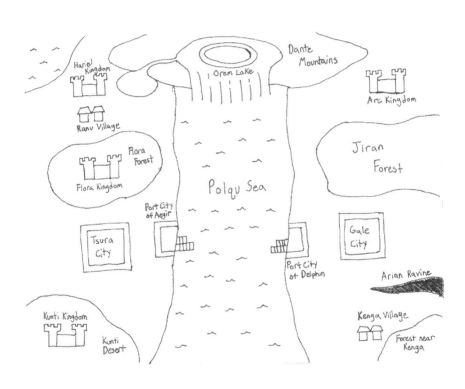

Contents

1 - Dawn of Realization

Pain.

That was the first thing I felt after I woke up. I had no clue why I was in such pain nor had any recollection of falling asleep in the first place. As I tried to get up from where I lay, my entire body cried out in agony over the sensation of being jabbed all over by hot blades. Unable to handle such pain, I stopped midway and just sat on what I felt to be the wooden floor of a home.

The reason I say "felt like" was that I had become aware that something was wrong with my sight. I could see, to a degree, walls and sunlight coming from a possible window, but they all appeared to be blurred. I couldn't even see my hands—which I held in front of my face—clearly.

When one of my hands brushed the sides of my head, I found the reason for my blurred vision: my eyes were covered by several layers of bandages. I was about to take them off when the sound of a door being opened interrupted me.

"Oh! So you're awake at last, I see," a dignified yet wise-sounding old man's voice spoke out.

A figure stood in the center of a doorway, but I couldn't see what he looked like. As he started to walk toward me, I heard a thumping kind of noise along with his footsteps.

The man stopped a foot away from me and said, "Please don't move so much. You are still recovering, so leave those bandages alone."

"Where am I? What happened to me?" Even speaking was too much for me, so I only spoke sporadically in a low tone.

"Where you are now is the small village of Kenga. It's just a few days' journey from the City of Gale. As for what happened, I was hoping you could tell me," said the man.

"What… do you mean?" I replied.

"Someone found you just outside the village, unconscious and severely wounded." As the mystery behind the source of my pain was solved, the man continued, "They brought you to my home, where I managed to patch you up quickly before you lost any more blood. What happened?"

I tried to remember the last thing I did, but I couldn't remember anything.

I had no memory of what I did the last few hours, the day before that, or even the week before that. I couldn't even remember if I knew of any of the places the man spoke of.

My mind was completely blank.

"I… I can't remember." I could hear my voice tremble while I spoke. "I can't remember anything."

"It's okay. Just tell me what you can remember," said the man.

Trying hard to think through the constant feeling of pain, I was finally able to remember something. "My name… My name is Shirai."

"Shirai, huh? I'm Elder Giram."

Upon learning the man's name, I wanted to thank him for helping me. However, while in the process of moving slightly forward, I noticed something.

My whole body felt weird. I knew I had one, yet I knew it wasn't mine.

"My body… something's wrong… it doesn't feel right."

"Is that so?" I could detect a hint of confusion in Giram's voice.

"Why are my eyes covered?" I placed both hands on the bandages. "Did something happen to them?"

Giram didn't say anything at first. Assuming that he was thinking, I waited. It was so quiet that I could hear him breathing. Finally, he replied, "Before I answer that, I must know something. This may sound weird, but do you remember what you looked like?"

I thought that was a weird question, but he sounded serious when he asked me, so I told him, "I know that I'm just an ordinary young man. What does that have to do with anything?"

Again, there was silence. Only this time it didn't last as long as before.

"I knew it was a good idea to do what I did," said Giram, who sounded relieved for some reason. "Listen, Shirai. At first I thought I should cover your eyes up because they were probably damaged, but now I think it is best if you never take those bandages off."

A lump instantly formed in my throat.

"*What* are you talking about?"

I felt Giram's hand being placed gently on my shoulder. "If you could see what you look like now, I think it would do more harm than good."

A rush of fear and anxiety quickly overcame me.

"Do you have anything that can reflect my image? Anything?"

"There is a small lake not five feet away from my home, but—"

Not letting Giram finish, I sprang up and felt my way to the door, ignoring the man's calls and the pain that overwhelmed my body. I found walking to be difficult, but I finally found my way to the door and went outside.

Through the bandages, I could see the bright sunlight, but everything else was still blurred. I lowered myself to the ground and began to feel for water. The second I felt wetness on my hand, I ripped off the bandages and looked down at the lake's surface. What I saw made me scream in shock and horror.

While Giram was right about me being severely wounded, that was not what made me cry out like that.

Instead of the face of a man looking back at me, it was the face of a *dragon*! In fact, in all outward appearances, I was a dragon. Yet at the same time, I looked human.

My red face, now a long, smooth snout, extended in front of golden reptilian eyes. A scar I never had before ran over the top and bottom part of my left eye. Copper-colored plates lined the top of my forehead and snout while tiny fangs lined the inside of my mouth.

I ran my fingers, still human in appearance except for the new talons I had, over the seven-inch-long horns that jutted out the back of my head. Still attached to one of my newly longer and pointed ears was my golden hoop earring. I felt the strands of my now longer, dark blond hair as it ran down my slightly elongated neck.

The sight of that thing staring back at me was so shocking that the last thing I remembered before I blacked out was screaming to the heavens, "*What happened to me?*"

When I awoke again, I found myself leaning against a wall inside a small house. The walls were made of large logs placed on top of each other, and the ceiling was made of wooden planks. A single bed sat in one corner, under a small window. Across from there was another window, only larger and wide open. There was a small fireplace with a pot over a roaring fire. In the center of the house was a wooden table with two chairs.

Since there was still sunlight streaming through the window, I realized that only a few hours had passed since I had fainted. Looking down, I found I was covered with a blanket. The first thing I thought was that what happened earlier was nothing but a dream.

When I took off the blanket, I looked down, and to my horror, my whole body, except for the front of my neck and my chest, was covered in small red scales. The scales were so tightly packed that it gave the appearance of human-like skin. The front of my neck and my chest were covered with tan-colored plates.

As I turned my head, I noticed that, a couple of inches from where my neck ended, a pair of vibrant red, thin, leathery wings had sprouted from out of my back. My whole upper body was now much more muscular than before, especially my arms.

Sticking out from behind a simple white cloth wrapped around my waist was a slender tail, long enough to wrap around my legs. My legs had become the hind legs of a dragon, and on my feet were three large toes each. They had thicker talons than my fingers.

Seeing my new body made me want to scream again.

"I see you're finally back with us."

The kind voice that suddenly spoke belonged to a young woman who stood at the front door. She was in her early twenties just like me; I was instantly struck by how beautiful she looked. With crystal blue eyes and shoulder-length, golden blond hair, she wore a simple light green dress with yellow edges. It reached down to her knees to reveal a

What happened to me?

pair of low, leather boots. She held a small bowl filled with water with a small cloth hanging over its edge.

"Where… am I…?" I barely stuttered. That was all I could say. This time I didn't just feel the same pain I felt before, but now for some reason, I felt lightheaded.

"Please don't try to speak. I was about to tell you anyway. I'm Tansu, and you are in my house. Giram brought you here after you fainted near the lake." Putting the bowl on the table, she smiled as she looked at me.

"So I hear your name is Shirai?"

Looking away, I said, "Yes."

Tansu looked me over slowly from where she was. "Elder Giram told me what happened to you. Even though you say you are a human, I never expected you to look like this."

When she said that, I instantly felt disgusted, because I remembered what I saw at the lake. I covered my face with my hands just so she didn't have to see it.

"Please… Please don't look at me." I was close to tears by this point.

Tansu slowly came over and gently removed my hands from my face. I was surprised to see that she was still smiling. I could also now clearly see the pink headband that held back her bangs.

"I don't think worrying what you look like now is what you should be doing. Right now, I need you to get well. Now get up from the floor."

I didn't want to move from where I was, but the look in her eyes told me I had no choice, so I tried to get up. However, I wasn't accustomed to walking on my new legs, and I almost fell over. Luckily, Tansu managed to catch me before my face met the floor. She helped drag me to the bed where she made me lie down. This was hard to do when one has horns, wings, and a tail that get in the way. I was forced to lie on my side with my head near the end of the pillow so my horns would hang over the edge of the bed.

"Now I want you to stay in that bed until I say you can get out." Tansu made it sound like an order. "Not only do your wounds need time to heal, but you now have a fever—probably from the shock you gave yourself. You need to sleep and let your body and mind get some rest."

She walked back to where I left the blanket that was on me earlier and draped it over my body. After making sure I was comfortable, Tansu walked over to the table. Picking up the cloth that was on the bowl's side, she dipped it in. After wringing out the extra water, she brought the wet cloth over and placed it on my forehead. Considering the fever I must have had, the wet cloth made my head feel refreshingly cooler.

She pulled up one of the chairs near the table and sat down, looking at me.

"You must have been through a lot," she said while smiling compassionately. "I'm sorry about your memory being lost."

"You…" my voice was almost a whisper.

"What is it, Shirai?"

"You're not afraid of what I am?"

She looked at me with a sympathetic look on her face. "The way I see it, you can tell what kind of person someone is just by looking into their eyes. And your eyes are telling me you are kind and gentle, yet with more courage than anyone I've ever met. They're also telling me that right now you are scared of what you are and afraid of being an outcast because of it. At times like this, you need the company of a good person to help see you through it."

Somehow I could tell that she was genuinely worried about me. I wanted to ask her some more questions, but before I could, she said in the same commanding tone, "Now, enough talk. Get some sleep. I don't want you to get any sicker than you are now. I'm heading out to run a few errands. I'll make sure to wake you when dinner is ready."

With that, she walked outside and gently closed the door behind her. Sleep was the furthest thing from my mind, but for some reason I felt tired and immediately dozed off.

I was roused by a wonderful smell. Glancing out of the window, I saw the sun was just starting to set, setting the sky ablaze with reds and oranges. My attention then focused back on the smell, which was coming from where Tansu was. She was busy cooking a bunch of fish over the fire. On the table I could see there was bread, a small bowl of fruit, and two cups. I slowly pulled myself up, surprised to find that my body wasn't hurting as much as before. I just sat there, watching her for a moment.

"That smells great," I finally said.

She turned her head around and saw me sitting on the bed. "I see my cooking can still wake anybody, no matter how hard they sleep. Are you strong enough to get yourself to the table?"

I nodded as I slowly got up, taking my time to walk over to the table. I looked at the small chair and knew I couldn't just sit down because of my wings and tail. Maneuvering the chair around, I sat as Tansu came over, carrying the fish she cooked on a plate, and joined me.

After cutting one of the fish, she gave it to me. "Well, go on and eat. There is plenty to go around."

At first, I just stared at it. Even though I was hungry, I didn't feel like eating any protein at the time. So I took an apple and quietly bit into it. As I chewed, I could feel the tiny fangs in my mouth chopping on the piece of apple quickly.

"It's good. Very good fruit," I muttered softly.

"I'm glad you think so. I grew the fruits myself. In fact, everyone in the village eats the fruits and vegetables I grow here."

I continued to eat the apple as I watched Tansu eat her food. Despite my new appearance, she had been nothing but kind to me and had not once shown any fear.

I finally got enough courage to ask, "Tansu, why are you being so kind to me? I'm a total stranger who wandered into this village. I doubt anyone would have taken me in with my... condition."

She stopped eating and gazed at me with a gentle expression. "Truth be told, when I first saw you, I *was* a little frightened. However, when Giram told me you had no memory of your past, I realized that you must have been the one most afraid. You shouldn't have to suffer alone."

She then smiled a little as she added, "Besides, I needed the company. It gets lonely here. Now please eat up. Tomorrow, I need to get some herbs from the village's healer so I can change those bandages."

Tansu returned to eating her food. I looked down at the table at the uneaten fish in front of me. I still didn't feel like eating it, so I picked up another apple. However, when I looked at the clawed hand that held it, I didn't feel like eating it either, so I put it back on the table.

I began to think of all that had happened so far, and the more I thought about it, the more I began to feel sad. Before I knew it, I could feel tears pooling in my eyes. I covered my face as I wept softly.

"Shirai? What's wrong?"

"I'm sorry. I can't stop crying. I just don't know what to do."

As I continued to cry, I heard the sound of a chair being moved. Tansu's arms suddenly wrapped themselves around me. I could smell the sweet aroma of flowers coming from her as she continued to hold me while I let the sadness come and go.

"It'll be okay, Shirai," she said in a motherly way.

She remained by my side throughout the evening until I finally fell asleep again.

2 - Knowledge Renewed

The next morning, I felt a lot better, despite the fact I still looked half-human, half-dragon. Looking toward the table, I saw Tansu sitting there, sleeping peacefully with her head resting on her arms.

I didn't want to disturb her, so I quietly got out of bed and made my way to the door. Incredibly, I wasn't in as much pain as before, and I was no longer lightheaded. Now I felt sore all over, but I didn't mind it as much.

Opening the door, I was greeted by a beautiful sight. A few yards away from the house was a field of nature's bounty—all kinds of fruit trees and berry bushes. Near them were rows of vegetables growing in the ground. *Tansu must really be dedicated to her gardens,* I thought to myself, *to be able to grow so much on her own.*

As I felt the warmth of the sun bearing down on my new body, I started to feel relaxed. While I was stretching a little, I discovered that by moving certain muscles on my back, I could actually unfold my new wings. Feeling the sun's rays hit them was like being covered by a soft blanket during the winter.

I sat down as best as I could and just stared at the bounty of fruit trees. I didn't know how much time had passed before Tansu came outside and saw me sitting where I was.

"Good morning, Shirai. You must be feeling a lot better if you were able to get out here."

"Yes, I am." I turned my attention back toward her garden. "Did you grow all these by yourself?"

She laughed lightly. "Of course not. I couldn't do it by myself. Some of the villagers come by to aid me."

"Even if that's true, it's still amazing that you can look after so many plants like that."

Again Tansu laughed. "When you put it that way, I guess you're right."

Then she walked past me. "Now you stay there. I need to get those herbs for your wounds. I'll be right back."

I continued to sit there as Tansu walked out of sight. A light breeze came in, bringing with it a cool wind. The sound of rustling trees and the occasional melody coming from tiny gray birds sitting on the branches were the only sounds I heard. This peaceful moment almost made me forget the events of yesterday.

While I watched the sunlight coming through the leaves of the trees, my stomach began to rumble a little. I could see a peach tree nearby with some of its fruit hanging on a low branch. Getting up, I slowly walked over to the tree, hoping I could pluck a few for me and Tansu.

However, when I got closer, I saw that the branch was higher than I thought. Fortunately, I was lucky to see that the peaches were just low enough for me to reach without putting a strain on my injuries.

I was alarmed to find myself jumping higher than any normal human could. I went flying through the branches of the tree, and just as I neared the top, I came crashing back down onto the ground, bringing along with me several peaches that landed on my head.

I was recovering from my fall when Tansu finally came back, accompanied by an eldery man. Seeing me lying on the ground, Tansu quickly came over and helped me up on my feet. "Shirai! What happened?"

I was still a little dazed after that incident, but I answered, "I just wanted to get some peaches for us, but when I jumped, I somehow reached the treetop in one leap. The rest is as you see."

The old man who came with Tansu remarked, "I see. So your new body isn't just for appearance. I thought it might not be, which is why I also came over to talk with you."

He was at least in his seventies. He had short, white hair and a face old with time that spoke of wisdom. He wore a blue robe that reached his ankles. In one hand, he was carrying something wrapped in a large bundle that I assumed were clothes, and in the other, a simple wooden stick to help him walk.

When I heard him speak, I quickly recognized who he was. "Are you Elder Giram?"

The man chuckled heartily. "I see you remember me. It's nice to know your memory loss isn't severe. Let us continue this discussion inside, before you further injure yourself, okay?"

Despite the joke Giram made, I agreed, and after picking up the peaches that were on the ground, I followed Tansu and Giram into the house.

Inside, I was instructed by Tansu to sit down on the bed. I did so, and she began to remove one of the bandages from my chest. She then took a couple of herbs and placed them on the wound. Compared to the pain I felt yesterday, this was a *lot* worse. Covering both the herbs and the wound with a clean roll of bandages, Tansu continued to do this with the other wounds.

As she worked, my eye traveled to the bundle that Giram had with him.

"What is that you have?" I said.

"This is one of the reasons I came over. These were the clothes you were wearing when we found you. Of course I doubt they would fit you anymore," replied Giram.

I thought that comment was uncalled for, but I didn't say anything.

"You also had something gripped tightly in your right hand. You were holding onto it as though it were more important to you than anything else in the world."

Giram unrolled the clothing to reveal a strange sword underneath. The blade was three feet long and was emerald green in color. It sparkled, even though there wasn't much light coming through the windows into the house. At the bottom of the blade were ancient-looking runes. The hilt was made of silver with two cat's-eyes imbedded at each end of the cross-guard.

"That sword!" I suddenly felt as if my mind was going to explode. I placed my hands on the sides of my head, hoping to keep my brain from jumping out of my skull.

"Shirai, what's wrong?" Tansu asked, sounding very worried.

I couldn't answer because my mind was being bombarded with visions of places and things I didn't know. Images of me using the strange sword started to surface. Finally, the pain stopped, and I found that I could remember more than what I had yesterday.

"Yes! I remember that sword! I remember I'm a swordsman, and that sword *is* important. I had to protect it…" I began to trail off a bit. "But… I can't remember why."

Giram said reassuringly, "At least we're off to a good start. If it is important to you, then you should be the one to keep an eye on it."

He placed the sword on the table before facing me. "The second thing I came here to tell you is that since yesterday, I've been researching your condition to help answer why you look the way you do. Since you are half-dragon, I began my research on that subject."

Pulling out a book he had in his robe called *Dragon Legends*, Giram explained that it was the *only* one he could find that talked about dragons. He told me that no one knew much about them anymore, since for some reason they moved to a place called the Dante Mountains over a thousand years ago. No one had seen any since.

"But there was an interesting note in the same book." Opening the book, he began reading a passage. "'One who is blessed by Ska, Lord of All Dragons, shall have divine protection from all who threaten them, the chosen.'"

He looked up. "I think this somewhat explains what happened to you."

"Ska? Lord of All Dragons? I don't know who that is or what the Dante Mountains are." I pointed to myself as I angrily added, "Is this what you call 'divine protection,' being changed into this?"

"I don't know why you're like that, either. I wish I could have found more information for you." He shook his head as though he was disappointed with himself for not being able to help me more.

"No. It's okay. I'm glad you went to so much trouble for my sake."

Giram smiled as he slowly got up from his chair. "I'm glad to be of service. Anyway, I need to get back to my work at home. We can talk another day."

He then headed for the door. When he reached it, he turned to face me again and said with all seriousness, "Think of your new form as a blessing, not a curse."

After my talk with Giram, I spent the next two weeks recovering. During that time, Tansu continued to look after me, changing my bandages, cooking meals, and making sure I wasn't feeling depressed.

She also helped me get used to walking on my legs. It wasn't what you call a smooth process, as I kept falling over most of the time, but eventually I got the hang of it.

I soon found out that, in addition to gardening, Tansu was an expert seamstress. In no time flat, she made me new clothes that would accommodate my wings and tail.

My new wardrobe consisted of a white sleeveless shirt with half of the cloth missing in the back and three strings there to close it. That, along with large half circles also cut in the back, helped to make sure my wings were free.

The wood-colored shorts were constructed like the shirt, but instead, she cut a hole for my tail. Once through, all I had to do was clasp the opening closed.

Life continued on uneventfully until one day when Tansu had to take ten buckets of produce picked from her garden to some of the villagers. She needed my help, since she couldn't carry it all. Despite my not wanting people to see me, she convinced me to help her.

When we got there, I finally saw how Kenga looked. It consisted mainly of the same kind of houses as Tansu's. Some of these were constructed of stone instead of wood, and some of the roofs were built out of straw. My guess was that there were at least twenty buildings in the entire village. To the north of the village I could see the small lake where I first saw myself, and to the south, a section of woods thrived.

Upon our arrival, the reaction that I got from the villagers was that of shock. Everyone made sure to keep their distance from me. They stared at me as though I was a monster. I soon felt like going back to Tansu's house and hiding there.

"I should go, Tansu. Everyone is obviously afraid of me."

Tansu quickly countered, "You can't, Shirai. I told everyone that you are nice, even though you look like a dragon. Give them a chance."

I glared at her, feeling slightly annoyed. "Was that supposed to make me feel better?"

We continued with our task of handing out the food we had, but still no one came near me or even said anything. When I thought I heard one of the townspeople call me a freak, I was ready to go back to Tansu's house.

That's about when a little girl came up to me, despite her mother warning her not to. In her hand she held a small blue and yellow iris.

"Uh… hi there," I said, trying not to sound like I *was* a freak.

The girl smiled. "Hi there! I heard you were hurt badly! Are you okay now?"

"Um … Yes I'm better now, thanks."

Still grinning, the girl said, "I'm glad! I got this for you. I hope it will make you happy."

She held the flower toward me. I looked at Tansu, who smiled as she nodded. I got on my knee and took the flower.

"Thank you very much… it's already making me feel happier. Here, take these as my way of thanking you." I gave her a few apples, and she eagerly took them and brought them back to her family.

"Told you it would be okay, didn't I?" Tansu happily said.

Beginning that day and in the weeks that followed, the villagers accepted me more and more, until they finally considered me a friend. I was having such a good time being in the village, sometimes I didn't care that my memory was gone. Whenever I looked at the green sword that sat near my bedside, however, I realized I needed to restore my memory.

Giram was a big help with that problem. He educated me on the basics, starting with world history.

He told me that the land we live in is called Lu' Cel. Legends tell that when the world was nothing but emptiness, monsters of darkness ruled. It was then that Asteron, God of Creation, and Ska, Lord of All Dragons, came to this empty void and drove the monsters to the netherworld.

Afterward, they breathed life into the void, creating not only the land and the heavens themselves, but also the wildlife, elves, dragons, and humans. Asteron left shortly after, leaving Ska to watch over Lu'

Cel. But before he left, he created the twin moons, Urula and Nege, to shine during the night, making sure that the darkness never returned.

All species lived together in peace until a thousand years ago when Ska and the other dragons suddenly departed for the Dante Mountains, and none of them have been seen since.

Next, he brought out a map and showed me what Lu' Cel looked like.

To the far west of Kenga village is the Polqu Sea, separating the land into west and east sides, with Kenga on the east. To the north is Gale City, the center of trade on the east side.

The Arian Ravine, between Kenga and Gale on the east edge of the map, is steeped in mystery. Some say that it has no bottom, others say it is where Asteron and Ska imprisoned the monsters of darkness that ruled the void before life came to Lu' Cel.

Farther north of Gale lay the Jiran Forest, extending far to the east. Past Jiran is Arc Kingdom, where the royal family rules over the east side.

The Port City of Delphin connects our side with the Port City of Aegir on the other side of the Polqu Sea. Past Aegir to the west is Tsura City, home of the Institution of Magic, where those gifted with magic learn how to control their powers.

To the southwest of Tsura is the Desert Kingdom of Kunti, which sits in the middle of a large desert spanning most of the bottom left corner of the map. Surrounded by several ancient ruins, Kunti sits in a place where an ancient civilization once lived. They were dedicated to a form of magic that has long since been lost.

North of Tsura is Flora Kingdom, nestled in the middle of a large forest. In the far northwest corner of Lu' Cel is the Hariel Kingdom, which is near the edge of a large ocean with vast unexplored open plains to the north. The Village of Ranu is a short walking distance from Hariel.

Finally, extending over a vast amount of area near the Hariel Kingdom all the way to Arc Kingdom are the Dante Mountains. Right next to the Polqu Sea, there is said to be a large lake in the center called Orem, the waters of which cascade down from an incredible height to empty into the Polqu Sea. They also feed into a river that ends at a lake near Hariel.

When I commented on how small Lu' Cel was, Giram said that no one knew what existed beyond what was known today. The dragons helped the people travel to other places, but since they left, everyone was afraid to go out any further. They didn't even know if there is life in the outskirts.

Finally, Giram brought me up to date with current events.

For decades things were peaceful in Lu' Cel. Then, six years ago, King Grant of the Hariel Kingdom, normally a peaceful man, suddenly invaded the Flora Kingdom. He brought the entire kingdom to its knees using some strange power. Some said it was like magic, but not any power that they knew about. He mercilessly slaughtered the royal family when he was finished.

He moved onto the Kunti Kingdom next and did the same thing there, except that kingdom was destroyed in the end. When he tried to invade the Arc Kingdom, he met with incredible resistance from the people and soldiers there. For three years, the two kingdoms had remained at war.

I hoped that the effects of the war wouldn't reach this peaceful place. Thankfully, our days passed by without incident. However, something started bothering me. During the time I spent with Tansu, learning everything about her, she never once mentioned anything about her family.

I could not know that the day I asked about it was the day that would change everything.

It was evening, and we were eating the dinner that Tansu made. I finally got up the nerve and asked, "Tell me about your family. You have never once talked about them."

She was drinking some water when I asked. She stopped midway and placed the cup back on the table, "Well... my mother and father used to own this house, but Father died two months before I was born, due to an illness. Mother died giving birth to me, so it was just me and my older brother, Dai. He was the one who actually started that garden outside. It was tough raising me and trying to earn enough money to care for us from the things he grew, but we managed to do well."

Stopping for a moment, she glanced out the window next to her. "One day, a year ago, word reached the village that Grant had his sights on Gale City. Dai went to join the resistance to stop him. They managed to fend off his advance… but… Dai was killed by General Lorimar, the best soldier in Grant's army."

I felt terrible for making Tansu relive such painful memories. "I'm sorry. I should never have asked. It must have been hard losing your family like that."

She looked like she was going to cry, but she shook her head, "No, it's okay, Shirai. I've learned that life can be tough sometimes. Please don't worry about it. You have a right to know about me." She looked out the window again and added, "I think it's time we went to bed."

I wanted to point out that it was still early evening, but when I saw her face, I decided not to contradict her. She then went outside, telling me she needed to do something. That left only me to clear up the table. I did so and went to bed afterward.

It was later that I was awakened to the sounds of someone crying nearby. I quietly got up and looked outside the door. One of the moons was high in the sky, and its light bathed the entire area in moonlight.

I saw Tansu, her head buried in her hands as she sat against one of the fruit trees. In one hand she held a small pendant in the shape of a rose. The way she had a gripped on it, I knew it must have been a gift from her brother. She had tried so hard to act happy when she really needed to be sad. I went back to bed, not wanting to bother her.

I was rudely awakened the next day as Tansu frantically shook me.

"What? What is it?"

I could see fear in her eyes. "You need to hide," she told me, "Please hurry! Grant's knights are heading for the village!"

3 - The Starting Path

From my hidden space I could see that it was just as Tansu said. A company of twenty knights came marching into the village. Their plate armor looked dented and worn from continuous fighting. On each of their chest plates was an emblem of a snake wrapped around a sword. While some were pulling empty carts behind them, all of them wielded a sword, spear, or a crossbow.

Leading the troops was a young knight with dull gray eyes and brown, spiky hair that looked as though it hadn't been washed in a while. He rode a silver-colored stallion. Attached to the back of the saddle was a small flag with the same emblem the knights had.

Everyone had come out to see the knights who soon filled the town square. The young knight signaled his men to halt. He then got off his horse and gave a small salute to the people.

"Attention all people of Kenga. We are emissaries of His Majesty Grant. I am Sergeant Russ, and we have come here to acquire supplies needed for our troops. You will comply with this request without any resistance."

There were quiet murmurings from the villagers. While they talked among themselves, Giram came forward to speak with Russ. "Kind sir, with what we already trade with the people of Gale and Arc, we have just enough to keep us going. We can't spare—"

"Silence!" Russ struck Giram in the chest with his sword's scabbard.

Tansu and I were watching behind a small wooden house just out of the knight's range during all of this. Some of the villagers helped

19

him up. I was relieved to see he was fine, but at the same time, I was angry. I wanted to charge in with my sword clutched tightly in my right hand and go after Russ. Before I could act, I felt Tansu hold onto my shoulder very firmly.

"Please don't, Shirai. I hate what they are doing too, but if you do anything rash, you could put the whole village in danger."

Despite my desire to try and help the people of Kenga for their kindness toward me, I knew she was right, so I held my ground.

"Let that be a lesson to you," Russ told the rest of the villagers. "I don't want to, but I have orders from my general to get the food we need by any means."

He then ordered his men to go into each hut, take whatever food they found, and load it on the carts. As the soldiers began pushing the villagers aside and entering their huts, one of the knights who had been sent further ahead in the village came running back all excited.

"Sir! There is a garden full of all kinds of fruit and vegetables over there! It has enough to feed us for a week!"

Now they were threatening Tansu's garden, one of the few precious things she had left. I was about to come out from hiding and make sure they stayed away from the garden when the same little girl who gave me the flower threw a large rock at the knight. Since he didn't have a helmet on, the rock left a nasty gash on his forehead.

"You leave Tansu's garden alone! You can't have it!" she angrily shouted at the knight.

The mother of the child came up to her and quickly pulled her back. "No, little one! You shouldn't do that!"

The knight put his hand down from the gash and glared at the mother furiously. "What kind of mother are you letting that brat go around doing things like that to people?!"

"I'm sorry! She didn't know what she was doing!"

The girl quickly replied, "They can't just come in like this just because some stupid person says so!"

I watched in horror as the knight drew his sword. With greater speed than I ever had before, I sprinted toward the knight and sliced into his armor with my sword. I didn't think my sword would do anything to his plate armor, but somehow I was able to slice through the metal *and* the knight's chest. He fell dead to the ground.

"What's going on?"

Russ pushed through the crowd onto the scene and saw me standing over his dead trooper. His eyes grew wide from shock as he looked at my face.

"What in Lu' Cel is that thing?"

Using that moment, I instructed everyone, "Everyone, get inside your houses, now!"

No one hesitated as the villagers all rushed inside.

I then turned back to Russ. As I stared at him angrily, I readied my sword to block any attack, "I don't know who you think you are or who your king is, but no one has the right to kill an innocent mother and child, or to take things by force, for that matter."

Russ quickly recovered from his shock. Pulling out his sword, he faced his men, "Go! Kill that... that thing!"

Several knights came rushing toward me, their swords out, ready with the intent to kill me. Before they could make use of them, I jumped high in the air, just as I had done when I tried to grab the peaches. This time, though, I had more control of how high I went and how much force I used to do so.

Coming down, I swung my tail around hard. My tail knocked each of the soldiers to the ground, and from the way they were grabbing their now heavily dented chest plates, it broke a few of their ribs in the process. I had no idea how I did that. It just came to me.

"Take this, you monster!" I heard shouting coming from behind Russ.

Several knights launched their crossbow arrows at me. I could hear the arrows whistling through the air as they came closer. As they came within a foot of puncturing my body, I dashed around them, passing by Russ with such speed that I doubt he saw me.

As I approached the startled knights, I began slashing at them with my claws. Each strike not only shattered each archer's bow, but tore through their armor and severely cut into their arms.

I had my back turned so I didn't see the knights carrying spears until one ripped across my back. Even though my body was covered with tiny scales, they didn't seem to protect me as much as I hoped it would.

As the blood trickled down my back from the wound, I spun around and let loose a small blast of fire from my mouth. The fire instantly heated up the spears the knights were holding, and they threw them down. Using that moment, I struck them all down with my sword.

"How did I do that?" I thought aloud.

"Fools! And you call yourself the Army of Grant? I'll show you how it's done!"

Hearing Russ behind me, I spun around just in time to see him coming at me with his sword. I brought my own sword up and blocked his first attack, tiny sparks appearing as our two weapons connected. My wound from the spear slowed me down. All I could do was block each of Russ's attacks.

Finally, he had me pressed against one of the houses. He was going to deliver the final blow when he looked down at my sword.

"The Sword of the Wyvern?" his eyes widened, "It can't be! That was lost three years ago! It disappeared, along with Shirai!"

"How do you know my name?"

When Russ heard my question, he froze like a statue. Composing himself, he looked at me as though he was trying to really take in my face. Finally, he relaxed and sheathed his sword, the desire to continue battling faded from his eyes.

"So that's it," I heard Russ say softly to himself. He turned and walked away from me. I stared at him as he shouted orders.

He ordered them to leave the village. Some naturally wanted to know why, but the stern glare in their leader's eyes told them the decision was final. The knights quickly filed out of the village.

Getting on his horse, Russ turned and faced me. "Go to the Dante Mountains. You may find the truth there."

It was clearly obvious by his behavior that he knew something about me. I tried to go after him, but my wounded back wouldn't let me. I was forced to watch as he then shouted to the villagers, "I'll go and tell General Lorimar that you didn't have anything. He will probably leave you alone, but be careful anyway! Men, let's go!"

He served under the man who had killed Tansu's brother? Now I really wanted to stop him, but by then he had already galloped ahead of the knights, leaving all of us bewildered as to the sergeant's sudden change in attitude.

When they were finally out of sight, Tansu came out of hiding and ran over to me, "Shirai, are you crazy? You could have been killed!"

"Nice way to ask if I'm all right."

I was sure I was going to get a long lecture from Tansu, but she just sighed heavily, "Let me see your back."

She took off my now cut shirt to get a better look at my wounded back. She was cleaning away the blood when everyone came out of their houses and formed a half circle around us.

Giram stepped forward, holding a bundle of herbs, "When I saw you going after those knights, I figured you would need these."

"Thank you, Giram." Tansu took the herbs and placed them on my cut. It stung, but I was too busy replaying Russ's message in my mind to care. He knew something about me, and I needed to find out what.

"Giram, do you have an extra map of Lu' Cel I can borrow?"

I heard Tansu let out a small gasp as she finished up covering my wound, while Giram stared at me with a serious look in his eye, "You plan to follow that man's words?"

I nodded. "I have no idea what Grant is thinking or what the heck the Sword of the Wyvern is. I don't even know how I did any of the things I did while fighting the knights. So if it means I have to go through his army and personally see Ska to get the answers, then I have to go."

Mutters rose from the crowd. Most thought I was crazy to go up against Grant while others worried about my safety. In fact, I was expecting Giram to refuse me. Instead, he sighed softly before giving me a kind smile.

"If you must go, please remember what I said. Think of your new form as a blessing."

I also smiled. "Looks like I'm going to need it after all."

I thanked Tansu for her help and was finally able to get up. It was then I noticed the bodies of the knights I'd slain. Even though they were working for Grant, they were just following orders. I couldn't just let their deaths be meaningless.

"I have a request to make of you all," I asked. "We should give these men a proper burial so their souls may find rest. Despite everything that is happening in the world, they are human, after all."

No one really agreed to my suggestion at first, but then Tansu spoke up, "He's right. If we cannot show kindness even to the dead, we are no better than Grant."

With that, everyone began preparations for the burial rites. It was near sunset by the time we had buried all of the bodies. The prayers were said, and flowers were placed on the graves. During the ceremony, I could see that Tansu looked preoccupied.

The ceremony ended just as night fell. Everyone headed back to their homes while Tansu and I went back to her house. When we got back, I sat at the table, thinking about what I needed to do. Tansu sat quietly on the other chair as she patched up my shirt. Every few moments, she would look out of the window.

"Tansu, is something on your mind?"

She said nothing as she continued her work. I had a pretty good idea what was bothering Tansu.

"This wouldn't have anything to do with the fact that that Russ character works for the person who killed your brother?"

Stopping her sewing, Tansu put my shirt on the table and gazed up at me. I could see she was clearly upset.

"He must be so close that the thought of it makes me sick. I wanted to kill Russ to even the score. But I—"

Tansu didn't finish speaking or go back to work on my shirt. Instead, she stared out the window. I knew how she felt. When Russ mentioned who his superior was, for a split-second, I also felt like killing him. However, unlike the knights I killed to protect myself and the villagers, I knew killing Russ wouldn't accomplish anything.

"Tansu, this may sound harsh, but you really think killing Russ would make you happy? Would it bring your brother back? If you let that desire linger, it'll slowly change you."

When I didn't see any change in her attitude, I got up from my chair, walked behind Tansu, and gently wrapped my arms around her. I was half-expecting her to object, but she didn't move or say anything.

"You were the only one willing to take me in when I first came here. You made me feel welcome and happy. I don't want you to change because of hatred. I like you the way you are now."

Tansu sighed softly and held my hand with her own. Looking up at me, I saw her comforting smile, "Thank you, Shirai."

The next day came, and the sun was shining brightly as I was readying to leave, but Tansu wasn't around. She left my newly repaired shirt and a scabbard for my sword on the table. I didn't have time to go and look for Tansu. She knew I planned last night to leave as soon as I woke up. Taking the things she left me, I headed to the road that led out of the village. I saw everyone gathered to see me off.

Giram was at the front of the crowd, smiling and holding a scroll in his hand. "Please take care, Shirai. Remember that you will always have a place here in Kenga if you don't find what you are looking for."

He handed me the scroll. I opened it and saw the map I had asked for. "Thank you for all you did for me, Giram."

He moved back into the crowd. The mother of the child I saved came up to me next, holding a large bag, "Take this with you. I figure you might need it for carrying food or anything else you'll need."

"Thank you." I slung the bag across my shoulder. When I placed the map in the bag, to my surprise, I found there was something already inside it. I didn't want to waste time seeing what it was. I would check later.

My little friend came up to me next. "Please come back when you can."

I picked her up and held her in the air, "Of course I will come back. After all, you are the third one who made me feel welcome here."

She laughed happily as I put her down. I searched the faces. Tansu wasn't among the crowd. I was really hoping she would be here so I could personally thank her for everything she had done for me.

"If you see Tansu, Giram, could you tell her I'll miss her most of all, and that I thank her for all her help."

"I'll relay that message for you, Shirai. Now go, before you decide to change your mind!" He made it sound like an order, but he was right.

I waved goodbye to everyone and headed off toward the Dante Mountains.

A mile later, I was looking out at the vast plains that stretched in front of me. It was going to be a long journey, I thought. As I continued on my way, I noticed something ahead of me. Next to the trail was a large boulder. There was someone sitting on top of it. At first I thought it was just another traveler like me sitting on the boulder to rest, but as I got closer, I nearly let my bag slide off my shoulders.

It was Tansu.

Wearing new clothing, she had a tanned leather vest on top of a green short-sleeve shirt and an amethyst-colored skirt. She wore leather gloves and the same boots she always wore. Around her neck was the rose pendant that she had wept over that night I saw her in the garden. There was a small pouch on her belt, and slung across her back was a bow and a quiver full of arrows.

"What are you doing here?" I called out to her.

When she saw me, she leapt off the boulder and walked up to me, looking straight into my eyes, "What does it look like I'm doing? I'm coming with you! You may be a fierce dragon swordsman, but you can never seem to keep from getting hurt. Somebody's got to make sure you make it to the Dante Mountains in one piece."

"Are you crazy? I don't know what's waiting at the mountains! Not to mention the fact that Grant's army is still trying to take Arc, so I may run into tons of knights! Besides, who's going to take care of your garden?"

Taking the bow from her back, she held it out in front of her. "I can take care of myself. Gardening isn't the only way I get food, you know. My brother taught me how to use the bow and arrow, and I'm quite skilled. As for the garden, last night I asked everyone to watch over it for me."

As she lowered her bow, Tansu suddenly looked a little upset. Her tone had also changed, "But the real reason I want to come … I'm hoping that maybe we will meet General Lorimar so I can at least see the person who killed my brother. Maybe that way I can finally make peace with my past."

I wanted to argue some more, but I could tell she was serious. How could this be the same girl who was always so happy? Then again, the way she acted a moment ago was more like her.

"You know," I said with a sigh, "you may be a great host, but you *really* need to work on your negotiation skills."

I then put my hand on her head, "You just make sure to have plenty of herbs at hand, okay?"

She gave me the same smile she had the first time we met. With that we started down the road together.

Tansu prepared for travel

4 - Reunion

Our journey to the Dante Mountains went on for days. We only stopped for rest and food. As we continued, I learned when Tansu said that she was skilled at hunting, it *wasn't* an understatement.

I told her no one could be that good with a bow. However, she quickly made a fool out of me by shooting down a wild bird that flew high above us—so high even I couldn't jump to get it. And to add insult to injury, the arrow she used hit the bird right in the center of its chest!

I learned other things as well. I was amazed at how beautiful the countryside was. The sun shone down on huge fields of grass while the wind blew across them, making them shimmer like a crystal. The wildlife went on with their simple lives, unaware of the changes that were happening in the world, especially now. Even the small ponds we came across were as untouched as the day they were formed. It was hard to believe that at this very moment, far away, a war was going on that could ruin this tranquil place.

During the time we spent in the wilderness, I also discovered things my new body had given me. My strength had increased, so I could now lift something like a medium-sized boulder with ease. In addition, I was able to exert more strength in simple actions such as jumping, running, and pushing, which helped explain how I was able to fight like I did.

Not only that, my sense of smell, hearing, and sight had been affected. I could now detect smells a normal person couldn't, see things over a mile away, and hear the faintest sounds. I even learned how to effectively use my body as a weapon, such as the way I used my tail as a whip on the knights back in Kenga.

The one thing, however, that I couldn't figure out was how I was able to bring out the flames I had used. I brought that subject up with Tansu one night as we set up for camp.

"I don't understand it. How was I able to shoot fire like that? And why can't I do it again?"

"I don't know myself, Shirai," she replied, trying to reassure me, "but I'm sure you'll figure it out soon. Besides, you have already found out a lot of good strengths your new body has given you."

Even though she may have been right, it didn't make me feel any better. As things stood, and if what people were saying about Grant being as powerful as he was now, we were going to need all the help we could get.

Later, we were passing through a small forest a short distance from Gale City. Nothing out of the ordinary happened while we made our way through. We saw only the occasional deer and tree squirrel. It was when we were nearing the other side that I stopped in my tracks.

I felt something wasn't right.

"What is it, Shirai?" Tansu asked.

I held my hand up to signal her to be silent. I listened to the sounds of the forest for anything out of the ordinary. I heard the usual sounds at first—the leaves of the trees rustling as tiny animals ran across the branches and the birds singing their songs. It was when I heard the snapping of a twig directly above us that I sprang into action.

"Get out of the way, Tansu!"

I pushed her out of the way and something came down from the treetop at a high speed. A weird-looking spear entered the ground right where Tansu was a moment ago. Holding the spear in his hand was a young man.

He wore his long black hair done in several braids in the back of his head, with a gray bandana wrapped around his forehead. He had a sky blue jacket with a fluff collar over a dark blue, long-sleeved shirt. His long, brown pants with diamond patterns on the side of the legs reached his high black boots. His green eyes looked at us as though he was impressed. I could tell he was going to be trouble.

Bandit

"That's impressive how you sensed my attack coming. 'Course if I had ears like that, I'd probably be able to hear anyone coming a mile away too. So what are you, a man or a dragon?"

The man pulled his spear from the ground. Now that I could get a better look at his weapon, I could see it was no ordinary spear. Thinner than the spears I had seen back at Kenga, it ended in a sharp tip. Running the entire length of the spear were ancient magic runes. In addition, I could see a faint aura surrounding the spear.

"Who are you and why did to try to kill my friend?" I pulled out the Sword of the Wyvern.

The man pointed his spear at me, looking smug. "The name's Nova. And I wasn't trying to kill her. It's not my style. My real target was the small bag on her waist. I was hoping for an easy target, but I wasn't expecting someone like you to be with her."

I laughed a little. "Think you're pretty confident, do you? Let's see how good you are with that spear."

I charged Nova and brought my sword down, only to have him block my attack with his spear. I tried to slice through his weapon... only to find I couldn't! Whatever the spear was made of couldn't be broken so easily.

To make matters worse, I soon found that Nova was a *lot* stronger than he looked. To prove my point, he pushed me backward easily.

"How did he manage to do that?" I heard Tansu ask.

I quickly regained my balance, "Looks like he's no ordinary thief, Tansu. Stay back, okay?"

She nodded, and I once again engaged Nova. I tried everything I could think of to get to him, but no matter how I attacked, he managed to block every move I made. Lucky for me, even though he obviously knew how to handle a spear, I was able to dodge his attacks with ease.

Nova was looking at me weirdly. Then, without warning, he pulled away and put his hand up, signifying that he was stopping his attack. "Hang on. The way you use that sword. I've seen it before."

I looked at him, a little baffled by his words, "You have?"

It was strange hearing someone say they knew my style of fighting, considering I didn't even know how I had learned it in the first place. But what was even stranger was I realized I'd seen his style of fighting also.

Nova slowly came closer to me. I kept a defensive stance, but I could see he had no intention of fighting. He was more interested in looking at the earring I had on.

His eyes suddenly widened in shock, "That earring! That's the exact earring I gave my friend Shirai back when we were teenagers!"

I was too shocked to say anything.

"You know Shirai?" Tansu asked.

Nova nodded as he kept looking at me. "But it can't be... you can't be him. Not looking like that!"

He closed his eyes like he was trying to think. Moments later, his eyes sprung open, and he snapped his fingers. "There *is* one way I can be sure of who you really are! Shirai and I always greeted each other with a special handshake. Let's see you try it."

Nova lifted my arm up and then pressed his arm against mine. He waited for me to do something, even though I had no idea what to do. I looked at the way our arms were positioned, and suddenly remembered something. I clasped my hand around the area below Nova's elbow, and he did the same thing. We shook our arms, let go, and took each other's hand and shook them too.

When we finished, that same pain I felt when I remembered about the importance of Sword of the Wyvern, but it wasn't as painful as before, and it lasted only a split second. I looked at Nova and smiled.

"Nova? Nova of Ranu Village?"

Nova's face lit up. "Shirai, it is you!"

We gave each other a friendly hug.

"It's been ages! You sure have changed since I saw you last!"

Nova laughed, "Look who's talking about having changed! What happened to you? Why do you look like a... a dragon?"

"It's a long story, Nova."

"So is he your friend, Shirai?" Tansu came foward, "Maybe he can tell you who you are."

Nova turned to Tansu and eyed her carefully, "And who is this lovely lady? Your girlfriend?"

Tansu's face turned beet red while I scratched my head nervously. "Girl... No! She's a friend who has helped me out for the last few weeks."

Nova let out another laugh, "Relax! I'm just kidding, but what did she mean, I could tell you who you are?"

We all got comfortable as I explained everything to Nova: how I awoke looking like a dragon, the Sword of the Wyvern, and the raid on Kenga Village. At the end, I asked if he knew anything about me that could shed light on my past.

"Sorry. Unfortunately, I don't know anything about you either."

Tansu looked more surprised than I was at his answer. "But how can you know Shirai and say that you don't know who he is at the same time?"

Nova held up a hand in defense. "Let me explain. When I was twelve, Shirai came to our village. He looked like he had no idea where he was. I offered to show him around. We were soon having a good time, and he didn't notice it was getting late. He left quickly, saying he would be back soon."

Again I remembered something. "That's right. I had to be back at someplace, but I can't remember where and why."

A big smile grew on Nova's face. "And just like he promised, he did come back, regularly. We had such a great time together, playing all kinds of games, getting into all kinds of mischief."

I grinned also. "Those were good times indeed. We were known as 'Twin Trouble' by the villagers."

Tansu snickered a little when she heard our old nickname. I couldn't blame her. Even I thought it was funny when it first came up.

"About that time, I wanted to learn how to use a spear like my dad. Lucky for me, Shirai was also learning how to use a weapon at the same time."

I nodded in agreement, "It was nice to have someone to practice with."

Nova looked at me and added, "But during our time together, he never once told me about who his parents were or where he lived. Sure, I would have liked to have known those things, but at the time, I didn't have any other friends, so I didn't pry."

Tansu also looked at me. "I don't know what you were thinking back then, but now I bet you wish you told him."

"How can you say that, Tansu, knowing I don't remember anything?" I replied, feeling a little hurt by her comment.

Nova patted me on the back, "She's right, you know. It's your own fault."

"Not you too, Nova."

Both Tansu and Nova laughed together. My face would have been red from embarrassment if it wasn't already red to begin with.

Nova became serious. "Then, seven years ago, you just stopped coming by. I had no idea where you were or how to find you. It was a blow to me, losing the only friend I ever had."

"I'm sorry, Nova. I wish I could tell you where I've been, but at the moment I don't even remember where I was,"

Nova shook his head, "It's not your fault, pal. I managed to get by in life, but it *is* great seeing you again! You've gotten better with the sword since the last time I saw you."

"And you certainly have gotten better with the spear. I remember at first you couldn't even hold one properly." I winked at the end.

Nova countered while laughing. "Look who's talking, considering I managed to defeat you in every duel we had! Every time you lost, you would say that the next time you would beat me. And you never did!"

"Why did you have to bring that up, Nova, especially around Tansu?"

Tansu now looked at me slyly. "What's the matter, Shirai? Afraid I might learn more embarrassing stuff that happened to you?"

I would have told her it wasn't her business, but I couldn't tell her that. I just turned my attention back toward Nova. "Nova, I know it's short notice, but why don't you come with us? We could use all the help we can get."

Nova suddenly became enraged, "I can't."

"What? Why not?"

He explained that, when King Grant was on his way to lay siege to Flora Kingdom, he stopped by Nova's village. Grant thought they were harboring Flora knights who were sent by their king to attack the Hariel Kingdom, and he had an unknown sorcerer use some kind of power to burn his village to the ground. He lost his parents in the fires that followed.

"How could Grant even think Flora would want to attack their neighbor?" Tansu asked.

"I wish I knew, Tansu," he replied angrily.

"Thanks to Grant, I had to steal just to get by. Normal thieves hurt or threaten their victims, but that wasn't my style. I took what I needed and left the rest."

He ended by angrily stating, "This war has brought nothing but pain and sorrow, so I want no part of it."

"But, Nova!" Tansu said.

"Quiet!" I said. I quickly got up. I sensed something wrong. Nova must have sensed it too, because he also got up. His body stiffened as he held his spear tightly.

"What's wrong with you two?" Tansu asked us.

"Someone is here," Nova said quietly.

Suddenly the air was filled with the sound of evil chortling. From the treetops, someone leapt down to the ground.

It was a man dressed in a deep purple robe with chains attached to clasps on each shoulder that met at a small black crystal that was just below the collar. The large hood that he wore concealed his entire face except the mouth, which was curled in a malicious sneer. I could literally feel something evil emanating from him as he continued to chortle.

When Nova saw the figure, he looked ready to kill, "It's him! The one who burned Ranu and killed my parents!"

The man didn't pay any attention to Nova, but looked in my direction and replied in a chilled tone, "So you are still alive. I'm so glad, Shirai."

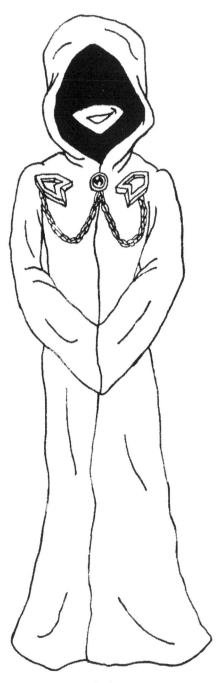

Concealed sorcerer

5 - The Concealed Sorcerer

The second the man said my name, I had my sword out and pointed at him, "Who are you? How do you even know me?"

Again the man chortled. His grin sent a chill up my spine the second I saw it. "So what I heard is true. You have no idea who you really are. Well, this is something I don't have to tell General Lorimar at the moment."

Tansu was quick to respond, "General Lorimar? What does he have to do with this?"

The sorcerer shook his head while holding up his hands. "My, my. So many questions, yet so little time to truly answer them. I suppose, for the time being, you all can just call me Ignotus."

"Ignotus? What kind of a name is that?" Nova scoffed, holding his spear with both hands with the front end pointed at Ignotus.

The sorcerer continued to pay no attention to Nova. When he looked toward Tansu, she moved slightly behind me. "As for how General Lorimar is involved, little lady, he was the one who sent me here. I am here to take back the Sword of the Wyvern that Shirai took three years ago."

My fingers tightened around my sword's hilt as I raised it up for battle. "You really think I'll give this sword to a murderer like you, let alone the right hand man of King Grant? You'll only get it if you can pry it from my fingers."

Ignotus laughed so loudly, his voice almost echoed through the woods. "Oh, Shirai! You've become so defiant! You never used to be like that! You always did what you were told!"

Swallowing his laughter, he raised his right hand up in the air, and a ball of flames formed in his palm.

"Unfortunately, my orders were to bring the sword back, no matter what. So I will take it back now."

Ignotus then threw the fireball straight at us with incredible speed. We all managed to get out of its path, and it flew past us and hit a nearby tree. The tree wasn't as lucky, however, as the fireball exploded on contact, completely destroying it.

"Everyone, be careful!" Nova warned. "I've seen how powerful his magic is!"

"It doesn't matter what he throws at us! We can't let him get the sword!"

With that, I quickly charged at Ignotus. My blade was an inch away from going through his body, but at the last second, he vanished and somehow reappeared behind me.

"You may have the Lord of All Dragons's blessing, but you are obviously inexperienced in using that power to the fullest!"

He conjured up a stone spike from the ground. It barely missed my leg as I quickly jumped out of the way. I swung my tail at the spike, reducing it into rubble. I made sure the debris flew toward Ignotus. Using this distraction, I came at him with my sword.

"Such childish attacks are useless!"

Ignotus quickly countered with a wave of water that came out of his hand. The force of the attack pushed me back against a tree. I tried to bring forth the same flames I had used in Kenga. Eventually I succeeded, but I only managed a small flame. Ignotus easily dodged it and retaliated by bring down a lightning bolt from the air. It struck an inch away from where I was.

That was too close! I thought to myself. *We need something new.*

It was at that exact moment I remembered something that Nova and I had done once, a maneuver we came up with that just might work.

"Nova, let's show him the old move we used before!"

He must have been thinking the same thing, because he gave me a thumbs up. "With pleasure!"

Using both hands, he held his spear in a horizontal position and waited for my next move. With great speed, I jumped on top of the spear. The second my foot touched it, Nova used the spear to throw me upwards into the canopy and out of sight.

"What sort of trick are you up to?" Ignotus asked impatiently.

"Let us show you!" With a single motion, Nova dragged his spear so it would bring up dirt from the ground and quickly fling it at Ignotus.

He reacted by covering his face with his arms like we hoped he would. "Dirt throwing? Is that supposed to impress me?"

When Ignotus brought down his arms, he saw Nova coming at him. However, he only managed to slice into the cloth of the robe. Ignotus countered, bringing forth a small blast of wind that pushed Nova backward.

"Was that the best you can do?"

Nova smiled. "What makes you think that was the main part of the plan?"

"What?" Ignotus sounded surprised.

He had forgotten all about me, but it was too late. I dropped down from the treetops and imbedded the Sword of the Wyvern into Ignotus's heart.

"The 'Old Bait Trick' works once again!" I said with pride.

"That was amazing, you guys!" Tansu praised.

I was going to agree with her, but our victory was shortlived, as the sound of Ignotus laughing maliciously came from the limp body at the end of my sword.

"What the!"

"Clever, Shirai," Ingontus's voice sounded, "but *ineffective*!"

I felt something cold hit me in the back. I fell forward on what should have been Ignotus's body, only to find that it was nothing more than a robe with nobody in it.

The real Ignotus stepped out from behind a tree after firing an ice bolt at me.

"Shirai!" both Tansu and Nova shouted.

"One who has command of a dragon's powers can't even tell a real from a fake!" Ignotus cackled. "And after you trained so hard too with the sword! Maybe you're just not good at using such a weapon!"

I staggered to my feet, growling softly as I glared at Ignotus with anger.

"I see it's going to take a lot more than that to bring you down. Let's see if this will—"

Before Ignotus could follow up whatever threat he was about to say, he suddenly lurched forward as something came out of his chest. It was the end of one of Tansu's arrows! She had gotten behind him and shot him in the back.

"Maybe you should have kept your eyes on all of us!" she said triumphantly.

I hoped *that* would finally take Ignotus down, but once again, luck wasn't on our side. He just took hold of the arrow and ripped it out of his body. A small amount of blood was on the arrow's shaft. In a burst of flames, Ignotus turned it instantly to ash.

"A good effort, little girl." He actually sounded impressed. "If your arrow was just a few more inches to my left, you would have pierced my heart. I was planning on doing something different to get rid of you, Shirai. But I think I know a better way."

Ignotus once again disappeared. To my horror he appeared behind Tansu, quickly locking his arm around her neck.

"Shirai!"

"Tansu!" I tried to get closer to them.

"That wouldn't be wise, boy, unless you want your ladyfriend to die before your eyes," Ignotus's free hand was close to Tansu's face.

Any sudden movement on my part, and he would kill Tansu with a single spell. Realizing that I had no choice, I let the Sword of the Wyvern drop from my hand.

"Good. Now how to deal with you? General Lorimar said that I should try to bring the dragon man back too." Ignotus formed a dark ball of energy. "But seeing your hostility toward King Grant, you must be taken care of before you find the truth!"

He fired the black energy at me.

"Shirai! No!" Tansu cried out as she tried to get away from Ignotus.

I didn't have time to duck. Even if I could, I wasn't going to risk Tansu's safety. I waited for Ignotus's spell to take me down.

I had completely forgotten about Nova. Out of nowhere, he came in front of me, his spear out in front of him. I wanted to push him out of the way, but as the energy neared Nova, his spear started to glow. As the glow grew brighter, the ball of dark energy just vanished.

"What is this?" Ignotus demanded. "My magic stopped by a mere spear? It's impossible! Unless—"

Nova was now slyly grinning. "I see you know your legends, Ignotus. This is indeed the Tao Spear, said to have the power to neutralize nearly every kind of magic. So unless you want to know what it's like having a spear go through your heart, let Tansu go and get out of here!"

"Seems I have no choice but to depart for now." Ignotus let go of Tansu, who was quick to distance herself from him. "But be warned. We will not be stopped, and Shirai will die for his actions!"

With that, Ignotus vanished into the shadows. I was going to say something to Nova when Tansu ran over to me and hugged me tight. "Shirai, I'm so glad you're all right."

I winced as I felt a stinging sensation from my back. "Not so tight please! My back was just struck for the second time, remember?"

Tansu quickly let me go and apologized while Nova came up to the two of us. "Are you okay, Shirai?"

I nodded, "Thank you for coming to our rescue, Nova. I owe you."

"I thank you too, Nova," Tansu added. She then gave Nova a small kiss on his cheek. For some reason, I felt jealous, but Nova didn't seem to mind it.

"What impresses me more is that you have the Legendary Tao Spear," she went on. "Even in my village we know about the spear made ages ago by unknown methods and lost for ages. Where did you find it?"

"Accidentally, actually. While I was in Kunti after my village was burned, I stumbled on a secret chamber just on the outskirts of the city. Inside I found the final resting place of the spear. I know taking something like that is wrong, but I figured if it was used for good, it wouldn't matter."

"Oh, and I suppose robbing people is what you call good?" I happily countered.

Nova just gave a little cough and continued, "Anyway, looks like there is something going on, and it involves you and that sword of yours."

I nodded. "That Ignotus character... he knows me too, just like Russ. However, something else about him bothers me. He's not your typical magic user. It is as if he wasn't even human."

No one added anything to my statement. I figured they were thinking the same thing. As I contemplated that matter, I suddenly felt Nova placing his hand on my shoulder, "You know, I was thinking. Maybe I should come with you guys. Seeing as you now have Ignotus as an enemy, you're going to need help. I can't very well let my friends face him alone."

"You mean it, Nova?" Tansu asked.

He winked at her, "Of course I do, Tansu. After all, someone needs to make sure Shirai doesn't screw up again."

"What does that mean?" I automatically shouted, "You want to start something, Nova?"

Tansu and Nova began to laugh. It took a moment for me to realize how I sounded. When I did, I couldn't help but laugh at myself too.

6 - The City

The day after our encounter with Ignotus, we finally reached the outskirts of Gale City. I could see the outside of the city was surrounded by high walls made of smooth, white limestone. There were entrances into the city at the west, east, and south ends. Each corner of the wall had a turret where a lone sentry stood on guard, ready to shoot arrows at any enemy coming toward Gale. Dozens of horse-drawn carts were seen either leaving or entering the city, each one packed with crates or supplies.

"That's Gale City? It's huge!" I said in amazement.

"Well it *is* the second largest city in the land, next to Tsura City," Tansu explained.

"It's also the best place to get a good drink. I can't wait till I hit the bars!" Nova said excitingly.

I looked at Nova in complete surprise, "Since when did you start drinking? You told me once you'd never touch a drop of alcohol as long as you lived."

Nova was grinning as wide as possible. "Well, things change, Shirai. Things change."

One didn't need good sense to tell by his expression that he didn't just like drinking—he *loved* it.

"Well that's going to have to change too, Nova," Tansu told him. "We can't afford to spend our money just so you can get loaded. It's only going to be used to get things we really need."

To further make her point known, she dangled the pouch that had our money in front of Nova's face, her fingers tightly gripped on the strings that closed it off. Nova looked discouraged while I was secretly relieved that Tansu was with us.

"Well we better get going..." I was about to walk forward when I felt someone grabbing my arm and pulling me back hard.

"Whoa there, Shirai. Have you forgotten that you are not exactly someone that anyone would welcome?" Nova told me.

In my eagerness to get inside Gale, I had forgotten that I was a dragon man. The people of Kenga liked me because Tansu was there to help, but this was a big city. If I went in like I was now, there'd be a riot.

"So what do we do now? Wait until it's dark and sneak in?"

Without asking, Tansu suddenly took the big bag I had received from the woman in Kenga. Opening it, she pulled out a giant, hooded cloak, large enough to cover my entire body, tail, and wings, plus shield my face.

"That's what was already inside?" I asked. "When did—"

"I had a feeling we would need it, so I made this the night before you were going to leave. I made sure to give it to my friend so that you'd be sure to get it."

Once again, Tansu continued to amaze me.

"You are quite the woman, Tansu. Not only beautiful and tough, but smart also," Nova complimented Tansu, flashing a big smile. "Any guy would be lucky to have you as a girlfriend."

I quickly donned the cloak, and we headed toward the city gate. There were four guards clad in simple armor checking everyone who came and left the city, making sure Grant's men didn't sneak in. We were let by without any trouble, despite the fact that I knew I probably looked like someone evil.

What I saw behind the walls made my jaw drop.

The city was far larger than I had originally thought, divided into four major sections, each taking up a different corner. There were all kinds of buildings down every street, including small residential homes, medium to large stores, or a combination of the two.

At the end of each block stood a tall tree to mark where a street was. Down one street, I saw street vendors selling jewelry, food, fish, and clothing. Down another there were businesses with people coming and going as they checked to see what was for sale.

Even the air smelled wonderful as the aroma of all kinds of food from vendors filled it. In fact, I was getting really hungry just taking in the different smells.

"So many buildings. How do people keep from getting lost?" Tansu asked while she took in the sights.

"You just have to know where certain landmarks are, and you'll find your way around this place in no time," Nova explained.

Ignoring the aroma of food, I asked, "That's nice and all, but what are we going to do while we're here?"

Nova gave both of us a wink. "Well, the way I see it, since Tansu can use her arrows to stay a safe distance, you and I are going to need some armor. I happen to know someone here who can make it for free. Just follow me."

Nova went on ahead. leading the way. I looked at Tansu, who was just as confused as I was. We followed him as he led us to the northeast section of the city.

The section was made up of mostly workshops. There were all kinds of smiths: a blacksmith, a blade smith, and a tinsmith, to name a few. Each one was busy, given the black smoke rising from the smokestacks on top of the workshops. With my new senses, I could hear the sounds of the smiths as they struck the metal or other materials they were using on their anvils, even among the other noises of the city.

"We're here," Nova announced as he stopped at a workshop.

The shop Nova pointed us to wasn't like the others. In fact, it was *far worse*. The place looked run down and in desperate need of renovations. Not only that, but from what I could see, it looked abandoned.

"This old place? Someone you know lives here?" I was quickly becoming skeptical of Nova's so-called friend.

"He's not what you would call a normal smith. He does special custom orders. Don't be fooled by its appearance. This place is famous in Lu' Cel."

Nova opened the door and went inside, followed by Tansu and then me. He was right about appearances. The outside looked awful, but the inside was as tidy as a workshop could be. There was a large forge on one side of the workshop and a giant tub of water next to an anvil for tempering the hot metal on the other side. Hanging on the wall were displays of swords, armor, shields, and other kinds of equipment. A door leading into a small kitchen lay on the opposite side of the workshop, right next to stairs leading to the second floor.

"Hey, Chent! Are you here?" Nova suddenly shouted very loudly.

Moments later, movement was heard coming from upstairs. Pretty soon, someone was descending the stairs. It was a large, muscular man in his early forties. His dark red hair was messy, his face was covered with soot, and his beard was long and held together with a band. The overalls the man wore were just as dirty as his face. The man's brown eyes were half-closed, as though we had roused him from sleep.

"What is it? Can it wait until tomorrow?" the man asked in a gruff tone while rubbing his eyes.

"I see you're still sleeping your life away, Chent."

Chent looked at Nova, and his face lit up, "Well Nova, you old softie! I thought for sure your lifestyle would have you in jail!"

Both Nova and Chent shook each other's hands firmly.

"Guess I'm just lucky." Nova then faced toward Tansu and myself. "Anyway, I want you to meet my friends. We have Tansu from Kenga Village."

Tansu bowed to Chent, "A pleasure to meet you, sir. Forgive me for saying this, but you don't exactly look like someone who would be friends with Nova."

Chent laughed wholeheartedly. "Yeah, well I owe him for helping spread the word of my business for me."

He then looked toward my direction. I made sure to cover my face so he couldn't see it. "And who is that character? A new partner in crime?"

That remark got me miffed. Nova must have sensed my mood change, because he quickly replied, "No, that's an old friend of mine from my teenage years. He's Shirai."

Chent came over and extended his hand toward me, "So you're the old friend he kept mentioning. Nice to finally meet you."

I didn't take his hand as I answered softly, "Nice to meet you too."

"Not very friendly is he?" Chent asked Nova.

"He has his reasons, which is why we are here. We were hoping you could fix up some simple armor for me and Shirai?"

Chent went over to Nova and gave him a swift pat on the back. "For you, Nova, no problem!"

"Good. But before you begin," Nova suddenly sounded serious, "I need you first to promise you won't say anything about us or what you see."

Chent stared at Nova, looking unsure as to what he meant, "What I see? What do you mean by that?"

"I think you better sit down for this."

Shrugging, the smith pulled up a chair and sat down. Nova looked toward me and nodded. I feared this might end badly, but if we were going to get armor, I'd have to eventually show myself to put it on, so it might as well be now. Reluctantly I removed my cloak. Chent took one look at me and almost fell backward off his chair.

"Wha… is that a dragon?"

"No. I mean, not exactly." I felt like hiding again, but before I could put my cloak back on, Chent came over and stared at me with excitement.

"Amazing! Simply amazing!" He sounded as if he was seeing something spectacular. "All my life I always wanted to see a real dragon up close, and this is the next best thing!"

He kept looking at me like I was something to be gawked at. Tansu saw how upset I was quickly becoming, so she stepped in. "Mr. Chent, please stop. You're upsetting Shirai."

Realizing that he was acting like a fool in front of me, Chent said with an apologetic smile, "Sorry lad. I shouldn't have acted like that. Forgive and forget?"

He again extended his hand toward me. I could see he was really sorry, so I shook his hand, "It's okay, Chent. I know I look weird."

He pulled his hand away from me. "Which makes me wonder. If you are not a dragon, then what are you?"

Nova volunteered to tell Chent the short version of my situation.

"I see. Sorry to hear about what happened to you, lad."

"Thanks Chent—" I was cut off when my stomach growled loudly. I had forgotten I'd gotten hungry earlier from smelling all that food on our way here.

"Excuse me," I said, embarrassed by it.

47

Chent took in stride. "I think before I get started on that armor of yours, you all could stand to be fed, am I right?"

We all nodded. In quick order, Chent had prepared a large meal for all of us. We all ate as we told him the full version of what had happened to us.

"So *you're* the one who sent Russ running back to his general."

"Has he been by here?" I asked.

He shook his head, "No. He just went straight toward Delphin. Didn't even bother us."

"What could he be thinking?" Nova wondered.

"I don't know," I replied. "All I have to go by is that message he gave about heading toward the Dante Mountains."

"Not to mention the fact that it seems Ignotus wants to keep you from getting there," Tansu added. "This just keeps getting more mysterious by the second."

We all agreed on that. After our meal, Chent took our measurements for the armor and got straight to work. Nova decided to help out a little, leaving me and Tansu to do whatever we wanted. She wanted to explore the city, so I ended up back in my cloak, and we left Chent's place.

Everywhere we went there was something exciting. There was a meadow in the back of the city where families took their children to play. We spent a few minutes just watching the people, but as I watched, I got a little depressed. I wondered if I had any parents or if they were wondering where their son was. With my memory gone, though, it was impossible.

Tansu told me she wanted to see what was for sale, so we went back to the business section. We went in all kinds of shops where she spent most of her time browsing. She looked at new dresses, admired all kinds of jewelry, and browsed through a bookstore. After the many hours she had me waiting for her, in the end all she bought was a book and a new bow to replace her old one.

"All of that time spent here, and *that's* all you want?"

"What's with the attitude?" she quickly countered. "I only bought what I could actually use on our journey. It's not my fault that there are so many great things here."

Despite making a point, I was still miffed from waiting for her to make a decision, so I looked over her shoulder instead. It was then I noticed something on a nearby vendor table. Without thinking, I took the pouch that held the money we had from Tansu and went over there to make my own purchase.

"What's with you?" She came up right behind me. I didn't need to look at her to tell that she was mad. "First you whine about me taking so long, and then you take our money without asking, and now I find you buying something too. What in Lu' Cel did you find so interesting?"

Instead of answering her, I took her right arm and showed her by slipping a gold bracelet around her wrist. On the bracelet were designs of little flowers.

"I just thought this would look good on you."

At first she didn't say anything, but just looked at the bracelet. Finally, she said, "You didn't need to do that."

I had a small smile while replying, "Think of it as my way of saying thank you for taking care of me back in Kenga. Besides I wanted to get it for you."

Again Tansu stared at the bracelet for a moment. Then, looking at me straight in the eye, she smiled also. "Thank you."

Afterward, we wandered the city, taking in all the sights until we came to a huge fountain. It sat in the center of the city, spouting out water from the mouths of two statues of dragons next to small angels. We sat down on the edge of the fountain and watched as the sun disappeared behind the city's wall.

"It sure is peaceful here," Tansu said, looking up at the stars that had started to appear.

"It sure is. You would never know that there was a war going on, living here."

Tansu stated, sounding depressed, "Peace like this can't last. It could change any day soon."

I had a hunch she was thinking about her brother being killed in this very city. It was about then I noticed what looked like a small temple to the north of the fountain.

"Why don't we go into that temple over there? We can give a prayer to those whose lives were lost during this war."

Tansu half smiled and agreed with my idea.

The outside of the temple was simple. Above the entrance was a stained glass window. Two birds carved from stone sat at opposite ends of the temple. The inside was calm and serene with rows of wooden seats and tall pillars supporting the ceiling. Several candles hung on each pillar, illuminating the inside. In the back of the temple was a large statue of a man standing on the back of a dragon.

In front of the statue, on her knees, was a priestess dressed in religious clothing, praying. She must have heard us coming, because she stopped praying, got up on her feet, and turned to face us.

"Welcome," she said warmly. "This is the temple of Asteron, God of All Creation, and Ska, Lord of All Dragons. We don't get many people at this time of day."

"Sorry for interrupting your prayer, miss," Tansu apologized.

The priestess shook her head softly. "It's okay. I was just praying for the same thing I've been praying for the last six years: for this terrible war to end soon."

"Everyone wants this whole mess to end too."

I was busy looking at the statue of Ska. "Miss? Is this what Ska really looks like?"

The priestess shook her head. "I'm afraid that's just an artist's interpretation of what the two look like. No one knows exactly what Asteron was like, and no one has seen Ska in a long time, so people have forgotten what he looked like also."

She stared at the statue for a moment and then let out a sigh. "Six years. I can't believe it's been that long since the prince went missing."

"The prince?"

"That's right," Tansu exclaimed. "I never told you that. They say that the prince, King Grant's only son disappeared shortly before he began his attack on Flora Kingdom. No one knows what happened to him."

The priestess added, "Right, miss. Maybe if the prince returned, he could talk some sense into his father."

"What's the prince's name?"

"I believe he was called… oh yes, Aynor!"

A strange thing happened then. When I heard the name of the prince, I felt the same pain I felt every time I remembered something about myself. This time, however, it was stronger. I fell to my knees and grabbed my head for the pain was too much.

"Sir! Are you all right?" I heard the priestess ask.

"Shirai! What is it?" Tansu was by my side quickly.

A moment later, the pain was gone.

"I'm okay." I got up from the floor.

"Are you sure, sir?" the priestess asked.

I nodded, "I'm fine. It's nothing. Just felt dizzy for a moment. May we pray here?"

The priestess nodded. I got in front of the statue of Asteron and prayed for those I killed back at Kenga and for the safety of everyone there. Tansu also prayed, though she was obviously worried more about me than praying for her brother. We thanked the priestess and left the temple. It was night by the time we got back to Chent's workshop.

"Shirai, what happened?" Tansu asked just as we reached the door leading inside, "Did you remember something about yourself?"

I said nothing as I tried to make sure what I said next would make sense to her, "In a way... yes and no. I feel as though I know someone named Aynor, and yet at the same time, I know I never met anyone by that name. Even so, this Aynor feels close to me. I don't know what to make of it."

I felt Tansu hold my hand, "What you should do right now is not worry about whether you do or don't know this Aynor person. You should be more worried about getting enough sleep tonight, okay?"

I nodded happily in agreement. We finally entered the workshop for a good night's sleep.

7 - Invasion

Over the next few days, Chent and Nova continued working on the armor, while Tansu and I had a lot of free time. Most of Tansu's free time was spent cleaning Chent's home, which I couldn't blame her for. The rooms where we slept weren't what you'd call dirt-free, and that was saying something, considering Chent lived there alone. In addition to also taking charge of cooking our meals, she managed to set aside time for target practice so her archery skills didn't go to waste.

As for me, I spent my time practicing with my sword. Seeing how my fighting would be against someone as powerful as Ignotus, I needed to get better. Thankfully, Chent knew of an empty lot near his place where no one would see me practicing.

Since it was large enough for two people, I asked Nova to join me in a sparring match. It felt like old times back when we used to practice with our first weapons. Since that time, however, Nova's skill with the spear and his strength had gotten much better. He bested me almost every time, which did nothing for my self-esteem.

"That's the tenth time Nova has beaten you. Are you sure you're even trying?" Tansu watched from the sidelines. She clearly enjoyed how I was constantly losing.

"Very funny, Tansu." I picked myself off the ground from my recent defeat. "I don't understand it. I'm a lot stronger than Nova, so why I am losing so much?"

"You want my opinion, I think it's because your style of fighting is easy to read," Nova explained. "Besides, I'd already seen most of your maneuvers back in Ranu."

"He's got you there, Shirai," Tansu joked.

Personally, I didn't think it was funny.

Nova twirled the Tao Spear around. "Now me, I was never instructed on how to handle a spear, but I eventually learned how to by myself. That way, I developed my own style. I'm also constantly thinking of different ways to attack while I am on the move."

"Well that's your way, Nova, but I—" I stopped mid-sentence as I thought of something important.

"Shirai?" Tansu asked.

"I just remembered something. It never came up before, but I was being taught how to use the sword from someone. He was such a master of the sword that no one had ever beaten him. In fact, he'd have put you in your place in a minute, tops."

I made sure Nova knew that last part was meant for him, just so I would feel better about my numerous defeats.

"You're exaggerating," he laughed awkwardly. "No one can be *that* good."

"This is something I would never kid about. I wanted to be just like him."

"Well, maybe you never finished your training with this guy. That would explain things. What was the person called?"

I tried to remember the person's name. When I wasn't able to answer, Tansu and Nova didn't ask anymore about the subject. I figured they wanted me to remember things on my own and not try to force them out.

The day finally came when Chent finished our armor. For Nova, he prepared a lightweight hauberk, a sort of chain-mail shirt, which he wore on top of his dark blue shirt so his movements wouldn't be hampered. He also made some arm guards and a pair of greaves to protect his arms and legs.

Making my armor had been a bit trickier, even for Chent, but he came up with a modified brigandine, a cloth garment made with leather with small oblong steel plates riveted into the fabric. This was the only way he could think of to accommodate my wings. Along with the brigandine, he gave me some greaves and a pair of leather gauntlets with the parts that covered each finger removed for my talons in case I needed to use them.

"Amazing work, Chent. I can see why Nova came to you."

It was true. It was like I wasn't even wearing armor.

Chent strutted around the workshop, "There isn't anyone around here who knows how to make effective armor while making sure it's flexible at the same time."

"Careful there, Chent. You don't want that big head of your to get any bigger."

Tansu and I laughed a little at Nova's joke.

"I'd be careful with your words, boy." Chent gave Nova a stern glare. "Unless you want to find yourself someone else who would do this kind of thing for free, and for a thief, no less."

The two got into an argument after that comment, but I wasn't paying attention to them. I felt that something was wrong in the city. I also thought I heard something, but I needed the arguing to stop so I could hear better.

"Quiet, you two!"

Everyone stared at me.

"What is it, Shirai?" Tansu asked.

I concentrated on the noises that were outside. A second later, I heard something.

It was the sound of something heavy coming from the sky!

"Something's heading for the city!"

"What are you—?" Nova was cut off mid-sentence as the sounds of several crashes filled the workshop.

We all ran outside. Some buildings in the city were on fire. From the sky, boulders were falling, crushing the roofs of buildings. The sounds of people screaming pierced the air.

"What the hell is going on?" Chent shouted.

"It's has to be Grant's army!" I placed my right hand on the hilt of the Sword of the Wyvern. "They must be trying to take over the city again!"

"Well, why are we standing here yapping?" Nova got out the Tao Spear. "We have to do something!"

"Are you crazy?" Tansu asked, "What can we do against a whole army?"

"The first thing we can do is not panic, Tansu!" I advised. "The second is we make sure that the citizens are safe while we try to drive out as many knights as we can! If worse comes to worse, we may have to evacuate everyone!"

"Sounds like a plan, Shirai! Chent and I will take the southwest and east sections of the city!" With that, Nova and Chent were off.

"Come on, Tansu! We'll take the northwest and east!"

We hurried into the city. It was pandemonium everywhere we went. The fires that were already blazing were spreading to other buildings while people were fleeing from a squad of knights heading into the city.

Knowing that her arrows wouldn't pierce their armor, Tansu deliberately shot at their feet to slow them down enough for me to attack with a frontal assault. Soon five knights fell before I heard more knights coming in our direction.

"If we keep stopping to fight every knight we see, the townspeople will probably be all killed!" I yelled to Tansu. "Tansu! You go and find any civilians who need help and get them to a safe place!"

"And what about you?"

"I'm going to go and find where the majority of the knights are and stop them there!"

With that, I leapt onto a nearby roof, leaving Tansu behind, trusting that she wouldn't let me down. Jumping onto the roofs of nearby buildings, I scanned the city for any signs of serious trouble, such as a group of knights trying to kill some of the people, but I didn't see any. Whoever was in charge of the knights must have been sending them inside the city a few at a time. Such a method would prepare them for a final assault, one that could overtake the city in a matter of minutes.

Near the fountain I saw that the temple where Tansu and I had prayed a few days before was burning. Near it some knights were harassing a group of people who must have been in the temple when it caught fire. I quickly leapt down and made short work of the knights. The people I saved were shocked when they first saw me, but they were more grateful for being saved.

"Thank you, whoever you are!" an old woman said.

"You're welcome. Are there any others in trouble?"

"The priestess who works in the temple was still in there when we ran out!" a young man spoke out.

I looked at the burning temple. I didn't have much time. "Get to safety, now!"

Everyone quickly ran off to somewhere safe while I ran into the temple. The inside was an inferno, with fire and smoke everywhere. My new body managed to keep me safe from the flames, but it wouldn't last long. Through the blaze I saw the priestess, coughing from the smoke as she lay in front of the statue of Asteron.

"Asteron," she said in between coughs, "please save me."

The statue began to crumble at the base and fell toward her. I ran, scooped her up, and jumped away as the statue crashed right where she had knelt a second ago.

I turned to leave out the front when some of the pillars near the entrance fell and blocked our way out. I looked around for another way out, and when I looked up at the ceiling, I decided to try something crazy.

I made a giant leap, bashing my head against the ceiling and going right through it. We landed right in the fountain just outside. Even though I was glad to find my skull was as tough as the rest of my body, I knew I wouldn't be doing anything so reckless again soon.

As I recovered from the blow to my head, the priestess finally saw my face. She leapt out of my arms in fright, "Asteron! What are you?"

"I don't think that's important right now. I saved your life. You could at least thank someone who came to pray at your temple."

The priestess said nothing as she was obviously trying to remember something. Her face then lit up, "The man in the cloak with the young woman. That was you?"

I nodded.

"I'm sorry for the way I was a second ago." She bowed her head, "I *do* thank you for saving my life."

"It was nothing. Now we better get you to a safe place."

Instead of looking relieved, the priestess's face was suddenly filled with fright as she shouted, "Behind you!"

Something blunt hit me in the back of my head. The force of the blow sent me flying a few feet away from the fountain. The priestess quickly ran over to see if I was fine. Of course I wasn't all right. My head was pounding from going through a roof, and now this. I slowly got up and looked around at the person who had knocked me down.

I wasn't prepared for what I saw.

A middle-aged man, twice the size and build of Chent, towered over me by a good foot and a half. His massive body was covered in silver armor, with the emblem of Grant's army etched into the chest plate. His gray eyes looked down at me, as if judging. Below his shoulder-length silver hair, his full face braided beard fluttered in the breeze. His hand clenched a large, curved sword with a big hilt, which I guessed was what hit me.

"So what Russ told me is true," the man said in a calm tone. "A dragon man has the Sword of the Wyvern. I'd hoped I would never find it, but now that it's here, it must be returned to the king immediately. I do not want to kill you to get it, even if you are a monster. Hand it over peacefully, and I shall spare your life."

At that moment I looked over my shoulder and whispered to the priestess, "Run! Look for the woman who was with me and tell her to get over here with help quick!"

She was extremely worried, "But... do you not know who that is?"

"Don't worry about me! Please just go!"

Reluctantly, she ran off at top speed. I sighed softly, knowing I didn't have to protect someone at the moment. My attention focused back on the man who stood where he was, as still as a statue. His calm state in spite of being in the middle of chaos told me that this was someone who knew how to fight well.

"And who might I be addressing?"

"I am General Lorimar, Chief Soldier of King Grant!"

My stomach flipped when I heard his name, "So you're the one who killed Tansu's brother, Dai!"

"Dai... yes I knew him. He fought his best. He was a good fighter... but war is war."

His detached demeaner made me even madder.

He pointed his sword at me, "And what is the name of the one who holds the king's property?"

The giant soldier

I held out my sword as I yelled, "I'm Shirai, and I'm not going to be that simple to defeat!"

I thought I saw a slight change in Lorimar's expression when I said my name, but I couldn't really tell. He then got into a battle stance, "If you really are Shirai… then prove it with your blade!"

He then charged at me. He was fast despite being so large. He brought down his sword at full force, but I sidestepped the attack, which was a good thing. The ground where I had stood was smashed when Lorimar's sword struck it.

I went at him with a thrust of my sword, but he did the same sidestep I had done earlier. Lorimar attacked again, this time with a wide sweep of his sword. I managed to duck in time, but he did slice off a few strands of my hair.

"You're wide open!" I aimed at his legs with a powerful flick of my tail, trying to knock him off his feet. When I succeeded, I tried to plunge my sword hard into his armor, but he blocked my attack with his sword. Afterward, he kicked me hard in the chest, throwing me backward. I was lucky to have armor on at that moment, or his kick would have broken all of my ribs.

Quickly getting up, he launched a fury of swipes at me. Each one I blocked with my sword, but soon I found myself against a wall with no possible way to get out.

"This can't be the best you can do, is it?" Lorimar asked with a hint of disappointment.

He tried to thrust his sword into my stomach, but with a quick slide, I managed to get behind him. Using all of my strength, I flung Lorimar over my shoulder into the air. While he was unguarded, I tried once again to bring forth the flames I used before. I was able to let loose a larger blast of fire, but the armor Lorimar wore proved to be heat-resistant. The fire didn't seem to bother him.

He soon landed back on the ground and on his feet. I couldn't believe how good this man was. As I tried to think through my options, I realized something.

"You … you use the same style of swordfighting I use. How can that be?"

Lorimar looked at me with disbelief, "You truly don't remember anything, do you? It was I who taught you how to fight in the first place!"

I felt as though someone had stabbed me in chest. This couldn't be the same person I admired. Not someone like him.

"It… It can't be… you liar!"

I stupidly let my anger get the best of me and recklessly charged at Lorimar. He easily knocked the Sword of the Wyvern out my hand, and with a strong punch to my face, he knocked me into the wall. I could feel the bricks behind me break as I slammed into the wall at full force. I fell to my knees afterward, breathing heavily.

So strong. I don't know if I have anymore strength to win.

As I was thinking this, Lorimar came up to me and looked down with pity. "I'm sorry, Shirai. You meant a lot more to me than you could ever know. But even so… I have to follow His Majesty's orders."

He tightened his grip on his sword as he slowly brought it up.

I suddenly began to feel a rush of power build in my body.

"Farewell." Lorimar started to bring his sword down on me.

I… I must live!

Things were moving as if in slow motion. I held my open palm toward Lorimar. A ball of red energy formed in front of my hand and flew straight at him. The ball exploded in a flash of red light and made a giant hole in Lorimar's armor. He was flung backward and landed at the base of the fountain.

I suddenly felt drained of energy. I would have hit the ground face first if Nova hadn't caught me in time. Tansu, Chent, and the priestess were with him.

"Shirai! Hang in there!" Nova yelled.

"I'm fine… just tired."

"What was that attack you used?" Chent asked.

"I could feel a fierce aura coming from it," the priestess observed. "It was not something a human is capable of using."

"I don't know what that was either." I tried to look toward where Lorimar landed. "More importantly… is Lorimar dead?"

"Lorimar?" Tansu cried out as she quickly faced the man who was lying on the ground.

To my horror, he was getting up, but I soon saw by the hole in his armor that my attack almost went right through his chest. The skin on his chest was burnt slightly, and small trails of blood were coming from the edge of the hole.

"That… that power. So you were the one to whom Ska entrusted his will. Since that is the case… we will back off for now. I can't risk the safety of my men."

Lorimar slowly lumbered away.

"Wait!" Tansu shouted.

Lorimar looked at Tansu. Her rose pendant flashed in the light. "That pendant. Are you Tansu, the younger sister of Dai?"

Tansu didn't speak, but just nodded her head.

Lorimar sighed as if he was relieved to learn who Tansu was. "Thank Asteron. I can now honor that man's last wish."

"What are you talking about?"

He gazed at her with a serious expression. "Before dying, he asked that if I ever met his sister that I should not harm her in any way. Now that I know who you are, I shall definitely leave this place."

Tansu didn't say anything in response. Lorimar next looked at me with the same serious look. "Shirai. You must live, not just for the sake of the world… but for my sake too."

He started off again. Tansu suddenly became angry and was about to go after him when I took a hold of her arm.

"Let him go. There's no need for more bloodshed right now." That was the last thing I said before darkness overcame me.

I awoke to find myself lying on the bed I had been using at Chent's house. I looked around the room. My armor was next to the Sword of the Wyvern, which was next to my bed. I felt the place where Lorimar punched me. It was slightly swollen, which I had expected it to be from his sheer strength alone.

As I pulled my hand back, the bedroom door opened, and Tansu entered the room. When she saw me awake, she quickly came to my side and said, "Thank Asteron. I thought you would never wake up."

"What happened? The last thing I remember was Lorimar walking away."

"He did. He took all his troops and just left. That was two days ago."

"And the city?"

"The city is safe too. Thanks to our quick acting, there were only a few causalities."

I breathed a sigh of relief. "I'm glad."

Just then, Nova entered the room. "So the sleeping dragon is finally awake. You had us all worried, especially Tansu."

Tansu started to blush while I smiled. "Well, I'm glad you all care about me so much."

Nova grinned. "I know you just woke up, but there is something you should see. Come on!"

With that he grabbed my arm, pulled me out of the room, and led me downstairs, with Tansu behind us. We stopped at the front door as Nova said, "It's outside."

I didn't know what he was talking about, but I decided to go along with the gag. I opened the door and was greeted by hundreds of the town's citizens. When they saw me, they all started to cheer. In front of everyone were Chent and the priestess.

"Wha... What is all this?" I asked Chent.

"The townsfolk wanted to see the one who saved their lives and the city."

"I believe Asteron brought you to this place at that time to save us. We all wanted to thank you for all you did." The priestess bowed her head.

Tansu and Nova had at that point come outside too and were waving to everyone. I would have joined in too, but I was busy remembering the last thing Lorimar said to me.

For his sake? Just what was going on? Who was he, really?

✶✶✶✶✶

"My Lord Grant, General Lorimar has been seriously injured in his attempt to take Gale City. The raid was thwarted by Shirai and his companions."

Ignotus was speaking to a man with white hair, a slightly wrinkled face, and royal clothing. The man was quiet for a moment as he sat on his throne.

"Lorimar defeated? I can't believe he was beaten like that."

"He was defeated because Shirai has begun to realize the power that he possesses."

Grant scoffed, "It would seem that the fool had a backup plan. No matter. In the end, he will soon fail. Ignotus, I need you to go after them again soon. We still can't take any chances that he may reach the Dante Mountains."

Ignotus nodded and vanished. Grant got up from his throne and pressed a stone on the wall behind it. A secret door opened, and he went through it. Past the door was a massive room. In the center, tied down with hundreds of chains, was a giant, golden dragon that took up almost all of the room. It was asleep as Grant came near it.

Grant grinned maliciously. "That young man will never make it here in time. It was futile placing hope in someone like that. It will soon be over."

8 - The Hidden Ones

We helped with what repairs we could and left Gale to continue our journey. Walking north, I brought out our map to take a quick glance at it.

"If we stay by the coastline…" I traced an imaginary path along the map, "we'll get to the Dante Mountains faster."

"I don't think that's a good idea, Shirai," I heard Nova remark. "In Gale, I heard rumors that Grant's troops are positioned there. We go there, and we'll be walking into a force of maybe hundreds."

"Are you sure about this rumor, Nova?" Tansu asked skeptically.

"If there's one thing I'm never wrong about, it's making sure my facts are right."

"And where did you get this rumor from exactly? Down in the pub from some drunkard?"

Nova just huffed in response.

"Rumor or not, we can't dismiss it as a possibility." I glanced again at the map to find an alternative route. "It looks like our only option is to head through Jiran Forest and sneak our way past to the mountain's edge."

Neither Tansu nor Nova said anything. In fact, they both looked a little worried.

"Is there something wrong?"

"Shirai, no one goes through that place," Tansu explained. "It is home to the elfin kind, and they haven't made an appearance in fifteen hundred years."

"Not only that," Nova added, "it's said the forest is like a natural maze. We may get lost forever."

The elves disappeared before the dragons did? That was something Giram had forgotten to explain, but we didn't have time to dwell on such matters.

"Even if that's true, you guys, the only other way I can see to get to the mountains is to swim the Polqu Sea. Besides, I'll make sure we won't get lost, I promise."

Realizing that we had few options, Tansu and Nova agreed with the plan, and we headed toward the Jiran Forest. Two days later, we had arrived at its edge.

I saw what Nova meant by natural maze. The inside was covered with low-hanging vines that blocked paths. Tall trees with large tops prevented almost any sunlight from getting into the forest. If one didn't constantly check the surroundings, he or she could spend forever trying to find the way out.

We started our way into the forest slowly. Using my dragon senses, I led everyone through the thicket of trees, bushes, and vines. Hours passed, and we still hadn't made it to the end of the forest. Even with my senses, it was difficult to tell one tree from another.

The one thing I did notice was that the air seemed fresher than the other places I'd been to so far. I also saw fleeting glimpses of animals I had never seen before—even one that looked like a cross between a wolf and a bear.

Pretty soon we were exhausted from walking, so we sat down in a small, open field.

"This is insane. What kind of place is this? It feels like we've been walking around in circles!" Nova complained.

"It's like they say." Tansu sounded worried. "We may never find the exit."

"I don't know about that."

Nova was confused by my statement, "And what does that mean?"

"While we were walking, I've been sensing something around the entire forest."

"You mean, like hidden knights?" Tansu asked.

I looked up at the trees. "No. It's more like some unseen force is covering the entire forest. I think this force is what makes people's sense of direction go disarray. Someone doesn't want anybody finding out what's in this forest."

"Oh yeah?" Nova replied, still unconvinced, "Like who?"

As if on cue to answer his question, there was loud rustling in the treetops. We immediately jumped up from the ground and into battle stances. Suddenly, twelve figures dropped from the trees and surrounded us in a semicircle with the arrows notched in their bows, all pointed at our chests.

Even though I had never seen one, I knew our foes were elves because they looked like humans, but with very pointy ears. There was also a sense of magic coming from them. An elderly looking elf with long, shimmering, silver hair and golden eyes, dressed in simple leather armor from head to toe came forward from behind two elves who had their sights on me.

"It's incredible that someone figured out the secret of why this forest will not let anyone out," he said, sounding very impressed by my deductions, "but it won't matter. We can't have anyone tell the world of our secret place."

He then commanded the others, "On my mark, fire! Ready?"

"Got any ideas on how to get out of here?" Nova asked me.

The elves had blocked every possible escape route. "I guess we have no choice but to fight. Get ready for my signal."

Tansu and Nova nodded and got ready.

When I drew out the Sword of the Wyvern, the elderly elf took one look and quickly cried out, "Hold your fire! Lay down your arms now!"

Everyone, including us, was confused by his sudden change in attitude, but the elves did as they were told. He then came over to me and actually bowed to us. "Forgive my rudeness. I didn't know we were in the presence of the one chosen by Ska himself. I'm Tybal, Commander of Her Highness's Guards."

I looked at both Tansu and Nova and saw they also didn't have a clue as to what was going on. However, seeing as the elves didn't want to harm us now, I sheathed my sword.

"Uh… okay. I'm Shirai, and these are my friends Tansu and Nova."

Tybal smiled. "Ah, so you're the one who took on General Lorimar and unleashed the Power of Ska. Our Highness said you would be coming through soon and that we must bring you to see her."

"Bring us where? How did she know we would be coming? And what is the Power of Ska?"

"Be patient, my friend. All will be revealed soon."

Tybal signaled his troops, and they began muttering under their breath. From what I could hear, it was a language I had never heard before. As they muttered, I felt a wave of what I could only describe as pure magic filling the air. The feeling must have been strong, because from the way Tansu and Nova were looking around the area, they must have felt it too.

Finally, the elves stopped, and when they did, the entire area changed. Instead of a dense forest, we were now standing at the entrance of a large village.

"What was that all about?" Nova asked Tybal.

"The home of the elves, Elruan, is hidden from the eyes of man with elfin magic. Come, Her Highness is waiting for you."

Tybal led all of us into the village while his soldiers stayed behind. After another chant, the entrance to Elruan again closed.

I was in awe at the things I saw.

Unlike the trees we saw before, the ones in the village were spaced further apart so plenty of sunlight could come in. Built in the very same trees were houses, each one done in a style both beautiful and mysterious.

Connecting the houses were sturdy rope bridges linking each tree with another. Some trees had wooden ramps that went to the ground so people on the ground could get to the treetops.

While there were buildings on the ground, the ones in the trees must have been residential homes. A lot of elves were looking down at us from up there. They were all staring at us like we were criminals.

"Amazing! To think all this is hidden by magic!" Tansu exclaimed.

"I know, Tansu, but why is everyone staring at us?" I asked Tybal.

"They haven't seen any humans since the last one was willingly admitted here. It was the great-great-grandfather of the current ruler of the Arc Kingdom. He had saved our last queen from falling into the hands of a group who wanted knowledge of how we elves utilize our magic to use in a plot to overthrow Arc. Such an event left an unpleasant impression of how humans are."

"Well, now I can understand why you elves are not so keen on us humans," Nova said carelessly.

"Nova! Watch what you say! We're guests here!" Tansu scolded.

Nova went quiet after that.

We were eventually led to a large building, almost like a castle, built between two large trees. The inside was filled with flowers of all kinds, lined against each wall like a rainbow. Light came from large windows and bathed them in much needed sunlight. Small canals allowed water to come into the building that ended up in pools beneath the flowers.

We came to a pair of giant wooden doors where Tybal shouted, "Your Highness, it is Tybal, your loyal commander."

A soft, elegant voice replied, "You may enter."

We entered the throne room. The same flowers as in the other chamber lined the walls. They went all the way behind a throne sitting in the back carved from a tree that may have once stood in the middle of the palace. Two large windows sat high above both sides of the throne.

There, waiting for us, was a regal-looking woman. Since I had no idea how fast elves aged, from what I could see, she looked to be in her early thirties. Her long, smooth, shining blonde hair hung down to her knees and seemed to glow. She had the greenest eyes imaginable that seemed to judge our every move. Her long, flowing aquamarine-colored robe reached down to the floor, covering her feet.

Tybal walked up to the woman, got down on one knee, and humbly said, "Your Highness, I have brought the ones you have been waiting for."

"Thank you, Tybal. You may resume your duties. I would like to speak to the three alone."

Tybal nodded his head, got up, and left the room, leaving us alone with the queen. We just stood there rigid, not wanting to do anything to upset her.

"I'm Queen Eri, Leader of the Elves." She must have sensed how tense we were, because she smiled kindly. "You have no need to be so tense around me."

After we loosened up, I replied politely, "Thank you, Your Highness."

"Please, Shirai. No need to be formal. I get tired of hearing that all the time."

I looked at the queen, puzzled, "How did you know my name? We didn't tell you who we are."

Again, Eri smiled. "I know a lot of things. For instance, the young lady's name is Tansu, from Kenga Village, and the young man is Nova, former resident of Ranu Village. Right now you are trying to find the dragons of the Dante Mountains to find a clue as to who you are."

I was speechless.

"How do you know about all that, Lady Eri?" Tansu asked.

"My people's magic is tied to the very land itself. We can feel any changes going on from even the farthest reaches of Lu' Cel." Eri stopped talking for a moment as her expression suddenly became serious. "And for a while, we've been sensing that something horrible is going to descend on Lu' Cel… and the starting point will be at Hariel."

"You mean the fact that Grant has been invading other kingdoms?" Nova asked.

Eri shook her head. "Grant is just a part of the problem. I believe there is something more sinister behind this. Despite our power, we can't sense this unknown player. Ska may be the only one who knows what evil is happening to Lu' Cel."

"If your ties to Lu' Cel are that strong, couldn't you use your magic to contact the dragons from here so we can find out what is going on?" I asked Eri.

Again, she shook her head. "If it were possible, we would have done so. In order for us to communicate with the dragons, their minds must be open. In the past their minds were open to us, but six years ago, they closed them off. We have no idea what has happened to them."

I couldn't believe that even the dragons were being affected by this war. It must be something big if they refused to talk with even the elves. "That time again? Everything seems to point toward Grant: the disappearance of Prince Aynor and my sword. If that's the case, I'm afraid that we must be going if we're to make it to the Dante Mountains so we can get the answers we need in time."

The queen again sounded serious. "I'm afraid that would be risky at the moment."

"Why is that?" Tansu asked.

"Two days ago we had sensed that Grant's army was on the move. They are currently heading for Arc Castle. If you go now, they may get their hands on the Sword of the Wyvern."

All three of us gasped in silence.

"Arc is going to be attacked soon?" Nova shouted. "They might not be able to stop this raid like always! Why don't you elves help them?"

"Unfortunately, I must put the wellbeing of my people first. Even though my family is in debt to the royal family for saving our past queen's life, we personally do not want to become active in the war."

Looking out the nearby window that had a view of the elves that lived in the treetops, Eri looked despondent. "Aside from that, as you probably saw on your way here, most of my people dislike humans and wish to not have anything to do with them. I can't very well force them to consider helping them if they think like that."

"So you're just going to stay neutral until Grant does the same thing he nearly did to Gale?" Tansu angrily asked.

"Both of you calm down!" I spoke as sternly as possible.

"But Shirai…"

"I know how you both feel. However, Eri has a point. She can't risk her people's safety."

While I too thought that Eri should help the people of Arc, the way the two were going, I was afraid that they may do or say something they might regret. To my relief, they calmed down.

"I'm sorry about that, Eri." I bowed to her. "They shouldn't have talked like that."

She shook her head. "No, they are right in what they say. A good leader makes sure to take everyone's feelings into consideration."

I could tell by the way Eri sounded that she *did* want to help Arc.

"While I can't do anything for Arc, I can at least make your stay more comfortable. You may stay in our village as our guests, as long as you don't leave Elruan until it is safe to continue. I'll have Tybal show you where you can stay."

When she mentioned Tybal, I quickly remembered there was one more thing I needed to bring up. "Thank you, but there was something I wanted to know first."

"What is it, Shirai?"

"Tybal mentioned something about the Power of Ska. What is that?"

Eri said nothing for a moment. Finally she answered, "I'm afraid all we know about that is what was left in ancient elfin lore. The Dragon Race is known for possessing powers that exceed any other on Lu' Cel. Ska's power is so great, he could literally convert his strength into a force that could create life, change it, or eradicate it completely. So far, we know he has only used it for peaceful purposes and not once for evil intentions. I hope you found what I explained useful."

I didn't. In fact, it only made things worse, but I couldn't tell her that after she'd been so kind to us. "Thank you."

We started to leave, but before we even reached the door the queen suddenly spoke up, "One more thing, Shirai."

We all faced her again.

"What is it?"

"Be wary of using that power. It is neither good nor evil. Only the one wielding it can make it either. If you're not careful, you might end up causing harm to others, including yourself."

I paused to take in her warning. I thanked her, and we left.

It wasn't until we were at the castle steps that my friends decided to speak, starting with Tansu. "Are you just going to let this happen, Shirai?"

"You don't think I want to do something to help? But right now, I think we should take some time to think things through."

I was trying hard not to get angrier than I was. I had thought I could get some clue as to who I was from the queen, but I had just been subjected to more questions.

Nova came next with his own opinion. "I can't believe you, Shirai! You were the first one to jump at helping the people of Gale but now you're acting like a…"

His comment finally got my temper up. "That's enough, Nova! I can't be at two places at once! It also doesn't help matters that everything the queen explained was too much for me to grasp! I just don't know what to make of anything anymore!"

When I realized I had snapped at my friends, I told them, "I'm sorry, you guys. It's just I'm stressed out from everything that has happened."

Nova replied, "No, we should be sorry too. We forget that you have been through a lot. We should have been more supportive."

Tansu agreed with him.

I smiled. "Maybe we *should* take a little time off and relax. I wonder if we can get someone to show us around the village."

"I can help you with that!" an energetic voice suddenly spoke out right before I felt my arm being grabbed and pulled me off the stairs to the ground a foot below.

9 - The Elfin Girl

When I recovered from my fall, I looked at who had my arm and saw a young elf girl holding my arm in a death grip as she smiled at me. "It's nice to finally meet you!"

She looked the same age as Tansu, with shoulder-length, brilliant orange hair with a yellow hair band. Her green eyes looked at me with such eagerness. Whereas the other elves I saw wore plain clothing, she had an orange red, short-sleeve top made of silky material with a rose-colored vest of the same material over the first. Long, amber-colored pants, with a picture of a dove sown on the right pants leg, reached down to the sandals on her feet

"Shirai! What happened?" Tansu asked. She was bending slightly over the edge of the stairs so she could see me.

"I'm sorry about pulling you down like that," the elf girl said, "but it's my first time to see humans up close! Especially one who has Ska's blessings."

She finally let go of my arm.

"It's okay… uh…"

"My name is Sara. And what are yours?"

"I'm Shirai." I saw that Tansu and Nova were now standing next to us, so I motioned to them. "They're Tansu and Nova, my friends."

"Kinda clingy for an elf, aren't you? You always greet strangers like that?" Nova asked as he helped me up to my feet.

Sara too got up from the ground, "Sorry, it's just…"

Mystery elf girl

She stopped mid-sentence as she looked toward the castle entrance. She suddenly sounded edgy as she quickly said, "Sorry to cut this short, but I've got to move! I'll come by later!"

Before anyone could stop her, she had disappeared behind the castle just as the gate opened. Out came Tybal. "There you are. Is something wrong?"

"Uh no… Everything's fine."

"Very well. The queen has explained everything. Follow me, please."

Tybal led us to a medium-sized building on the ground level nearby. The inside was simple, but different than any room we'd seen. There were three beds and a large table with three chairs. On two of the walls were open windows. But what made this room different was the fact that on another wall was a small spring out of which water flowed.

"These will be your quarters until it is safe for you to leave. Food will be brought to you shortly. The water here is so you may wash up or to get a drink. If you need anything else, please call for me."

"Thank you, Tybal," Tansu said.

He bowed slightly and left. As soon as he was gone, Nova plopped himself down on one of the beds, "Man, this place is something, isn't it?"

"I'll say." I, too, sat down on one of the beds. "The elves seem to be able to coexist with nature. I bet if they shared their secrets with others, life would be better for a lot of people."

I looked at Tansu, who seemed was deep in thought.

"What is it, Tansu?"

"Oh nothing, Shirai. I was just thinking about that strange girl, Sara."

"Did someone mention my name?" We all leapt in fright when Sara's voice came out of nowhere. A second later, she jumped into the room through one of the open windows.

"Haven't you ever heard of knocking?" Nova shouted.

She grinned. "I'm so sorry, but I need to make sure no one saw me come here."

"Is that why you just left like that back at the castle?" Tansu asked as she sat down on one of the chairs.

Sara also sat down. "Yep. Anyway, it's cool that Her Highness is letting you three stay with us for a bit."

Sara was talking like she was excited by the news. She wasn't acting like the elves we had seen. In fact, she was the exact opposite.

"We have no choice," I told her. "If we left now, we'd risk the chance that Grant's army will ambush us and try to take the Sword of the Wyvern from us."

Sara didn't say anything as she suddenly got up and, without warning, took hold of my sword. I tensed up, but I felt as though she wasn't going to do anything with it. She just stared at the blade for a moment.

"So this is the sword I heard the queen talk about," her tone suddenly sounded bitter. "She said that Grant has been looking for it everywhere, and he is willing to do anything to get it."

We all just looked at her. As she stared at the sword, a small frown appearing on her face.

"Is there something wrong, Sara? You look like you're seeing someone you detest," Nova asked.

It looked like she was going to say something when she suddenly froze just like she did before. "Uh-oh! I've got to go!"

She handed me back the sword and ran to one of the windows. Before she left, she turned to us. "I'll come back and show you around our village, so don't go anywhere with anyone else!"

With that, she was gone again. At that moment, the main door opened, and two elves came in, holding plates filled with different kinds of food, some things I had never seen before. There was fruit that was a bluish color—even though it looked like apples, silver-colored berries, and too many others to describe.

Without saying anything, the two elves bowed their heads quickly and left the house, leaving us alone with the strange food in front of us.

"So… who's going to taste first?" Nova asked, obviously reluctant to try them.

"What do you think, they put something in the food, and you're afraid to try it? That's not like you, Nova. You used to eat anything given to you, no matter what it looked like."

Nova eyed me slyly. "If you're so sure of yourself, why don't you go first than?"

"Okay, I will."

I started to pick up the blue apple, but for some reason, my hand stopped an inch away from it. I began to think of what might happen if we *did* eat elfin food, and I quickly took my hand away from the apple.

Nova laughed when he saw me pull my hand back, "So you're afraid to do it too!"

I felt like giving him a good beating when Tansu suddenly spoke up, "You guys are impossible! I'll try it!"

She quickly picked up the same blue apple and took a bite out of it. The two of us watched for any changes that might happen to Tansu, but nothing did. Finally she swallowed, and with a big smile said, "Amazing! This is even tastier than the apples I grow back home!"

Seeing her react like that, I quickly took some of the silver berries and put them in my mouth. I couldn't believe how sweet and juicy they were. It was like eating honey and peaches at the same time.

"It is good!"

Nova still hesitated, but eventually he did eat some of the food, and his reaction was the same as ours. With that problem over, we finished what was left and afterward went to bed. I was so tired from walking through the woods earlier that I was sound asleep in a matter of minutes. The next day, Sara was true to her word, and she showed us around the place.

The things I saw in the elfin village were not like anything I had seen so far.

In the back of the village was a small lake with two waterfalls cascading from cliffs high above. What made even it more special was that, in between the two falls, there was a large rainbow, visible even from a distance. We took this opportunity to do some swimming. The water felt cool as we had a small water war with each other.

Sara won.

She took us to a giant archery range next. Several elves were already there practicing. However, they weren't using regular arrows. A few seconds after hitting the target, these arrows disappeared and reappeared in the archer's hand. Tansu took a turn and managed to outshoot most of the elves there. Despite the fact they didn't like humans, those she beat wanted rematches later.

Next, Sara took us to a holding pen for deer-like animals. While they looked like normal deer, their horns were a bronze color, and they had a horse's mane going all the way down their backs. Instead of a small tail, they had a cat tail. They were called Cerquline, considered sacred to the elves. Sara said they were supposed to like humans.

They didn't seem to like Nova, as they kept trying to bite him whenever he got close.

For the next couple of days, Sara continued to show us the incredible sights of Elruan, and during that time, we all became good friends with her.

One day, we were brought to a place high above the treetops. There was a bench so people could sit down and enjoy the view. One could see for miles away, or in my case, even farther.

I could see Gale City, and in the opposite direction, Arc Kingdom. However, I couldn't see Grant's troops. They must still be approaching from further away. The more I looked at Arc, the more I wanted to leave this place and go help the people there. Knowing the risk in that, I faced a different direction, and there in my view, was the place we were heading for: The Dante Mountains.

From what I could see, it was so bleak and dismal that I began to wonder how anyone, even dragons, could live there.

"We'll be heading there soon, you guys." I said.

Tansu and Nova came over and also looked at the mountains in the distance.

"Not exactly what you call a fun spot," Nova said ominously. "They say anyone who is foolish enough to try to climb them is never heard from again, nor are their bodies ever found."

"Even if that's true, Nova, we can't back down now," Tansu explained. "We directly interfered with Grant's plans, so we can't go back to our normal lives. We have to see this through, not only to get answers, but to help Shirai too."

"Thanks, Tansu." I turned back to Sara, "Hey Sara! Come and see this—"

I stopped when I saw her. She was just sitting on the bench, looking as if the world had ended.

"Sara? What is it?" Tansu asked as she went over and sat down next to Sara.

"That... that mountain. I wish you wouldn't go there. It's been nothing but trouble." She sounded extremely depressed.

"But we have to," Nova said. "We need to find Ska and find out what is going on; not to mention Shirai may finally remember who he is."

That didn't change Sara's attitude. She looked up at us with heavy eyes. "He won't help Shirai... none of the dragons will help. You think you're the first ones to try and ask them for help? Ever since the war started, many men have tried to see Ska, but they all failed. Even my father wanted to get his advice and... he..."

Tansu suddenly grabbed Nova by the arm and pulled him away from the rest of us.

"What did you do that for?" I overheard Nova complain.

"You need to learn when to be comforting and not just say whatever is on your mind, especially since you saw how upset Sara was already!" Tansu argued. "Now go apologize!"

I looked away as Nova passed by me to hide the small smirk I had. He walked over to Sara and he held out his hand to her, "Sara, I'm sorry for upsetting you. I should've asked why you were sad first. Will you forgive this idiot?"

Sara looked at Nova for a moment. Her face grew happier as she took his hand. "Just be careful next time. You make sure you know about somebody before you say things like that."

"Then I think we better start on that while we are stuck here. What *was* your father like?" Tansu asked.

Sara didn't answer immediately, as if trying to find a way to tell us. "Well, to tell the truth—"

My senses suddenly picked up something, something evil coming at us at a high speed.

"Everyone, get down from here, now!"

With great speed, Nova picked Sara up, and we all leapt from the area. As soon as we were off, it was engulfed in a fiery explosion.

We landed on the roof of one of the treetop houses. The elves inside came running out of their home to see what was happening. We jumped off the roof and landed next to them.

"What in Asteron's name is going on here?" a male elf demanded.

"No time to explain!" I told them, "Go! Tell your queen you're under attack!"

"What are you talking about?" the elf next to the male asked.

"Please don't argue with him!" Sara spoke out, "Go and tell her now!"

The two elves looked at Sara with shock, "You... you're—"

"Yes, I am. Now go!"

The two elves quickly leapt down to the ground below.

As I turned to ask Sara what was going on, Tansu shouted, "Shirai! Look!"

She pointed to someone on a nearby branch. When I saw who it was, I reached for the Sword of the Wyvern.

Standing on the branch, acting all innocent, was Ignotus!

10 - Evil Magic versus Good Magic

"**I**gnotus!"

The sorcerer chuckled, "So this is where you disappeared to. Hanging out with a bunch of nature-loving tree folk."

"Who is he? I sense evil magic coming from him," Sara asked.

"That's Ignotus, Grant's personal sorcerer," Nova quickly replied, the Tao Spear held tightly in his hand. Tansu had her bow ready to launch arrows, while I had my hand on my sword's hilt ready to bring it out immediately.

"*He's* the one who destroyed Ranu in a single day?"

"It was such an easy task. The best day of my life, listening to the screams of those pathetic peasants as they burned away!" Ignotus laughed. Nova's expression became more and more angry. Ignotus finally noticed Nova glaring at him, "What's wrong? Offended about the way I think how useless that eyesore of a village was, even though it's true?"

Nova lunged forward. "You bastard!"

Sara grabbed his arm tightly. "No, Nova!"

"Let me go! He must pay for what he said about Ranu!" Nova tried to break away from Sara, but she was stronger than she looked because she didn't budge.

"He's trying to make you angry so you'll make a mistake and then he'll kill you!"

"Maybe so but—"

Sara put her hands on both of Nova's arms. "Listen to me, Nova! My father once gave me some very good advice! You can't let his words interfere with your judgment! Think with your mind, not your heart!"

That was good advice indeed. I should have thought about that with my battle with Lorimar. It got to Nova too. He stopped trying to break away from Sara and calmed down.

"That's pretty good advice your father gave you, Sara," Nova said.

Again Ignotus chuckled. "Yes, very interesting choice of words, especially coming from the mouth of a half-elf such as you."

We all turned to face Sara, who now hung her head in shame.

"Sara, what's he talking about?" Tansu asked.

"My father was a human. He fell in love with my mother, and they were married despite the villagers' protest. Everything went okay from there till five months ago. My father left the village, hoping to try to make contact with the dragons, but he never came back." Small tears trickled down Sara's cheeks.

"Is that why you look sad sometimes?" I asked.

Sara quickly shook her head "Not just that. Because I'm a half-elf, I sometimes feel like I'm alone. My father was the only human in our village, and there isn't another half-elf like me. Even though everyone here is nice to me... I wanted real friends who don't care if I'm human or even an elf."

I felt like that when I found out about my transformation. I started to say something, but Nova interrupted, "Is that all? Why didn't you just say that? We're already friends, have been since we first saw you. I mean look at us! We're friends with someone who is half-dragon! You really think such a thing matters to us?"

Sara stopped crying as she realized that what Nova said was true. Despite my annoyance with that half-dragon comment Nova made, I was glad he had spoken.

"You're right. Thanks, you guys."

Suddenly Ignotus started to cackle hysterically.

"What's so funny, you bastard?" Tansu glared at him.

"You're the offspring of that wimp of a man who was the last one to try to climb the Dante Mountains!"

"And how do you know him?" Sara asked.

His mouth curled into a cruel smile, "Who do you think makes sure that no one ever makes it to the dragons, huh? His death was especially delightful, as he fell into a deep crevasse, screaming!"

That was it for me. Not only had this monster destroyed entire villages, but he was making sure no one could get to Ska.

Something inside me snapped. I flew at Ignotus with such speed I sliced into his robe and nearly struck his abdomen with my talons. I then landed on his branch like a cat, my claws digging tightly into the wood.

"You will never leave this place alive!" I roared, my hatred for him filling every corner of my soul.

"So you have gotten better," he sneered. "However, this time I came prepared!"

Ignotus snapped his fingers, and hundreds of strange, flying creatures flew down from the sky. They looked like distorted rats with tiny wings on their backs. They were only the size of a dinner plates, but from out of their mouths came balls of black energy that did incredible damage to anything they touched. They whirled past us.

"Tansu! Nova! You got to stop those things!"

Tansu started to speak, "But, Shirai—"

"*Go!*"

Tansu and Nova went after the monsters. Sara dropped from the tree and began running to the other homes.

I went at Ignotus with everything I had. I was in such a blind rage that I used all my strength to try and kill him. Ignotus tried different kinds of magic—fireballs, small flying boulders, even mini tornados. My desire to see him dead forced my body further, and I dodged every attack. We leaped from branch to branch, neither of us able to get at the other.

"Incredible! The Power of Ska is simply amazing! Such energy, such raw power!" He was more amused with the fighting than he was trying to actually hit me. I, on the other hand, was going to make sure that his head would be cut off.

But like Sara said, I was listening to my heart instead of my mind. I learned that when I saw out of the corner of my eye one of the flying monsters going straight at Sara, who was busy trying to help a pregnant mother escape. I couldn't get away to help them as the thing fired at her!

"Sara! Look out!"

But it was too late, and I was sure that she was going to die. Then, from out of nowhere, Nova came and blocked the incoming attack with his back. He fell to the ground, writhing in pain.

"Nova! Are you all right?" Sara shouted.

Nova's back was burned through his now badly damaged armor.

Seeing my best friend hurt pushed me further over the edge, "I'll kill you!"

I began to feel the same rush of power that I had felt before I unleashed Ska's power on Lorimar. Only this time, it came quickly and filled my body with overflowing energy. I began to wildly shoot off blasts of energy trying to get Ignotus.

"Kill me? The way you are acting now? You'll never even touch me! But then again, I was like that before. You and I are so much alike!"

"We are not alike!"

✶✶✶✶✶

Meanwhile, Sara tried to franticly revive Nova, "Nova! Nova! Wake up!"

She was relieved to see his eyes open.

"Do you have to shout like that?" he said in a low voice.

"You idiot! Why did you do that?!"

"It's like you say… sometimes I'm an idiot. What's happening with Shirai and Ignotus?"

Sara pointed to where the two were battling. Nova, being as observant as always, noticed Shirai's strange behavior. But it was when he saw Shirai use the same power that he used in Gale City that he began to worry.

"Sara! Please… if you can use magic like the others do, stop Shirai!" he said in a worried tone.

"But why…"

"That power that he's using. It doesn't feel right. It feels… too violent. It could destroy him. Please…"

He blacked out from the pain. At that moment, Tybal and a couple of guards came up from behind Sara.

"What in Asteron's name are you—"

Sara cut him off, "Tybal! Take Nova to our best healer now, then go help Tansu and the others get rid of the monsters!"

Tybal didn't say anything else as he made one of the elves carry Nova away, while Sara hurried to help Shirai.

✳✳✳✳✳

I began to feel exhausted from using Ska's power so much that I was beginning to slow down. Ignotus noticed the change in my movement and took this opportunity to get up close and blast me into a nearby tree with a barrage of sharp rocks.

I landed hard on the forest floor with a loud crash. Even though I was wearing armor, the parts of my body that weren't covered were so badly cut up from the spell; along with the fact that I had shot off all those blasts, I couldn't move. I had to watch as Ignotus slowly come over to me.

"In the end, this is what happens to those who try to foolishly use a power they were never meant to control. You'll never be able to defeat me if you can't grasp that concept. But it doesn't matter anyway ... for you will die right here and now!"

He began gathering streams of blood-red-colored energy until it began to form an orb in his palm. I waited for the end to come, cursing my own stupidity.

But it never came. Out of the tree that I was leaning against a giant fist made of wood came flying from the trunk and struck Ignotus at full force!

"What was that?" he shouted as he regained his balance.

From behind the tree, Sara slowly stepped out. "That was just a small sample of what elfin magic is capable of! So back away now if you don't want another taste of what I can do!"

"Foolish girl. Your magic can't hope to defeat mine!"

Ignotus launched a fireball at Sara. She immediately held one arm out and clenched her fingers into a fist. She brought her fist up, and a ball of water emerged from out of the ground and intercepted the fireball, which went up as steam.

He attacked with a huge icicle that he sent flying at Sara. She countered by quickly getting to ground level, and as if she was pulling something out of a bag, pulled up a wall of solid rock. It took the brunt of the attack.

"Impressive, little girl, but not good enough!"

Ignotus disappeared, but Sara didn't lose her cool. Closing her eyes, she stood still and waited for whatever he had planned to come. A split second later, her eyes snapped open, and quickly twirling around, she moved her hand like she was using a whip to wrap around something. A visible gust of wind appeared and did wrap around something, namely a hidden Ignotus. Sara flung him over her shoulder where he landed at the base of a large tree.

"Don't try to fool my instinct by trying such a maneuver," she scoffed.

"Very well then, let's see how you handle this!"

Ignotus tried to go for another attack, but Sara was quick to make some vines that hung in the treetops come and bind him. Before he had a chance to react, the vines quickly lifted him up into the air and flung him into the trunk, like what had happened to me. He made a loud crash as his body hit the tree. Ignotus staggered and struggled to get back on his feet.

"How? How can this—?"

Ignotus saw me coming at him at that moment. I slashed my talons down his chest, leaving five deep gashes. The attack forced away part of the hood that covered his face so I could finally see what he looked like.

When I did, my blood ran cold, and I felt nauseous. Ignotus took this free moment and knocked me back with his arm, and with his other arm covering his face, ran away. At this time, Tansu and Tybal appeared. They quickly came over to my side.

"Shirai! He's getting away! Why don't you go after him?" Tybal asked.

I didn't answer.

"What's wrong?"

"Stop it, Tybal! Something is wrong with him!" Tansu got down on the ground and held my hand.

"Shirai, are you okay? Did something happen?"

I still didn't answer. I was planted where I was, my whole body starting to shake with fear at what I had seen.

"You're shaking! Tell me what's wrong!"

I tried to get the words out of my mouth, "His... face... his face."

"You saw what Ignotus looked like? Is that what happened?"

"His face... I..."

Before I could get anything else out, I collapsed.

11 - Joining Together

"**W**hat's going on?"

When I opened my eyes again, I was standing in the middle of a burning village. Houses were on fire and the scent of fresh human blood filled the air.

I ran through the blaze trying to find anyone who was still alive. All I found were hundreds of corpses, all of them horrifically mutilated by something or someone.

Just then, the sound of a woman screaming caught my attention. Following the sound, I was terrified to see that it was Tansu who was screaming. Next to her, crumpled on the ground were Nova and Sara, already dead.

Standing in front of her was Ignotus.

"Tansu!"

I tried to move in, but some unseen force was holding me in place. I had to watch helplessly as Ignotus killed her. To make it more painful, he somehow used the Power of Ska to do it.

"No… everyone… Ignotus! You *animal*!"

Whatever had a hold on me finally lifted and I came at him. I practically ripped the hood from his head with every intention of tearing his throat out for what he had done.

I staggered back when I saw that underneath the hood the face was not who I originally thought… but me as I am now!

"What are you talking about? Ignotus didn't kill everyone … you did. After all, you're the only one here." Hearing Ignotus's voice coming out of my mouth further terrified me.

I thought he was trying to confuse me, but when I glanced down for a second, I saw that I was wearing the same robe he wore. Looking back up, I saw that the other person was gone, leaving me alone in the middle of all the carnage.

"No! I couldn't have!" I screamed. "I don't believe it!"

"But it's true," the disembodied voice of Ignotus replied. "You're the only one that has the ability to use that power. Calling yourself an animal doesn't suit you, though. Monster would have been better!"

His cackling was so deafening I covered my ears to block it out. The second I placed my hands on the sides of my head, I felt that they were moist. When I looked at my hands, I cringed. Both of them were covered in blood.

"See? You *are* a monster. Killing your friends wasn't enough, but to take pleasure in feeling their blood on your hands was too much. You're no human, but just a bloodthirsty creature."

I screamed so loudly that any other sound was drowned out.

It wasn't until I noticed that I was someplace else that I stopped screaming. I wasn't in the burning village anymore, but in the building that Queen Eri arranged for us to stay in. I could feel sweat from my forehead rolling down my head.

Was all that… a dream?

Looking down, I was relieved to see I was wearing the clothes Tansu made for me. Someone had taken my armor off, which was placed next to the Sword of the Wyvern, and had wrapped most of my body in bandages.

Why am I like this? And why am I here? It wasn't long before I quickly remembered what happened. *That's right. Ignotus attacked, and I fought him; but I totally lost it, and he got the best of me. Sara came in and saved me, and then I managed to get at Ignotus and—*

When the memory of what I saw under Ignotus's hood came back, I once again felt sick to my stomach.

What is going on? Why does he look like—

I was too tired and weak to try to figure out the reason, so I let it drop for now. Slowly, I got out of bed and walked toward the front door. As I was about to touch the handle of the door, I heard voices coming from the other side.

"It's been five days now. Is he still out, Tansu?" It was Nova speaking.

"Yes. We're lucky that the elves had expert knowledge in the medical arts." This time it was Tansu speaking. "But I'm more worried about what happened to Shirai."

"You mean the way he was acting?" Sara's voice came in. "Maybe he lost control of his anger. It happens."

Tansu again spoke, this time sounding a bit scared. "No. I don't think it's that simple. When I saw his eyes… he… was like a wild animal—so full of rage and murderous intent. I thought he was going to turn into a monster."

How can she call me that? I was shaken.

I thought back to the fight and then the dream. She was right. The angrier I got, the more I lost control of myself. When I was using Ska's power, I hadn't felt the same fierceness last time, only rage and hatred.

It was just like the queen had warned me about.

Nova came in, suggesting, "I'm starting to think maybe being blessed by Ska isn't that great. Who knows when or if Shirai will go off like that again? For his sake, maybe we should just stop this trip."

A shiver ran down my spine. *Stop?*

"How can you say that, Nova?" Sara argued. "You're his best friend!"

"I'm saying that because I *am* his best friend! I don't want to see him like that ever again!"

My fingers started to curl up into a fist. *You idiot! Because of your stupid mistake, they may just leave you! Damn it!*

Before I could put myself down even further, Nova said, "But I also know it's not fair to him if he is stuck like he is now, with no memory of his own life or of his parents or knowing if he even had any."

"No. It wouldn't be fair to him or to us," Tansu sighed softly. "Leaving him at this point would just truly be cruel. For his sake, I'm still going with him. Seeing what happened to him, he's going to need somebody to make sure he doesn't stray down that path again."

Nova chuckled, "Well, if that's what you want, guess the same goes for me. He goes off like that again, one good whack from my spear will guarantee that he'll be his old self again!"

"Shirai is so lucky to have you two as friends," Sara pointed out.

I couldn't believe that, despite everything I had done, they would still be at my side.

Sara was right. I had good friends.

When I heard them come closer to the door I quickly got back into bed.

"Shirai! You're finally awake!" Nova said.

"Yep. And I see that you're okay too."

"It was thanks to Sara's quick thinking that I'm still standing." He winked as he said that.

"Oh come now, Nova. A burn like that couldn't kill an idiot like you," Sara joked.

This started a friendly fight between her and Nova. Tansu ignored them and sat down by my side.

"I'm so glad that you are all right," Tansu said.

"Tansu."

"What is it—?"

Without any warning, I wrapped my arms around her and held her close. Nova and Sara stopped their bickering and looked our way.

"Shi … Shirai? What—?"

"I don't want to be a monster." I spoke in a low tone. "Please don't leave … and let me become one."

As I held her, I felt small tears running down my cheek. She didn't say or do anything for a moment. Finally, she wrapped her arms around me.

"I won't, Shirai. I won't."

The two of us sat there for a long time. Nova and Sara were about to leave the room to give us some privacy when Tybal suddenly came inside. "I see you are finally up, Shirai."

The second he came in, we pulled away from each other. Quickly wiping away the leftover tears from my face, I looked at Tybal. "Yes, I'm fine now."

Tybal was puzzled at first by what we just did, but he regained his senses. "Well, I'm glad. The reason for my visit is that Her Majesty has called a meeting with her people. She sensed that you had awakened, and she wants you and your friends to be there."

Tansu frowned. "Right now? But Shirai just—"

"It's okay, Tansu, I'll be fine. We should go see what this is about."

Seeing that she was outnumbered, Tansu didn't argue further. A few minutes later, we were standing in front of a huge crowd of elves in the front of the castle. Hundreds of soldiers stood in front of each side of the staircase, each one saluting Eri, who had come out of the castle.

"I have some important matters to discuss with all of you." She looked toward me. "First off, I am thankful for our guests' help in stopping Ignotus's onslaught on our home."

"It was nothing, Your Majesty." I replied humbly.

Suddenly turning toward Nova, she added, "And I want to give you special thanks, Nova, for protecting my daughter, Sara."

All three of us nearly fell backward as we shouted at the same time, *"Daughter?"*

"Oh. Did I forget to mention that the one my father married was the queen?" Sara acted as if she was the innocent one.

"It would have been nice," Nova replied angrily.

"I see she's still like her father, a fiery spirited girl," Eri said jokingly.

"Mother! How can you say that?"

Politely ignoring her daughter, Eri looked out at all of her people. "The main reason I have called you here is because, as of now, the elves are going to assist those being threatened by Grant."

There were loud mutterings coming from the soldiers and the other elves. Eri shouted, "Silence! This is not the time to be worrying about the reasons why we do or don't hate humans!"

All of the elves quickly fell silent as the queen continued her speech. "The attack by the one called Ignotus has shown me that Grant does not care who gets caught up in his mad plan. We must help Shirai's group and our neighbor Arc. Let us show this king that, despite our neutrality, we are a nation that will not allow such acts to go unpunished!"

A mighty cry filled the air as everyone cheered on their queen. Even we joined in. Eri raised up a hand so everyone knew to stop cheering.

"Our first priority is to send many of our warriors to Arc Kingdom to strengthen their defense. The next will be sending others to Gale City to round up volunteers to aid in a counterattack as soon as possible. Now go!"

Everyone left except Tansu, Nova, Sara, Tybal, me, and a couple of soldiers.

"Thank you, Your Highness, for coming through," I said to her.

Eri shook her head. "I should be thanking you for proving to us that sitting on the sidelines is not something that can last long."

Tybal stepped forward. "I have sent some of our most skilled magic users to cause a diversion so you can make it past Grant's knights and reach the Dante Mountains. With Ignotus indisposed of for now, you may finally succeed where others have failed."

"That's good to hear," Nova said happily.

"We would also like to give you something to help you." The queen looked at Tybal. "If you would please?"

Tybal nodded and signaled one of the soldiers to come over. The soldier handed something to Tybal. As he walked over to Tansu, I saw he was holding a quiver of the magic arrows she had used when we were at the shooting range.

"These arrows will always come back to their user's quiver so you never run out. I hope you find it helpful to your cause."

He handed it to Tansu, who thanked him and replaced the quiver she had with the new one. I thought that was the end of things at that point, but Sara suddenly got on one knee and looked up at her mother with a determined look in her eyes.

"Mother! With your permission, I would like to go with them on their journey!" she shouted.

No one was expecting her to say that, much less Tybal, who quickly shouted, "Sara! As your watcher, you can't be serious! Think of how this will affect your mother!"

Sara got up and faced Tybal. "I can't stand by and let what happened here continue somewhere else! I know it may be dangerous, but if we have even the slightest chance of succeeding, I want to be there when it happens and—"

"Sara!" Eri's voice was loud and clear, and the argument stopped right then and there.

"Mother."

Eri sighed. "If you must go, then you might as well wait until everyone is completely healed before heading out."

Sara smiled.

"But Your Highness…"

"She's not a little child anymore, Tybal. Sara's old enough to make her own decisions, and I can think of no better way to start her own life than to be with her friends. She might bridge the gap that keeps us elves from living among the humans."

The queen smiled as she watched Sara nearly jumping up with joy.

"This is great, isn't it, guys?" she said, excited.

"Welcome aboard, Sara," Tansu replied happily.

She must have been happy to have another girl to talk to, but Nova looked annoyed by the fact that Sara was coming along. However, for a moment, I thought I saw a small grin appear on his face.

As for me, I agreed with the queen. This war was something that all the people of Lu' Cel needed to band together against.

*****

"Lord Grant, Ignotus has returned," one of Grant's knights said humbly.

"It's been five days since he left. Why didn't he just come here himself?"

"I'm afraid he couldn't. He was seriously injured."

One of Grant's eyebrows rose up, "Injured? How?"

"He was targeting the elves in Jiran—"

The king immediately pounded his throne's armrest hard. "*What?* That idiot! Now the elves will get involved and retaliate! Why did he go there anyway?"

"He said he was going after someone and was injured by that person."

The king looked worried. "Shirai injured Ignotus? How is that possible?"

At that moment, a wounded Ignotus limped into the throne room, "My Lord, I have some news of importance to relay."

"I can't believe you screwed up so badly! What could you possibly have to report?"

"It's obvious Shirai lacks what it takes to fully control the Power of Ska."

Grant sat there quietly for a second. "That *is* interesting. What else do you have for me?"

"Unfortunately it's not good. He saw my face."

"What?"

"I was careless for a second."

"Damn. We have to speed things up now that he knows what you look like and before he finds the truth! I want you to get better fast! Take him to the infirmary."

"Yes, sir." The knight helped Ignotus out of the throne room, leaving Grant alone.

"Did you hear what happened?" he spoke to the shadows behind him.

"Indeed, Grant," a low voice spoke from the darkness.

"I'm afraid Shirai may soon realize what he is really capable of."

"Fear not. As long as *he* is under your influence, Shirai will never succeed. It won't be long before I am free and all of Lu' Cel is yours. Just a little while longer."

12 - Mountain of Darkness

True to his word, the magic users Tybal sent to buy us time did their job well. We made it through the area without any problems, and after a day of traveling, we reached the base of the Dante Mountains.

What Nova had said about them was an understatement.

The sky around the mountains was unnaturally dark. Unseen peaks were covered by a thick cloud bank. The air felt cold, damp, and dismal. How anyone could live here, especially the Lord of All Dragons, was beyond my grasp.

"*This* is where we'll find the dragons?" Nova asked.

"Unfortunately yes, Nova," Sara replied in an uneasy tone. "My mother said they chose this place to make sure no one except those who are worthy could get to them."

"Shirai, are you sure we can do this?" Tansu asked.

I wondered that myself, but looking at the Sword of the Wyvern at my side put those worries behind me. "We will make it, Tansu. I'm sure of it!"

With everyone's spirits raised, we began our ascent.

It was rough going at first, what with narrow ledges to grab onto and sudden gusts of strong winds trying to blow us off the mountainside. At one point, I told Tansu she could climb on my back and I would carry her, but she told me she needed to prove she could do this on her own.

Despite all the effort we gave, we only made it a third of the way up the mountain when we decided to find a place to rest. Luckily, we found a cave sitting in front of a wide ledge big enough for us to walk across.

"How did the dragons even make it up to this place?" Nova complained as he lay back against the cave wall.

I was outside, looking down the edge of the ledge, "I don't know, Nova, but they must be more durable than we are if this view didn't make them squeamish."

"What are you talking about? Let me see."

Nova came over next to me and looked down. When he did, he almost lost his balance and fell off. The bottom wasn't visible anymore due to the fact that the same cloud bank that was covering the peaks was now *below* us too.

"What's going on? Why are there clouds down there when they should be up there?"

"It must be the power of the dragons at work, just like Eri told us."

I looked up toward the mountain's peak. Even if what the queen said about the dragons' power was true, I wondered about something. If the dragons could command the very clouds themselves to move, why had they come here instead of finding a better place and using that same power to make it suitable for them?

A grunting noise turned our attention back to the inside of the cave. The noise came from Sara, who was busy trying to get a fire going by using her magic to light some branches she brought with her. For some reason, she wasn't having much success.

"It's no use." Sara threw up her hands in defeat. "I can't bring out a flame. The air must be too damp."

"Let me try and help, Sara." I let loose a small blast of fire, and the wood instantly ignited.

"Amazing, Shirai!"

By this time, Nova had gone back to lying against the cave wall. "Looks like you finally improved on handling fire there, Shirai."

"He has improved a lot since he first arrived at my place back at Kenga," Tansu added happily.

Sara perked up suddenly. "That's right. You never did tell me how this all began. While I get the food prepared, why not tell me about it?"

As Sara worked on getting the food ready, Tansu and Nova told her everything: the day I appeared at Kenga Village, Russ's appearance, and meeting Nova and Ignotus. This went on for an hour. As Sara listened intently to the two, I sat off to the side a bit, my mind going back over past events.

Well, I'm here just like you said, Russ. But why did you even tell me to come here if you work for Grant? As a matter of fact, why did Lorimar tell me to live for his sake if he too is the enemy? And how does Ignotus even know me or why he—?

I shook my head, trying to stop myself from remembering what I had seen back at Elruan. No one except me, Grant, and maybe Lorimar even knew what Ignotus really looked like. I didn't think telling everyone about it would help any either.

Instead of getting any kind of answer, I'm given more questions. Ska, why did you give me this power if I can't control it, or for that matter, why did you change me? Somebody please tell me what I am supposed to do!

"Shirai? What's wrong?" Sara's voice intruded on my private thoughts.

I looked up. Everyone was looking at me.

"Nothing… just thinking about—"

"Oh really?" Nova interrupted with a snicker, "I've known you for a while, and I've learned when you say something like that, you haven't told the entire truth."

"I am not lying, Nova! I'm just—"

Tansu came in at that time, asking, "Shirai, it wouldn't have anything to do with you seeing Ignotus's real face, would it?"

My body tensed up.

"You saw his face?" Nova anxiously asked. "When did this happen?"

"It was while you were being taken care of for your burns," Sara answered. "Whatever he saw really shook him up."

"Sara…"

Tansu hurried to my side. "You don't have to tell us what you saw, Shirai, but we are your friends. We want to help you, but *only* when you feel ready to tell us, okay?"

I looked at her, then at Nova and then at Sara. I finally let out a small sigh. "Something tells me you will see his true self soon. And when that time comes, I want you all to be prepared for what happens afterward."

With that, the subject was dropped and we finally got to eat our meal.

After finishing, we once again continued our way up the mountain. The further up we went, the more our way down was covered by clouds. It wasn't as smooth while climbing either. Some of the time, Sara had to use her magic to make stepping stones for us just so we could continue.

About halfway up, we came upon another large ledge and another cave.

"What were those dragons thinking, living in such a place?" Nova once again complained.

"Don't act like that, Nova," Sara argued. "You sound like a big baby."

"This coming from someone who's lived a sheltered life until now."

While the two went at each other, Tansu turned to me. "Shirai, why are there caves on every major ledge we come upon?"

"They must be for the dragons to use."

"Well, if that's true, why hasn't one dragon come out yet?"

That was a good question. Surely by now they must have sensed our presence and would have come out of hiding. I was pondering that subject when I sensed something was amiss. Before I could figure out what was bothering me, several icicles came flying at us from the darkness covering the sky.

"Watch it!" I shouted.

We ducked just as the icicles imbedded themselves in the mountain wall. When they made contact with the wall, the place they entered was quickly covered with a layer of ice.

Our attackers then came out of the darkness and showed themselves. They were medium-sized, demon-looking creatures, floating in midair, with no legs. I saw that one didn't have talons like the others, but a second later, new ones magically appeared. Their talons weren't really talons, but the icicles that nearly impaled us!

"More of Ignotus's monsters?" Sara growled. "How did they find us way up here?"

"They must have been left here to keep an eye on people who make it this far!" I quickly drew out the Sword of the Wyvern.

Tansu readied her bow. "Here they come!"

I managed to slice into two of them as they tried to send more projectiles at me. When I saw five icicles coming at me from up above, I let loose some flames, instantly melting them into harmless water.

Using the new arrows given to her, Tansu was quicker to attack than any of us as she was able to rapidly fire off arrow after arrow at the monsters. Not only that, but her new arrows were stronger than regular arrows. Instead of becoming stuck in the monsters' bodies, each one continued right through them!

Nova used the Tao Spear to neutralize the attacks of a couple of monsters, and then quickly cleaved them in a single slash. Sara used the surrounding area to her advantage as she made rocks shoot of the cliff and smash into the creatures. When one shot its icicle fingers at her, she moved her hand as if she was swatting the air, and a blast of wind blew the icicles back. The one who originally shot at her froze solid before it plummeted to the ground far below.

"There's too many of them!" Nova shouted as he destroyed two more.

"Not to mention the weather conditions are making it harder for us to fight!" Sara added as she also finished off a pair of monsters.

"Keep calm, everyone! Just make sure you watch where you are!" I dodged an onslaught of icicles being fired at me.

"Shirai!"

The feeling in my legs almost gave out. The scream was from Tansu, who was backed against the ledge's edge with three of the monsters blocking her way.

"Tansu!"

As I ran toward her, the monsters got ready to fire their icicles. Right before they launched their attack, the ground she was standing on gave way, and she began to fall. The monsters fired at Tansu, but I shielded her from the attack. As the icicles imbedded themselves in my right arm, a thin layer of ice quickly appeared around the wounds.

I ran past them, jumped after Tansu, and managed to grab her arm. With my free hand, I dug my talons hard into the rocky surface to keep us from falling farther down the cliff. Unfortunately, the arm I used to grab onto the wall was also the one that was hit by the monsters' attacks. Holding onto Tansu and the wall at the same time was putting an incredible strain on my body.

"Let me go! At this rate, you'll fall too!" Tansu cried out.

"Not on your life, Tansu! We will make it, the both of us!"

"Shirai! Tansu! Try to hang on a little longer! We'll try to get to you!" Nova called out to us.

I wanted to tell him to hurry, but I was already using what strength I had just holding onto both Tansu and the cliff wall. I tried to pull her up so she could hang on my back while I climbed back up to the others.

Only I found my attempt thwarted by one of the creatures. It launched another attack on me, this time sending the icicles into the shoulder of the same arm that was hit earlier. This caused my grip on the cliff to loosen, and both of us started to fall downward to the ground far below. I could see both Nova and Sara at the cliff's edge as they saw us plummeting.

"Shirai!"

Thinking of only protecting Tansu, I grabbed hold of her and held her close to me. I then flipped myself around so when we hit the ground, my body would act as a cushion.

"Don't do this, please!" Tansu cried out "Even if you are part dragon, this will kill you!"

"I want to make sure one of us has a future!"

Then there was silence.

As we fell, I became aware of something strange. Our falling was slowing down. Over Tansu's quiet crying, I was sure I heard a voice suddenly speaking in my mind.

Shirai... hear me...

Who's that? I thought to myself.

The power that was given to you is fueled by your hopes and desires! If you wish to save both the girl and yourself, believe you can!

Believe? How? Who are you? I asked, even though I had the strange sensation that somehow... I had heard the voice before.

I placed my hopes in you. Prove to me you can succeed! Believe in yourself and those who trust you!

With that, the voice fell silent, and our speed picked up again. I looked at Tansu, who had her head close to my chest. I then thought about Nova and Sara who were still above us, fighting for their lives. The voice was right. They never would have come here risking their lives if they didn't believe in me.

I... I must make it... I've come too far to just let my friends down! Ska, where ever you are, if you can hear me, give me the power needed to live!

As I thought that, I felt the same kind of strength that filled me when I used Ska's power, but this time it was gentle and warm. I felt it as it entered my wings. The next thing I knew, they started glowing for a moment before suddenly growing bigger. As they grew, silver-colored feathers started to cover each wing. I quickly opened them up, and our falling was reduced to a gentle floating.

Sensing the change in our descent, Tansu looked up and saw my transformed wings. "What... what is happening to your wings?"

"They're a gift from Ska."

I looked down and saw a ledge that I had never seen before. We floated down and made a safe landing right next to another cave entrance. I waited until both of my feet had touched the ground before I gently put Tansu down.

"Are you all right?"

"Yes, thanks to you," she replied smiling a little.

"I'm glad."

She then looked up, "But now what are we going to do?"

A dragon's wings

I saw what Tansu meant. The place where we landed was too steep for us to climb. I doubted my new wings, which I didn't even know how to use, could help us with the dangerous conditions that we faced climbing up the mountain.

"I don't know, Tansu. Even with these new wings, I don't know how to fly. Not to mention that Nova and Sara are by themselves against those monsters."

It was then I was quickly reminded about my injured arm as it started to throb painfully. Ice had already covered the area around the wound openings and the blood that escaped before that happened was still running down my arm.

"Your arm!" The way Tansu said that made it sound like it was her fault.

"Don't worry about it. It's not your fault I decided to be the hero."

"Let me help."

She pulled out the icicles in my arm, making sure not to freeze her hands off. After clearing away the ice that was still there and the blood, she pulled out some herbs and bandages from the small pouch she had at her side.

"When I said that you couldn't keep from getting hurt, I didn't think I would be right," Tansu laughed awkwardly as she wrapped one wound with bandages.

While she was busy patching me up, it gave me time to think. My thoughts eventually went back to the time Tansu and the others were talking about me back in Elruan. Remembering the conversation also reminded me of something else.

"Tansu, I need to know something."

She quickly replied, "This wouldn't have anything to do with the fact that you heard us talking back at Elruan?"

I chuckled sheepishly, "Was it that obvious?"

"You should know we wouldn't just leave you like that. But it's also not nice to eavesdrop like that!" As if to make her point known, Tansu put an extra helping of herbs on one of my wounds.

"*Ow*! I get it!" If this is what she did when she was annoyed, I'd hate to see what Tansu would do when she was angry! "But that's not what I was going to ask about."

Tansu stopped working on my arm and stared at me. "So what is it, already?"

"Why did you stick by me for so long? You said the main reason you came with me was to see Lorimar in person and you did, so you really have no reason to be here right now. So why?"

She said nothing as she went back to wrapping my arm. She only talked after she was done, "I stayed with you because when I first saw you … I don't know how to explain it, but I felt you would go on to do great things. Turns out my hunch was right. Not only did you save my village, you stopped the invasion of Gale and befriended the elves into helping out."

Tansu stopped talking. Turning around, I saw she had her head hung down.

"Tansu?"

"And there's another reason. I—"

Before the rest of her words came out, we both heard a loud noise coming from the cave nearby. It sounded as though something big was slowly walking toward us, but we couldn't see what it was because the inside of the cave was too dark. It wasn't long before the thing in the cave finally emerged from the darkness, and the moment it did, we both gasped.

It was at least four times taller than I was, sapphire in color with a huge body, a pair of giant wings, big claws, a long tail, two curved horns coming out the back of its large head with several small ones coming out its sides, and a mouth filled with sharp fangs. It looked at us with piercing, silver-colored eyes.

We had finally found what we were looking for all this time, but it didn't look too happy to see us.

13 - The Council of Ska

Tansu quickly got behind me as the sapphire-colored dragon came closer. Its heavy footsteps shook the ground all around us as it walked. Finally, it stopped a foot away from us and lowered its head so it could be at eye-level with us. Having a dragon this close had me on edge.

How is this possible? After all this time, mere mortals have survived the mountain's perils? The dragon's voice was speaking in my mind.

"How... how are you talking to us when your mouth doesn't move?" Tansu asked, still afraid to come out from behind me.

We of the Dragon Race have no need to use spoken words. Our minds can send messages better. The dragon got a look at me. *You... you may look like one of us, but you still smell like a human. Now what do you two want before your fate is decided?*

Regaining my bravery, I calmly stepped forward and brought out the Sword of the Wyvern. I held up the sword so the dragon could see it. "We seek an audience with your Lord Ska, on the matters of this."

That's...! So you are the one our Lord asked for help. I thought I detected his scent from your body. We've long been waiting for your arrival.

Ska was asking a human for help? Now I was *really* confused. "Why would the Lord of All Dragons want a human to help him? And what is the deal with this sword?"

I will take you to a place where your questions will be answered. Come. The sapphire dragon headed back into the tunnel.

"Wait!" Tansu came out from behind me. "We have two others with us! We need to get them! They are in danger!"

The sapphire dragon stopped walking and turned its head slightly so it was looking over its shoulder. *You mean the young man and the elfin girl? Another of my kin disposed of the things that intruded on our land, and they are safe… for now. We must make haste lest the others decide on what to do with them before you are reunited.*

The dragon continued into the cave. I didn't like the way it had said "what to do with them," and it was obvious that neither did Tansu, so we quickly followed.

The cave opening was actually an entrance to a network of tunnels that led throughout the Dante Mountains. They were big enough for the dragon to fully turn around and were lit by floating crystal spheres full of golden light. From the marks of the walls of the tunnels, I could tell these dragons had dug them by their own claws.

"Shirai, are you sure we should trust that dragon?" Tansu whispered.

"If they didn't want anyone to bother them, they would have probably killed us by now."

She gave me an annoyed glare. "Is that supposed to make me feel better?"

At that point, the dragon stopped at a massive gate carved out of the very mountain rock. On the wall was strange symbol-like writing.

"What are those symbols?" she asked.

"These are dragon runes, the dragon's written language—" I stopped when I realized I just answered Tansu's question. "How did I know *that*?"

In addition to great power, Ska's blessing includes the knowledge of our language, the sapphire dragon explained.

It must have been true, because I found myself reading what was on the door out loud. "It says 'Only the sound of the Dragon Race's voice may open the way to the Council of Ska.'"

Before I could ask what the message meant, the dragon let out a low, bellowing noise. A second later, the symbols lit up briefly, and the stone gate opened, leading into a very large open area.

It looked like a huge coliseum, except instead of human spectators, there were at least five dragons sitting on five of seven high perches. The place itself was carved from the mountainside and hung hundreds of feet above a huge lake, which must've been Lake Orem. As we walked forward, I saw that the very center perch, much larger than the others, was vacant.

Each one of the dragons was different in size, shape, and color. One was ruby-colored, another was emerald, and the rest were diamond, black, and silver. They watched as we entered the center of the arena where, to our relief, Nova and Sara were waiting for us.

"Shirai! Tansu! You're okay!" Sara came over and gave Tansu a hug while I walked over to Nova.

"Glad to see you two are okay too."

"Well, we thought we were goners when this dragon came out of the cave and blew away every last one of Ignotus's monsters," Nova said. He noticed my newly changed wings. "What in Lu' Cel happened to you this time?"

I looked over my shoulder at my wings. "You mean these? They saved us from falling to our death."

"Listen well, humans," one of the dragons spoke loudly. The one speaking was the ruby-colored dragon. It had purple-colored eyes, small, fin-like flaps on the sides of its head, and a long, slender, wingless body with a bushy tip at the end of its tail. "We, the members of the Council of Ska, wish to congratulate you all for your efforts in reaching here. We are especially glad that the one Ska himself chose has finally made it here."

"Thank you all, but we really came to meet your leader, Ska. We need to find out what is going on in the world and why I was changed into this form," I said.

"Before that happens, a more urgent matter must be covered," the emerald dragon spoke. It was like the sapphire dragon in shape, but it had bright brown-colored eyes and a beard of white hair, and its forearms were its wings. "Since you were chosen by Ska, you must be told something of importance vital for your well-being. It is about the truth behind the tale of how the world was created."

"The truth? What are you talking about?" Sara asked, "Asteron and Ska created this world, didn't they?"

The diamond dragon shook its head. It had yellow-colored eyes, no wings, brown-colored hair going down its head, and several spikes coming out of its shoulders and down its tail. "That is what your ancestors believed to be true. If humanity knew the truth, it would cause turmoil among those who live on Lu' Cel. That's the reason Ska moved all of our kind here long ago. It was to guard the truth. You see, Ska didn't help create Lu' Cel. He saved it from an evil that once ruled this world."

"What?" Nova sounded as confused as the rest of us.

The black dragon took the explanations further. This one had the same body type and wings as the sapphire dragon, but its eyes were as black as its color. Only a ring of reddish-orange-colored scales showed where its eyes were. Its body consisted of several protruding spike-like bumps coming out of several places of its body.

"Long ago, we dragons came to Lu' Cel from another world, one different than yours. Ours was a beautiful place, just like Lu' Cel is now. But then civil war broke out, and all changed overnight. The land was quickly ravaged, and many were killed. It became so severe that Ska himself led most of his people here in hopes of finding a peaceful place to live. Some stayed behind in hopes that one day the fighting would end."

The silver dragon picked up the story. This one could have been the sapphire dragon's twin, except its eyes were green. "However, when we came here, the populace of Lu' Cel was under siege from an incredible malevolent being that also came from another world. Seeing the inhabitants in such dire conditions, Ska fought against it while we and the others brought down its minions. Unfortunately, the evil was equal in strength to Ska, so he needed help."

The sapphire dragon, flying up to its perch, continued. "Using a special metal we brought with us from our home and a few of his own scales, Ska, a human, and an elf created the Sword of the Wyvern. Then, picking a human who willingly wanted to help, Ska infused him with some of his power transforming him into the very form you are now, Shirai."

"You … you mean there was someone like me before?" I secretly felt better knowing that there was someone else who looked like me.

"Yes." The ruby dragon spoke this time. "That human fought along side our lord, and in the end, they sealed away the evil using the sword. Alas, during this battle, the human lost his life, and afterward, Ska wouldn't speak of whom he fought."

Lost his life.

When those words were spoken in my mind, my head started hurting again. Once again I was bombarded with images of things I didn't know about. The pain was so great this time that I nearly fell over to the ground.

"Shirai! Is it happening again?" Tansu cried out.

"You mean this has happened before?" Nova asked.

"Yes. It seems to happen every time he remembers something from his past."

The dragons must have sensed my pain because I suddenly felt as though one of them entered my mind.

Relax your body. It was the voice of the emerald dragon. *Let your thoughts resonate with mine and share your pain.*

I closed my eyes and did as I was told. Right away I could feel the pain subside as images of unknown events kept on coming. Finally the images, along with the pain, vanished.

"Strange. It would seem that your mind wants to forget something that happened to you," the emerald dragon told me. "Even I cannot break the wall that keeps you from remembering everything."

"You mean his mind is forcing itself to forget everything?" Sara asked.

The dragon nodded. "Whatever has happened to this man, he alone must unlock the memories inside himself."

After hearing the dragon's words, I shook my head to clear the daze from the pain, and suddenly I remembered more about my past.

"I remember why I had the Sword of the Wyvern with me! I took it from Grant's castle to keep it away from him; but why exactly is unclear."

"You *took* something from Grant himself? You really outdid me when it comes to stealing!" Nova remarked proudly.

"I don't see how you can say something like that so casually, Nova," Tansu argued.

"There's more. I was hiding, fleeing from one place to another for a while after that until Ignotus and some of Grant's knights had me cornered and... I... I can't remember anymore than that."

"Ignotus... yes. We sensed his presence often here," the diamond dragon told us, "but he never came into the mountains. Each time he was here ... we sensed something corrupt coming from him."

"If you knew, why didn't stop him from killing all of those innocent people who tried to see you?" Tansu demanded.

"We couldn't risk starting something that couldn't be undone later," the black dragon explained, "especially against Grant's unusually strong powers."

While I thought they could have at least done something, I also knew the dragons were right in a sense,

"Maybe Ska can tell us what is wrong with him and Grant. Can we see him now?"

There was a slight, uncomfortable, quiet period as the dragons looked at each other, clearly talking among themselves with their minds. Finally, their conversation stopped, and the silver dragon said in a distraught tone, "We cannot. Unbelievable as it seems, Ska was captured by Grant."

"What?" All four of us shouted at the same time.

"We don't know how, but Grant somehow captured our lord six years ago, and we haven't been able to contact him at all," the sapphire dragon answered. "Where ever he is, there is something that keeps even us dragons from sensing him."

"Six years ago? The same time the whole war started. Everything seems to fit together," Sara thought out loud. "Grant captures Ska, he suddenly gains a power unknown to us, and he begins his conquest of all of Lu' Cel. But how is he keeping him captive if he's as powerful as you say?"

"That is something even we can't understand," the ruby dragon commented. "All we know is that Ska chose you, Shirai, for some grand task. We must rely on you and your companions to get to Hariel Kingdom and stop Grant himself."

I was about to say something when Tansu interrupted, "Why Shirai? Why don't you go and bring your leader back?"

"Do not think we haven't tried," the emerald dragon replied. "But something around Hariel prevents even us from coming near."

This time Sara objected. "So you're sending someone else? What kind of dragons are you, sending another to do something for you?"

I was afraid that remark was going to get all of us in trouble.

The diamond dragon calmly answered, "We have a duty to protect the others of our kind until Ska returns. We cannot just abandon our role. We are hoping Shirai, with both human and dragon powers, will be able to pass whatever is preventing us from finding Ska."

"What you're asking of Shirai is too much even for him," Tansu insisted. "You can't just ask him to do something like that. He's already been through so much—"

Wanting to finally say what was on my mind, I put my hand firmly on her shoulder, "No, Tansu. They are right. With the elves busy getting everyone ready for a counterattack, I'm the only one who can do this."

"But, Shirai—"

"It's okay. Besides," I added, "I want to meet Grant and ask him personally why he started this war."

"He's right, Tansu." Nova wrapped an arm around my neck. "But he won't go alone. I want to see what kind of treasure Grant has. Maybe I could 'convert it' to funds to rebuild Ranu."

"Joking aside, I agree with Nova," Sara said. "Shirai must be the one to face this problem, but he'll have us with him."

Tansu was quiet for a while. She must have been thinking about what to do, but I could understand how she felt. Anyone else in the same situation as we were now would probably wonder why they must do this and not someone else.

"Tansu, no one is forcing you to come with us. I know this is dangerous. You can go home if you want to. I don't want to be the one who is making you do this if you don't want to."

Still Tansu said nothing. Finally she looked at me and said, "You really are someone special, Shirai. I can tell by your eyes that you are just as afraid of this as I am, yet you have decided to go on. I'm beginning to see why Ska chose you as the one to help Lu' Cel. I'm going to see where the road you're following will take you until the end."

I smiled after she said that. The black dragon came in at that moment saying, "It seems you humans have more strength than we originally thought."

I looked up at the council. "That may be so, but Tansu was right about one thing: this is something one can't just sit around and do nothing about. The elves are joining the fight against Grant. I think you should too."

The silver dragon was quick to shake its head. "I'm afraid that is something we can't do. Ska has instructed us not to become involved with human life without his consent."

"You say that knowing full well what happened to him? If he was here right now, I imagine he would want you all to help the very people he risked his life saving instead of just watching on. Prove to him that you have the will to fight for a good cause."

Everyone was quiet. Again the dragons faced each other as though they were discussing among themselves. While they were busy, I was trying to figure out how I could say what I had just said in front of the council. I bet they never got such a lecture from a human, let alone one Ska chose. After what felt like hours, the council faced us again.

"It would seem not only are you all strong, but also wise," the sapphire dragon told us, "Indeed, we cannot just stand by while our lord is in trouble. We will help in anyway we can."

Today was a day of one surprise after another.

"That's great, but I think it would be unwise for all of you to just charge in while Grant holds your lord captive. The best thing you can do for now is to prepare in case anything goes wrong."

The diamond dragon nodded. "Indeed we will. In the meantime, there is something we can help you with right now. Everyone, stand together."

We did as we were told. The dragons started making the same bellowing noise the sapphire dragon had made to open the gate, only this time it sounded deeper, each dragon's call resonating with each other. As they bellowed, a ring of light appeared around us, and in a flash of light, we weren't on the Dante Mountains anymore. We were now just a few miles away from the Polqu Sea. Far down the way, we could see a giant city from which dozens of ships left.

"Is that… Delphin Port?" Nova said in amazement. "That's days from where we were! I can't believe the dragons have that kind of power."

"Their magic is even greater than mine," Sara remarked in awe.

"Looks like we have to take a ship to the other side of the Polqu Sea," Tansu observed. "Whatever is blocking their thoughts from Ska must be really strong if the dragons couldn't transport us directly to Hariel Kingdom."

"I hope we *can* get a ship. If not, we'll probably have to make our own. Let's go." I started down the road, followed by Tansu and Sara.

Nova, however, stayed where he was for a second.

"I can't believe I'm going back there," I heard him say in a low tone. He then quickly caught up to us.

*****

"It would appear an unforeseen problem has occurred, Grant," the voice in the darkness said.

"What is it?"

"It seems the one who holds the Sword of the Wyvern has managed to make contact with the dragons."

"How is it possible that someone like Shirai was able to do something we've been trying to prevent for six years? They must know about Ska now, and they are probably on the way here."

The voice laughed as lightly as that of a specter. "Be at ease, Grant. Even if he and his companions do make it here, he won't be able to stop us. Thanks to the Chains of Deist, Ska remains ours, and once that fool comes here, I will finally be free. Then the world will be at your mercy."

Even knowing that didn't put Grant's mind at ease.

"We can't take any chances. Even though Ska is incapacitated, Shirai is still somehow receiving help from him, and he may get too powerful."

"Fear not. I have already thought of a way around that. I have given our ace in the hole part of my strength, plus a little gift. He'll be ready."

14 - Boat Ride

Thanks to the members of the Council of Ska, we reached the Port City of Delphin in a matter of minutes. I found out quickly, though, that it wasn't what one called a normal city.

It did have its share of residents, but the majority of the people there were actually workers. Some were busy unloading cargo from trade ships while others were going out to sea trying to catch fish to sell to the market. Some of the sturdier workers stayed to work on constructing new ships.

At the time we arrived in Delphin, the place was filled with all kinds of activities. I wondered if we would be able to charter a boat to the other side of the Polqu Sea.

"Incredible! This place is so busy!" Tansu happily said.

"That's true, but I sense something is amiss here," I noted as we walked down the streets on our way to the harbor.

I said this while I had my cloak on. I didn't want to risk someone from Hariel recognizing me, as I was sure I had become an overnight sensation for my battle with Lorimar. I was thankful that, in spite of my now larger wings, the cloak still covered all of me.

"I know." Nova kept looking over every suspicious corner we walked by. "I felt tension the moment we entered this place."

Sara stopped for a moment to sniff the air, "Well, I sense something salty in the air."

"That would be the smell of sea water. We *are* at a seaport."

"Well, excuse me, Nova. This *is* the first city I've ever been to. I've never been outside Elruan."

"I remember my first time seeing the sea," Tansu reminisced. "My brother brought me here once when he was delivering our fruits. I never saw such a large body of water. I thought that it continued on forever."

"You think we have time for a quick dip in the water?" Sara asked, like an eager child begging their parent for something. "I've always wanted to know what it felt like swimming in the sea."

"I'm afraid we can't, Sara," I replied. "We need to get to Hariel Kingdom as quickly as we can."

"Well you certainly know how to take the fun out of everything."

I turned around and saw she had her tongue out like she was making fun of me. "If you have enough energy to make jokes, maybe you could help us find a ship?"

"Will do, leader." Once again acting as everything was a joke, she passed me and went on ahead. In spite of her joking, I couldn't help but think Sara was excited to be someplace new.

"Sara seems to be having a good time, doesn't she?" Tansu asked me.

"Well, this is the farthest she's ever been from her home. I think it's natural for one to act like that at first."

Confidentially, I was a little like Sara myself—not because I had never been anywhere except my homeland, but because with my amnesia, this felt like a new place to me too.

We continued our way toward the port. Along the way, I continued to feel something was amiss, but I couldn't put my finger on it.

I soon got my answer.

We were only a few feet away from the main port when …

"Um, Shirai?" Nova tapped me on my shoulder lightly. "I hate to interrupt, but I think there's something you may need to see."

I turned my head, "What is—"

I instantly saw what he was talking about. Standing right behind us was a group of five knights with their weapons out and pointed right at us. If that wasn't bad enough, five more appeared in front of us, blocking every possible escape route.

"Damn! What are Grant's knights doing here?" I quickly had my sword out, ready to use. Everyone else had gotten ready for battle too.

"They're here waiting for you, Shirai," a familiar voice spoke up from behind the knights in front of us. That person came forward, and when I saw who it was, I had mixed feelings of detest and confusion.

"Russ?" Tansu exclaimed.

"I knew there had to be a reason for the bad feeling I've had," I said with a hint of disgust. "Shouldn't you be back at Hariel, kissing up to your king?"

My remark didn't even faze him. "Lorimar had me stay here in case anyone tried to sneak aboard any of the ships illegally. But I had other reasons for being here."

Russ then signaled his men to lay down their weapons. I still kept a close eye on him, though. "And what reasons were those?"

"I thought by telling you to go to the Dante Mountains, you would find a way to stop Grant and come this way. And judging from the way you act, you must have, if you're this bold in trying to get a ship."

"I would say thank you for telling me, but I'm still unsure about you."

"And what is the other reason you're here?" Tansu asked.

Russ remained silent for a second before finally saying, "I want you all to take the ship I used to come here and get to Aegir as soon as possible."

My jaw nearly dropped as well as my sword when I heard Russ. I wasn't the only one, as everyone present had the same kind of reaction.

Nova came forward and asked, "Not to be rude or anything, but did I just hear a sergeant of Hariel ask the very group who's trying to stop his own king to take his ship?"

"I believe that's what I said, isn't it Nova, bearer of the Tao Spear," Russ answered calmly.

"Touché."

"Of course it won't be for free. There is a condition that has to be met first."

Sara sighed loudly. "I knew it was too good to be true."

"And what might that condition be?" I asked.

"You must take me and my men as hostages aboard the ship."

Russ's men began to mutter among themselves. I was still a little shocked from hearing Russ's condition so Tansu did the speaking for me. "I don't understand."

"It's the only way I can think of to make sure Grant doesn't know of our little deal here," he explained. "Besides, this way works for both of us. I keep an eye on all of you, and you get a free ride."

I thought about the idea for a minute. After coming to a decision, I quickly sheathed my sword. "If that's the case, I expect you and your men to be on your best behavior, or we'll have to take action."

Russ agreed without any counter-offer.

"Are you crazy, Shirai?" Nova argued. "Have you forgotten that he's the righthand man of Lorimar? How can you trust him so easily?"

"Because if he wanted to kill us, he could have done that earlier," I explained while I still made sure not to take my eyes off Russ in case it was a trick. "And I doubt he wants to cause a scene in the middle of the city where there could be a potential riot."

Russ nodded. "Well thought out, Shirai. Indeed, I don't want to spill blood unless it's absolutely necessary. I believe that's what you also want isn't it?"

I agreed with him. I didn't want any civilians hurt because of a possible fight just between us.

"Very well." Russ turned to his men. "We'll be leaving in ten minutes! All of you, fall back! These four must not be harmed in any way, and you are to do as they say without questions, or you'll answer to me! Understand?"

They all said yes, even though I could sense that most of them were wondering what their commander was thinking. With that, they all went on ahead, with us following behind.

"Why are we going along with this, Shirai?" Sara asked with a puzzled expression on her face.

"It's like Russ said: this way we can get a free boat ride, and we can keep an eye on the enemy at the same time, and …"

"And what?" Tansu asked.

"I have some questions I've wanted to ask Russ for a long time now. I can't let this opportunity slip by."

I turned my head to look over my shoulder while I kept walking. "If any of you feel they can't go along with this, you don't have to come."

"And let you have all the fun?" Nova argued, faking that he was hurt. "What kind of fool do you take me for? Like it or not, you're stuck with me until this is over with."

Sara nodded quickly. "Me too. I still want to see the new places on the other side."

When I saw Tansu looking occupied with something, I stopped walking. "Tansu? Are you okay?"

"I… I don't know if I'll be okay being on the same boat with that man. Not after what he did back at Kenga."

Hearing her worry, I walked over and placed my hand on her shoulder. "Then let's make a deal. While we're on the boat, I'll protect you if you protect me, okay? That way we're both safe."

She thought about that for a moment, and then smiled a little before agreeing.

We finally arrived at Russ's boat. It was a large warship with two large masts that each held up large white sails. The sails had the emblem of Hariel on them. The ship had a large open deck surrounded by railings, while the sides were lined with open cannons ready to fire on anything. It also had several oars to move the ship in case the winds weren't favorable.

Russ was waiting for us as we boarded the ship. "I have a favor to ask. I don't mean to be rude, but may I ask your elf friend if she could help us start a good wind going?"

A quiet growl left Sara's mouth. "For your information, pal, my magic isn't just here to do manual labor!"

"Sara, could you please do this just this once for us?" I asked nicely. "Don't forget, they're our hostages, so you have control over what you can do to them."

Sara calmed down, a sly look slowly appearing on her face. "Well, since you put it like that, I'm going to make sure you get your work cut out for you on this trip, my young knight."

Winking at us, she followed Russ to the deck where the wheel was. I could have sworn I saw him look worried for a moment when Sara told him what she would do with him. That left the rest of us to go to the bow of the ship.

"To think I would be heading back home after all these years," Nova grumbled with a hint of disgust in his tone. "Makes me sick knowing that there isn't anything left."

Tansu looked as appalled with Nova as I was. "How can you say that, Nova? Even if Ranu is destroyed, it's still your home."

He glared at Tansu with a serious glint in his eyes. "I told myself long ago that I wouldn't return to Ranu until I killed the one who destroyed it. I can't just break my promise like that. But it looks like I have no choice."

I could tell Nova was starting to act the same way he was back in Elruan when Ignotus tried taunting him. If he kept thinking like that, the next time we meet Ignotus, Sara might not be there to hold him back.

Quickly coming up with something to help cheer him up, I replied, "The way I see it, Nova, you're not breaking your promise. You're just making sure your home is still there. There's one more thing you should know. You can't go on carrying such a weight on your shoulders. You have friends to help you ease the burden."

Tansu nodded her head in agreement.

Nova looked off to the side laughing. "You are something man! You have no idea who you are, and yet you go out of your way to make others feel better instead of yourself! Sometimes I wonder if you're even for real."

About this time, the ship began to move away from port, thanks to Sara's magic.

It was a pleasant trip at first. Tansu spent her time watching the waters move back and forth across the surface and looking at the occasional sea dweller that came up for air. Each sighting made her even more excited to see the next one.

Sara was having fun bossing around Russ and the rest of the knights with every order she could think of. I was afraid she was going to push them too far, but for some reason, they never complained. Most, in fact, just did what they were told all the while looking at Sara in awe, probably because none of them had ever seen an elf before.

Nova spent his time drinking as much as he could and then taking the inevitable trips to the side of the railing as he tried not to throw up. It was getting to a point when one could know the exact time by his routine. Yet no matter how many times I told him to cut back, he still didn't listen to me.

I, on the other hand, spent the majority of my time working on new sword maneuvers so I could be prepared for anything that might come once we landed. In addition, I also trained hard on using the Power of Ska responsibly. It was imperative that I learned to control my emotions while using it so what happened in Elruan never happened again.

I was lucky one night to see the twin moons when they where both at their fullest. The reflection of their light shimmered on the water's surface so brightly that one could almost see the bottom of the clear, blue sea.

I was watching this sight while sitting near the railing, letting my feet dangle off the side. I was so preoccupied that I didn't hear the quiet footsteps coming up from behind me. It wasn't until I felt something come in contact with my shoulder that I reacted. I quickly turned, ready for action, only to find Tansu standing there.

"Tansu! Don't scare me like that! Do you know what I would have done if it was one of the knights trying to attack me?" I said.

"I'm sorry! I thought with your sensitive hearing you would have heard me coming beforehand." She was as startled as I was.

"No, it was my fault. I was enjoying looking out at the sea so much, I guess I didn't notice."

She walked over to the railing and leaned on it. "I can see why. It's not often you see the moons at their fullest, especially at a place like this."

"So what are you doing out here so late?"

Tansu sighed. "Well, Nova is having a drinking contest with a few of the knights, and Sara's refereeing the event. It wasn't my kind of place to be, so I thought I'd come up here."

I began wondering how anyone could hold that much liquor. Maybe Nova wasn't human at all. And how in Lu' Cel did Sara get caught up in his game?

"They must be having a good time. And what of our most gracious host, Russ?"

Tansu snickered. "Guess who was the first one to go down."

I couldn't help but lean back, guffawing. "That is rich! I needed that laugh! Thanks Tansu!"

Tansu sat down and let her feet dangle off the side too. "You know something, Shirai? Sometimes I wonder if this whole thing is nothing but a dream."

I stopped laughing as I asked, "What do you mean?"

"I mean the two of us, sitting here, looking out at the sea like this, on a boat owned by Lu' Cel's greatest enemy, heading for what may be the biggest battle of all time. I begin wondering if it's just a long dream I'm having, and I'm really back at Kenga with you, living out our lives in peace."

"That would be a nice thought," I said with a contented sigh.

She lifted up her right arm slightly, the bracelet on her arm reflecting the moonlight on its surface. "But then I look at the bracelet you got me and realize that everything is really happening. Our meeting with Nova and Ignotus, the fight between you and Lorimar, meeting the elves and the dragons. And then I begin to wonder."

"Wonder what?"

She turned to me with a worried look. "What's going to happen? How will all of this end? Will we die? Or will we succeed? We can only do so much. We're not gods. I worry that we might not get through everything that is going to be thrown at us."

I didn't answer her immediately. I looked out toward the water again, trying to think of what to say.

"We may not be gods, Tansu, but I think there is something only we humans have that not even the gods could have."

She looked confused "What's that?"

"It's the will to move forward and the strength we get when we fight for our dreams and loved ones. I believe that is what will see us through the tough times that are to come."

Tansu smiled "I suppose that's true. Thank you, Shirai, for being here for me."

She then gently leaned against my side.

"Tansu?"

"Please… let's just sit like this for a while, okay? I don't want to forget this moment."

I didn't say anything else, but wrapped my arm around her and held her close to me as we sat there, enjoying the night scene in peace.

I, too, didn't want to forget this moment.

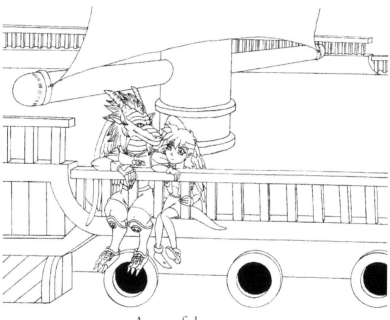

A peaceful moment

15 - Understanding of Power

We were still at sea, and I was beginning to get restless. I was hoping to get to Hariel as quickly as possible so we could finally end this madness, but I also wondered what would be waiting for me there.

Would the answer to who I am be there, or would I never find out the answer? Then a scarier thought came: if I did find out, would I want to be that same person again?

I was looking out at the water at the time I was thinking these things. I found that listening to the waves calmed me, but the sounds of the water were soon interrupted by the sound of boots walking on the deck.

The sound came from Russ as he walked toward me. I was a little surprised to see that he was not wearing his armor. Wearing a worn-out, brown leather jacket with sleeves that reached down to his elbow, he had on a gray leather brigandine on top of it. His black pants looked just as worn as his jacket.

"So this is where you have been all day." He acted as if we were friends. "You missed lunch. Your lady friend knows how to cook."

"I didn't think you were one who would worry about his enemy," I replied dryly.

"Believe it or not, I do have my kind side." He came over and leaned his back against the railing, looking at the sky. "I'm not a monster like that Ignotus fellow."

I was going to comment, but when I saw his face, I held my tongue. He didn't have his usual serious look on him.

He actually looked happy and relaxed.

"I truly miss days like this when one could just stare toward the sky without any care in the world."

I was a little confused. Ever since I had seen him push Giram back at Kenga, I thought he was just cruel. But now he was acting agreeable. I realized that I needed to learn not to judge people despite their first actions. While I was still unsure about Lorimar, however, my first impression of Ignotus still remained.

"I've been wondering about something since I met you again in Delphin," he said suddenly. "What happened to your wings?"

"They transformed in time to save the lives of Tansu and myself when we were attacked by your companion Ignotus's monsters."

Russ countered in a near-hurt tone, "I can assure you that whatever he is, he is no companion of mine! In fact, I haven't seen him since he was reported to have returned from his last mission severely wounded. Personally, I'm glad I don't have to listen to that voice of his for a while."

I didn't realize how serious I must have wounded Ignotus back at Elruan, but I agreed on one thing with Russ: I didn't want to hear his voice again either.

Or remember his face.

For a while we just stood where we were, not saying anything to each other. The rolling of the waves was the only sound.

I finally broke the silence. "Russ. Why are you going along with this senseless war? You seem more levelheaded than the others."

He remained silent.

"Oh, I'm sorry. I guess I'm not allowed to know such information, being the enemy, you know."

"I didn't want to be a part of this," Russ said. I didn't think it was possible at first, but I could tell he meant it. "Neither did my uncle."

"Your uncle? Who's that?"

"You've already met him, seeing as you managed to make such a hole in his armor."

I felt my stomach do a flip.

"You don't mean... Lorimar is your uncle?"

Russ nodded. "Of course, and the reason I know you is because he instructed both of us in how to use the sword."

My stomach did another flip, quickly followed by the now-familiar pain in my head. The combination of the two almost made me fall over the railing I was leaning against. Luckily, Russ saw what was happening and caught me in time. Dragging me away from the railing, he gently leaned me against one of the masts.

"Shirai? Are you okay? What's wrong?"

I couldn't hear him clearly because as my head pounded, I was hearing another voice—one that was inside my mind.

My own voice.

No! Don't remember! No more! Don't remember anymore! It's too painful! the voice kept repeating.

I must! I must remember! I argued with myself. *Let me remember! I don't care how painful it is! Let me remember!*

In the end, my mind only let me see a fragment of my memories. The rest it kept tightly locked away. It was like the emerald dragon had told me: My own mind was forcing itself to forget.

The pain quickly went away, and I was able to think straight again. "I'm... I'm fine, Russ. I was just caught off guard by your response."

After helping me back to my feet, I walked away from Russ and made my way back to the railing. I then made sure I had a tight grip on it for what I was going to do next.

Russ noticed the change in my attitude. "What's wrong, Shirai?"

"I... I remember. I didn't want it to be true... but Lorimar *did* teach me how to use the sword. And you were my sparing partner at the time. Weren't you?"

Russ's mood quickly changed. "So you remember that, huh? Yes, it's true."

"Then why? Why is the man I used to look up to as the greatest person ever going along with Grant's idea?" I was trying hard not to cry. I didn't want Russ to see me like that.

"You really think he's someone who gets pleasure of slaughtering innocent people?! He's tried on several occasions to persuade his brother to stop the fighting, but he doesn't listen!"

Again I was caught off guard. Lucky for me, I still had a grip on the railing. "B... Brother?"

Russ looked out to sea, heaving a depressed sigh. "You had no idea because you never entered the castle. Grant is Lorimar's older brother, which makes Lorimar the next heir to the throne since the prince disappeared. I'm related to them on my mother's side, but since she's only a noblewoman in the court, I'm just a knight."

I actually started feeling sorry for Russ. Not only was one of his relatives doing such cruel things, but he was forced by his status to aid in the same. I wanted to say something to him, but with what was going on between us, I didn't know what to say.

"I… I'm sorry. I didn't know. I didn't realize that there were people in Hariel who were also against this war."

"It's okay, Shirai." Russ tried his best to sound comforting. "What's really gotten to me was the rapid change in my uncle Grant."

"Rapid? What do you mean rapid?"

Russ explained that, six years ago, everything was normal in Hariel. One day, a strange crate appeared on the surface of the nearby lake and floated to the shore.

The crate itself looked very old, like it came from a time long ago. No one knew where it had come from or what was inside it. The people who found it tried to open it, but couldn't, so it was presented to the king in hopes that maybe his scholars could figure out what it was. The day after it was given to him, however, Aynor disappeared, and Grant began to act strangely. Then Ignotus appeared the day Ranu Village was destroyed.

"So no one knows what happened to the prince?"

"It's not just that. What was really weird is that no one except Grant and my uncle have even seen the prince. In fact, there were rumors going around that there wasn't any prince to begin with."

"Nothing is making any sense anymore. What is really going on?"

Russ was about to say something when the ship was suddenly hit by something large in the water. The whole boat shook as whatever hit us swam underneath the ship.

"Crowsnest! What in Lu' Cel was that?" Russ shouted.

"Sir! Something big just rammed us!"

"Go down below and see if it did any damage!"

The man quickly climbed down to the deck and was about to open the door below when it crashed opened and Tansu, Nova, and Sara came running out.

"What just happened?" Nova quickly asked.

"Something just hit us! We don't know what!" Russ answered.

"What do you mean, 'something'?" Sara asked.

It was then I sensed something moving toward us from under the water. "I think we're about to find out, Sara! It's coming!" I shouted.

As if on cue, whatever hit us jumped out of the water and landed on the deck of the ship.

It was fish-like in appearance, at nine feet tall. Its face looked as though someone had combined a man's face with a fish's and ended up with a jumbled mess. I stared at its fish eyes, human nose, fish mouth, and human-shaped head. The monster's upright body was big and brawny. It had fin-like arms with webbed fingers and stood on human legs with web toes. It also gave off a foul odor.

"What... what is that thing?" Tansu asked, trying not to gag from the sight of it.

"If I had to guess, I'd say it's one of Ignotus's monsters! It must have been waiting for us to pass here!" I replied.

"Whatever the reason, it doesn't look like it will let us go on!" Russ drew his sword.

"And you're not going to face it alone!" I also drew my sword.

Russ and I charged at the creature.

"Since when did those two become buddy-buddy with each other?" Nova asked.

"Does it really matter now? Help them!" Sara started toward the monster, followed by Tansu and a puzzled Nova.

While Russ and I managed to cut into the thing's sides before it had a chance to act, the assault didn't seem to bother it. It swung its fists trying to get at us, but it was slow, so we dodged them with ease. However, the deck boards weren't as lucky, as they were smashed by the creature's strength. I tried to chop off one of its hands, but the monster had good reflexes. I thought we could try to burn it to death. However, I scrapped that plan, as the ship would join it.

Tansu fired her arrows, hoping to get to the thing's chest, but it jumped out of the way and back into the sea. It then came out the other side of the boat, hoping for a surprise attack. Nova flung the creature onto the deck using the Tao Spear as a slingshot. It quickly recovered and shot green slime at us.

"Spread out!" Russ shouted.

Everyone managed to dodge the attack, but some of the slime grazed one of my wings. I felt a burning sensation coming from where the slime had made contact. A few of the feathers burned away, and the skin underneath it was smoking slightly.

"Shirai! Your wing!" Tansu called out.

"I'm fine, Tansu! Just watch out for that—"

The monster growled as it continued its assault on us with its barrage of deadly slime. Sara tried to use her magic to send the slime back at the thing. She only succeeded in burning several holes on the deck as it once again jumped back into the sea.

"At this rate, this ship will be reduced to scrap!" Nova looked for where the creature would appear.

"And my magic isn't as effective at sea against that thing as it would be on land," Sara added.

"I have a plan! Try to go along with it!" I instructed everyone.

They all nodded in response. We waited for any sign of the beast getting ready to emerge from the water for another attack. The wait came to an end as the thing surfaced. As it was halfway up onto the ship, I did a backflip and used my tail to launch the thing even higher into the air.

"Everyone! Strike!"

I fired off the Power of Ska at the thing. Tansu shot her arrow. Russ and Nova flung their weapons sharp-end first in the air, and Sara brought forth a gust of wind to push the weapons at incredible speed. Each of our attacks hit the creature's chest with pinpoint accuracy. It let out a loud squeal as it fell to the deck and didn't move.

"Nice plan, Shirai," Russ commented as he took a deep breath.

"It was the first thing that came to mind."

"I'm just glad it worked."

Nova walked toward the now dead creature to retrieve his spear.

But it was far from dead.

Without warning, several tentacles came out of the thing's shoulders and seized Nova, Sara, and Tansu.

"Everyone!" I cried out.

I dashed at the thing, hoping to slice the tentacles that held my friends. However, I didn't see the one coming out from the monster's back. It swatted me away like I was a fly, right into a nearby railing.

"Shirai!" I heard Tansu crying out through my pain.

Looking up, I saw to my horror that the monster was slowly squeezing the life out of my friends. Before I could fully recover from the blow I had taken, the creature fired another slime blob at me.

Russ shot forward and shielded me with his body.

"Russ!"

Russ fell down on the deck. I quickly ran to his side and held him up with my arms. He was hardly moving and moaned in pain. The blob had hit him dead center and eaten right through his armor. His chest was completely red from blood that was flowing from the places where the blob touched the skin.

"Why in Lu' Cel did you do that, you idiot!"

He half-opened his eyes. "It's a knight's duty... to protect those who can't defend themselves... and right now... your friends need to be protected..."

He passed out. I held back the tears that wanted to come. Gently putting Russ on his back, I slowly got up and stared at the creature that still had my friends in its grasp, anger rising in my body. But this wasn't the same kind of anger that I felt back in Elruan; it was more focused.

"I will protect them, Russ. And I will protect you too!"

A new kind of power began to fill my body. As it swelled up, I found myself understanding how to use it.

From out of the air, three swirling, razor-sharp wind-blades appeared floating in both my open palms. I threw them at the creature, and they sliced off the tentacles that held my friends. When they were safe, I focused all my attention on the monster that, at the moment, launched another blob straight at me.

I countered by magically conjuring a blast of icy wind, which instantly froze the blob in a case of ice. The monster roared when it saw its attack failed and recklessly charged at me. I delivered the final blow in the form of a powerful lightning bolt that came from out of nowhere. The creature fell on the deck in a smoldering heap of charred flesh and scales.

I turned to my friends, "Guys! Are you okay?"

"We're fine. Thanks for the rescue," Nova panted, "Shirai, what in Lu' Cel was that... you did?"

Before I could explain, I remembered about Russ. I ran over to him and was relieved to see that he was still breathing. However, I knew his good fortune wouldn't last long if we didn't do something for him quickly.

"Russ needs medical help now!"

"Why would you want to save him?" Nova asked.

"We can't just let him die, Nova! He saved my life!"

Nova held his hands out in defense. "Okay! Okay! No need to get so nasty!"

"I know a bit about healing. Let me see what I can do." Sara helped me to get Russ off the floor. "Tansu, can you help?"

"Okay, Sara."

Tansu went ahead to clear a way for us belowdecks. Sara and I slowly followed, leaving Nova to take up the rear after he recovered his spear and Russ's sword from the remains of our foe.

"If it's not one thing, it's another," he muttered. Before following after us, he pushed the body of the monster into the sea.

Despite the severity of Russ's injury, Sara and Tansu's fast actions saved his life. With the burns he received, though, he would be left with a bigger scar than mine. However, he was more worried, because with his injury he would be taken off the battlefield until he fully recovered. I was glad, not for my sake, but for Russ's because it meant he wouldn't have any part of this war.

For now.

After our encounter with Ignotus's sentry, the tension between us and Russ's men lifted, since we saved their sergeant's life. The last leg of our trip was uneventful, until the day came when I could see Aegir off in the distance. I was watching as the city came closer to us from the tip of the ship. I was thinking how great it was that we finally made it when Tansu and Nova came up behind me.

"Hey, guys. How is Russ doing?"

"He's doing fine, thanks to Sara's help," Tansu happily replied.

"I can't believe the way he keeps going on about how he needs to resume to his duties when he gets back," Nova commented.

"Incredible. He almost loses his life, and all he complains about is not being able to continue his work." I laughed a little. "I thought he would be happy that he doesn't have to be a part of the war for a while."

"What are you talking about, Shirai?" Tansu asked. "Did something happen between you two?"

"And for that matter, you never explained that power you used to save us back there," Nova added.

I told them everything that happened between Russ and me before the monster attack. I then explained that, during the battle, I tapped into a new power.

It was the ability to use magic the dragons could use.

"I... I can't believe you used to be Lorimar's apprentice," Tansu said in disbelief.

"Neither could I, but I clearly remember it, so it's true. I know how you feel about your brother, but please don't hold it against me or Russ, okay, Tansu?"

She smiled. "Don't worry, Shirai. I know you are a good person. And now I have a new opinion of Russ too. Especially considering the trouble he's had."

Nova huffed. "If you ask me, I think maybe Lorimar didn't try hard enough to stop his brother. You think someone that strong wouldn't give up so easily."

"I agree with you, Nova," I said.

Both of them gawked at me with a bewildered look.

"You what?"

"From what I saw of Lorimar back in Gale City, I could tell he was a man of strength, honor, and concern for his men. Yet he's willingly going along with his brother's plans. I think there's something else we're missing."

The problem was I couldn't think of what it was, and neither could my companions.

Soon we were docked in Aegir. We were all on deck, including Russ, as his men made sure the boat was tied up and the gangplank was brought up to the ship's side.

"I thank you and your companions for saving the lives of myself and my crew," Russ tried his best to still sound professional. He was back to wearing his armor, despite the fact he knew he didn't have a need for it immediately.

"You know you could be a little looser with this knight business and thank us like a regular person," Nova suggested. Russ gave him a quick glare.

"And I hope I don't see you anytime soon or I may have to do my duty and take you in." He smiled as he gave us this advice.

"We'll make sure to stay clear." Out of the corner of my eye, I saw some of Grant's knights patrolling the port. "Just to make something clear. The deal was that we had to take you all hostage so we could use your ship, right?"

"It was."

"Then please don't hold this against me!"

I gave him a good punch to his face. When he recovered from the blow, I made sure that he saw me winking at him, and then in a flash, I was off.

"Shirai! What was—?" Sara tried to finish when I grabbed her arm and made a dash off the ship.

Tansu and Nova stood where they were for only a second before following us. Behind me, I could hear Russ giving orders to go after us.

"What is going on, Shirai?" Sara demanded.

"This way, none of Russ's superiors will ever think that he was disobeying them by bringing us here on his own—just like what he had planned from the beginning! Now less talk! More running!"

With that, we continued our run through the streets toward the city's exit and our first official steps on the other side of the Polqu Sea.

*****

"My lord, General Lorimar has requested to see you," one of the castle guards told his king.

"My brother, huh? Probably trying once again to convince me to change my ways. Tell him that I will not see him and that, in the meantime, he is to do a check of the south section."

"At once." The guard quickly left.

"When will he learn that his constant pestering will not get him anywhere?"

The unknown voice came in. "He is a fool. He'll outlive his usefulness soon, but right now ..."

The voice grew quiet.

"Is something wrong?"

"I'm afraid so. Something with dragon blood has landed on West Lu' Cel. And it seems my barrier isn't affecting him."

"Damn! It must be Shirai! How could he even get here in the first place?"

"Even I don't know, but it's worse than that. I can sense that he has managed to gain more power than before."

Grant was close to chewing off his fingernails. "He is even more stubborn than Ska is. What should we do? It's not time yet."

At that moment, a knight came walking into the throne room. The knight was wearing dark green armor and a black cape. The knight's face was covered by a full helmet. In his hand was a blood red sword with runes at the bottom of the blade.

"Fear not, Grant. Our warrior is almost finished, and he'll soon be prepared for Ska's chosen."

16 - City of Magic

Things on the west side of Lu' Cel weren't the same as on the east side. For one thing, there were different kinds of animals than those we'd seen before. Another was the fact that there was less plant life filling the plains.

However, those were small differences compared to the problem I had at the moment. I felt there was something lingering all around us; and in addition, the air was filled with the scent of those who were killed in the early part of the war. Since I had a heightened sense of smell, one can only imagine how bad it was.

"Good grief, the air!" I covered my snout. "I can smell the dead all around me!"

"I know," Sara said. "I can also sense something unknown filling the air."

All of us had spent the last day trying to put distance between us and Aegir. Even though we no longer had Russ as an enemy, he still had to keep up the act so his superiors wouldn't find out about what happened between us.

I, for one, was starting to get tired, and having my sense of dragon smell being subjected to such odors wasn't helping matters. I wished we were already at Hariel.

"What did the two of you expect?" Nova argued. "Two kingdoms are gone, hundreds are dead, and there's the fact that somewhere, Grant is holding Ska prisoner here. Of course this side of Lu' Cel would be messed up."

"You could at least be a little more supportive of those who are more sensitive to these things than others," Sara remarked.

"And you could realize that you're going to have to learn to deal with it instead of whining about it."

I let out a loud sigh.

"And they're off. Sometimes I wonder if those two will get along long enough for us to finish what we came here to do. What do you think, Tansu?"

She didn't answer, even though I knew she was behind us.

"What's the matter? You don't agree with me?"

Again, no answer.

"Tansu? Is everything all right?"

Finally turning around, I saw she was way behind us, walking slowly. As she got closer, I also saw she was a little flushed. I frowned. It looked like she was having trouble breathing.

"Are you okay, Tansu? You don't look well."

"I'm fine, Shirai… I…"

She fell to the ground.

"Tansu!"

Nova and Sara stopped arguing. Quickly taking her in my arms, I was relieved to see that she was still breathing. It was, however, coming in short breaths, and she was perspiring a lot.

"What's wrong with her?" Nova asked.

Sara came to Tansu's side and looked her over carefully. Finally, after a couple of agonizing minutes, Sara just shook her head, "I don't know what's wrong with her. It's not something I ever saw before."

"Well, we have to do something!" I shouted frantically, "What if something happens to her? I…"

"Calm down, pal," Nova replied, "You're not helping her by getting worked up like this!"

"I know, but…"

He firmly grasped both my shoulders. "Listen to me. All of us look up to you as our leader. If you start acting like some frightened child, we can't work at our best. She'll be okay."

He was right. I needed to calm down so I could make levelheaded decisions.

"Thanks, Nova. Sara, take out our map and see where we can go for help."

She took the map from the big bag and unrolled it. After studying it, she said, "Tsura City! We're in luck! We can get great help there!"

"Which way?"

The moment she pointed us in the right direction, I was off running, Tansu in my arms.

Twenty minutes later, we were a mile from the city. From where we were, I could see a giant building that rose from the middle of the city. In fact, it practically took up half the place. I could also sense sudden bursts of magic coming from the same direction.

"What is that huge building?"

"That's our destination," Sara explained. "It's the Lu' Cel Institution of Magic. I'm sure that they'll have something that can help Tansu."

"If the building's as big as I think it is, you better put on your best clothes to impress them before we go any further," Nova suggested.

Carefully handing Tansu over to Nova, I donned my cloak, and we headed for the city. Luckily there weren't any knights to stop us, so we kept running through the city streets, people watching us as we sped past them. Finally we reached the gate that lead into the Institution of Magic.

Up close, it was even bigger than Queen Eri's castle. The walls were made of red-colored stones packed together tightly with cement. There were several sections to the school, such as a large circular arena off by itself away from the main building.

In another building nearby, several people were coming in and out, carrying books in their arms. In the front yard, an adult was busy demonstrating how to bring forth flames to a bunch of young students.

The front gate was locked, so I banged on it, hoping to get someone to come over. Someone did, and they didn't seem too happy about the noise I was making. It was a woman with long, red hair, with one side done in a bun and the other left untouched. She wore official-looking clothing, and her blue eyes stared at us with annoyance.

"What is the meaning of this disruption?"

"I'm sorry, but we need to see the person in charge."

"That would be me, young man. I'm Headmistress Luwina."

"Please, Miss Luwina! We need to come in! We need help!"

She shook her head. "I'm afraid it's impossible at the moment. We're having classes, and even if we weren't, you need to make an appointment."

"But Miss—"

Sara came up beside me. "Sorry for interrupting, but you said we could only get in by appointment?"

"That's right, young lady."

She fished something out of her pocket and held it up for Luwina, saying a little smugly, "How is this for an appointment?"

In her hand was a small metal medallion with an image of a Cerquline etched into it. Luwina took one look at it, and her jaw dropped. "That's…"

"Exactly. The Royal Seal of the Elfin Royal Family, the same family who long ago founded this school, and I'm Princess Sara, daughter of Queen Eri, current ruler of the elves. Since you also have an extensive library that rivals any known in any other city, you also know who this would be."

Without warning, Sara lifted up my hood, revealing my face. I was expecting a scream to come out of Luwina's mouth, but she stuttered, "Ska's chosen? I'm so sorry for the rude way I was before! What is the problem?"

I wanted to ask what was going on, but that had to wait. "Our friend suddenly became ill. We don't know what is wrong with her. Is there anyone who can help?"

"Of course. Come in quickly before someone from Hariel sees you." She quickly opened the gate and led us to the main building.

The inside was immense. Large pillars, each carved with intricate designs, held up the very high ceiling. Numerous corridors lined each side, each leading to different rooms.

Luwina led us to the infirmary, where Tansu was taken by the staff working there. While they checked on her, Luwina took us to a guest room so we could wait. For two grueling hours we sat there, waiting for news about Tansu.

"So why didn't you say the elves were the ones who made this school in the first place?" Nova asked Sara.

"You didn't ask. Besides that was a long time ago. I didn't think anyone would still remember."

"Well, for once it's a good thing to have a princess on our team, even if it's one who whines too much."

It was at that moment Luwina came into the room. When I saw her expression, I sensed that it wasn't going to be good.

"It seems that your friend is suffering from a disease that recently came up. Normally, it affects the young and old, has moderate symptoms, and usually goes away after two weeks. For some reason, however, her condition is severe."

"Can anything be done for her?" Sara asked.

Luwina shook her head. "I'm afraid not even our best healers can do anything for her. All we can do is try to make her comfortable, but if a miracle doesn't happen soon… she will not make it. I'm sorry."

With that she left, leaving all of us too stunned to say anything. Both Nova and Sara quickly became depressed, while I was hoping this was all just a horrible dream.

"Why?"

I was so upset I didn't realize I almost made a hole in a nearby wall when I punched it. The slight pain I felt afterward, unfortunately, made me realize it wasn't just some nightmare.

Were we truly going to lose Tansu?

"Calm down, Shirai. You want to bring the whole place down?" Nova said.

I growled viciously, "I don't want to hear anything from you!"

Nova fell silent.

"That was uncalled for, Shirai!" Sara yelled. "You think you're the only one who's upset, the only one who knows what it's like to lose someone special?"

I wanted to tell her that they couldn't possibly know how I felt—to hear that the person who had helped you through the most difficult thing you ever faced might not make it; how could they know how that felt?

But before those words could leave my mouth, I quickly remembered everyone had lost someone close to them. Feeling completely helpless, I fell to my knees and I just wanted to cry.

"Oh, thank Asteron, I finally found you!"

We all looked toward the direction of the new voice. There in the doorway, panting hard as though he had run all the way from wherever he had come from was a boy no more than fifteen. He was dressed in the clothing the other students wore. His short, brown hair was covered with a small cap, and behind a pair of small glasses were two gray eyes. In his tightly gripped hand was a worn book.

"Who are you, and what do you want?" Sara asked.

"The name's Zen. I'm a student here," he explained while catching his breath. "I'm sorry, but I overheard what was happening with your friend near the infirmary, and I had to find you as quickly as I could."

When he finished, Zen passed Nova and Sara and came directly over to me.

"So you're part-dragon, huh? That's amazing!" He then stared at Sara. "And an elf too! None of my friends will ever believe this!"

"Look, Zen. You came at a bad time to enjoy seeing what we look like," I said.

"Well, it would be nice to make notes, but I have a good reason being here. I know of something that can cure your friend."

We all stared at Zen.

"Look, kid, I find it in sick humor to come to us like that and say such things. Especially to Shirai," Nova advised.

"You think I'm *that* cruel?"

"As a matter of fact…"

"Wait a minute," I butted in. "I want to hear this. So what is this supposed cure?"

Zen smiled. "I'm sure you know about Flora Kingdom, right? My parents and I managed to escape from there before Grant's knights found us. We fled to this place and are trying to go on with our lives. Before that, though, they were working with the royal family to raise special plants that could be used to cure all sorts of diseases. I'm sure your friend the elf knows how potent plants can be."

"I do, and I'd watch what you say around people," Sara commented.

"Sorry. Anyway, this is the flower you need."

Zen opened the book he had in his hand. He turned to a page with a picture of a flower with pink and purple petals with large, green ones in the middle of each sequence.

"I don't know if there are any left, but I figure with your senses and the young elf lady's ties to the earth, you might be able to find it."

I looked at Sara. "What do you think?"

She asked if she could look at the book. She read the text that surrounded the picture of the flower, muttering to herself as she did so.

"Incredible! This is incredible!" she cried out in amazement. "This research could have saved a lot of lives! I don't understand why you don't show this to someone here!"

"You really think it's a good idea for someone who escaped being killed to go and tell someone who might go to one of Grant's knights?" Zen sarcastically replied.

Nova laughed. "For someone as young as you are, Zen, you really know how to survive. Unlike say, a certain elf."

Before an argument erupted, I asked, "Zen, could I ask you for a favor?"

"What is it?"

"Please help Nova watch over our friend? If this flower really can save Tansu, I need to go and get it."

"You may not be able to get it," he replied bluntly. "Last I heard Flora was crawling with knights."

"I know, but I can't let her die."

Zen took a moment to think about it. "I guess, but how are you going to get there? Flora's four days away from here."

"Leave that to me."

I opened a nearby second story window that overlooked the city. Then I looked to Sara. "I know this may sound weird, but I want you to get on my back, Sara, and hold on tight."

Sara glanced toward Nova, who stared quizzically. Deciding not to ask any questions, she quietly got on my back, making sure she had a good grip.

"Nova, keep a good eye out on Tansu."

Before anyone could react, I jumped out of the window.

"What are you doing?" Sara cried out, frightened.

Landing on the ground, I then leapt on top of one of the buildings nearby. This went on until we finally made it to the city's edge. When we landed outside, I started to run at top speed toward Flora Kingdom, with Sara hanging on for dear life.

I felt Sara tighten her grip on me. "Shirai! How in Lu' Cel are you doing this?!"

"One of the benefits of being part-dragon. We'll be at Flora Kingdom in no time!"

"If you don't get us killed first!"

"Don't worry about it!"

We were making good time crossing the land on our way to Flora. The ground was level, which was lucky for me, because I didn't have to do any sudden turns. After a while, though, I had to take a few seconds to rest.

"Shirai, I've noticed you've been looking out for Tansu a lot." Sara suddenly asked me at one point.

"Well, she was the one who helped me get through the shock of when I first found out about my new form. She spent so much time taking care of me that I want to do something for her."

"Do you love her?"

I nearly choked.

"What?"

"Relax. I can see the answer in your eyes," Sara giggled. "So why haven't you told her yet?"

"I can't. Not while I look like this. I know she likes me the way I am, but I'm afraid she may change her mind if I said that."

"If she loves you back, it won't matter what you look like. Look at my mom and dad. Do you think she married him just because he was human? You need to learn that love can be a very powerful thing."

I looked off to the side. *It's not that simple, Sara.*

After resting, we continued onwards. Two hours later, we finally made it to the immense forest where Flora resided.

It was filled with lush, green trees and different kinds of flowers. It was completely different than Jiran Forest. Wanting to make good time, I made our way to the treetops for a better look.

The castle was not far from where we were. While it looked like any castle, what set it apart from the others was the fact that the people had let the native plants grow everywhere. There were large vines creeping up the sides of the walls, branches from nearby trees hanging over the walkways on the top of the castle, and several flowers growing right out of the cracks.

"Wow! These people love plants even more than you elves do."

"I know. It hurts my pride in being an elf seeing something like this."

'Well, we can't just stay here gawking. How are we supposed to find a single kind of flower in such a big place?"

"Zen's notes said that the flower we are looking for has a unique smell of cinnamon and lavender combined. That shouldn't be too hard for that super nose of yours, right?"

"You don't have to make it sound like I'm some dog," I moaned.

We headed for the castle. Zen hadn't lied when he said the place was crawling with knights. It took our combined wits, not to mention timed use of magic by Sara, to sneak by them since there were so many.

Inside I started to sniff the air for any sign of the flower. We went through corridor after corridor, hoping to get its scent. Just when we were about to give up, we entered the throne room, the only place we hadn't looked.

"Wait! Yes! I smell it! It's definitely here!" I whispered.

"But there aren't any flowers here," Sara pointed out.

She was right. No flowers were growing anywhere in the room.

"I don't understand. I know I smell them." I looked around for anything out of the ordinary but had no luck. "Sara, can you sense them anywhere here?"

Sara got on the ground and placed her hand on the floor. She then closed her eyes and began to concentrate on feeling the surroundings. "You're right, Shirai. I can sense them, but the odd thing is that they're not in *this* room. It seems they're in a room that's connected to this one."

Aside from the door we had used to enter the throne room, there weren't any other doors. I then thought of something. Walking over to the walls, I began to slowly run my fingers on them, hoping for something to happen.

And something did happen.

When I came upon the wall next to the throne, I found a secret button made to look like one of the stones the wall was made up of. The section of wall the button was on opened up to reveal a secret room. There, sitting in a room that was being watered periodically by hidden springs, were miles of the flowers we came for.

"So that's how they kept this room safe!"

"We can talk about how remarkable it is later, Sara. Let's get one and go before someone finds us *and* this place."

"I think we should take a few with us. If Zen can somehow grow more of these, they can be a benefit to Lu' Cel."

Despite my wanting to get back to Tansu as quickly as we could, she had a good point. Luckily, the room had some small flower pots. We replanted some of the flowers and put them in the bag I had taken with us.

After taking as many as we could carry, we made sure the room was shut and made our way to the door leading out of the throne room. When we opened the door, we were greeted by the one person I didn't want to see at that moment.

17 - Hate or Love

"Lorimar?"

"Shirai?" Lorimar quickly pulled out his sword. "What in Lu' Cel are you doing here?"

"That's none of your business, old man. Besides, I could ask you the same thing!"

I also wanted to get my sword out, but I was carrying the one thing that could save Tansu's life. If we fought here, they might get destroyed. I began trying to think of another way out of this mess.

"If you must know, Grant assigned me to check on the perimeter for anything suspicious. I never thought I would find you."

Lorimar began advancing toward us. As he did, I glanced over his shoulder and saw something that could help us.

"Sara, when I say now, make a diversion, got it?" She nodded. I looked back at the advancing general. "Sorry, but I don't have time to deal with you or your brother at the moment. Now!"

Sara worked her magic on the ivy hanging just outside a window near Lorimar, causing it to quickly grasp onto his arm. Sara managed to get by him in the confusion, but when I passed him, he was one step ahead of me. Lorimar quickly sliced the ivy, and with his hand free, he took hold of my throat and pressed me against a nearby wall.

"Shirai!" Sara cried out.

"Where did you learn that?" Lorimar pointed the tip of his sword an inch from my face.

"Your nephew clued me in. I would have gladly been his pupil instead of having you as a teacher!"

"So you remember that, right? I'll have to deal with Russ later. As for that earlier comment, I want to tell you the real reason, but I have my orders to fulfill."

Lorimar was about to plunge his sword into me when Sara ran between us.

"Sara! What are you doing?!"

She showed absolutely no fear of Lorimar as she shouted right in his face. "Look here, pal! If it wasn't for Shirai and everyone else, your nephew would have been killed when one of Ignotus's monsters came after us!"

"What?" Lorimar actually sounded shocked.

"That's right! In fact, Russ got hurt trying to protect Shirai! Think about how much you are hurting both him and Shirai because you can't make your brother see reason! At any rate, we don't have time for this right now! Our friend Tansu is very ill, and if we don't get back to her soon, she'll die! So move it, or I'll make you move myself!"

This was a side of Sara I had never seen before. Her bravery facing possible death and arguing with one of Grant's most powerful warriors shocked me.

Lorimar looked as though what Sara said about him truly bothered him, but then he replied, "I'm sorry, my lady, but if I overlook this, I would be disgracing my homeland."

Lorimar tightened his grip on his sword, still holding it close to Sara's chest. I thought he was going to kill her, but to my surprise, he lowered his sword instead and let go of my throat.

"However, since I made a warrior's promise to the brother of Tansu that no harm would come to her, I did not see anything. Hurry to her now."

Lorimar sheathed his sword and started to walk away. We took this moment to try to get out of the castle.

"Shirai!"

We stopped in our tracks as we heard Lorimar call back to us.

"Twice now I haven't been able to do my duty. When the time comes, come to the ruins of Ranu Village. We have to settle this once and for all."

"I'll be there."

We left without looking back. Making it outside of the castle, Sara immediately hung on to my back and we were off. We were both quiet on the way back to Tsura.

"Sara, I have to say something to you."

"What?"

"What you did back there was not only stupid, but completely uncalled for! You could have been killed! How would I explained that to your mother?!"

"What? But Shirai, if I didn't—"

"However," I interrupted her, "what you did was also incredibly brave. I wish I had that kind of courage back there."

Two hours later, I jumped through the guest room window, startling both Nova and Luwina.

"What in heaven's name? Where did you come from?" Luwina cried out.

"I think my heart stopped!" Nova added.

"Sorry, but time is too valuable to use doors. Miss Luwina, do you know of a student here named Zen?"

"Yes, he's one of our best pupils here."

"Tell him to get in here as quickly as he can. Also tell him we brought *it* back."

Luwina quickly left the room.

"So you found the flower?"

We answered Nova by showing the numerous flowers we had in the bag, "I know Tansu is sick, but I don't think she's going to need *all* that."

"Sometimes, Nova, I wonder if you ever use that brain of yours," Sara commented.

I quickly braced myself for another argument, but it never came. At that moment, Zen came running into the room, and his eyes bugged out at the sight of all of the flowers. "Wow! You brought all these back?"

"Sara figured you could try growing them here for others to use when they need it."

"Are you kidding? With this many, we'll have a whole field of them in a month! But right now let's get one of them to the infirmary." Quickly picking up one of the flowers, Zen headed straight for the infirmary with all three of us right behind him.

Once there, we all watched as Zen instructed the staff how to prepare the flower for medical use, while the rest of us sat around the bed Tansu was in. As they were preparing the medicine, Sara joined them, taking notes and sharing her own knowledge of healing. The medicine was finally ready.

Instead of the staff giving it to her, Zen handed the cup holding the medicine to me. "Seeing as how you went through much trouble for her sake, I think you should be the one to help her."

Sara and Nova quickly agreed with him. Seeing as everyone was looking at me, I had no choice. I carefully lifted Tansu's head up and made the medicine enter her mouth smoothly. She coughed a little as it went down her throat. After that, I gently placed her head back on her pillow.

"It'll take a few hours for the medicine to work, but she'll be fine," Zen told us.

"Thank you, Zen, for your help."

"Let's say we're even for all the flowers you brought back. I have to get back to class. See you later!"

With that, he was right out the door.

"I'm glad everything's back to normal for now," Nova commented.

"Not everything." I looked at the people that were still with us. "Could you please leave us for a moment?"

I made sure we were alone before speaking. "Guys, I want to apologize for my recent actions. I acted like a jerk."

"Why the apology? You didn't do anything to hurt us," Nova replied. "You were just really worried about Tansu."

"Let me say this, okay? I know that you have all lost someone important to you, but all I cared about was her. I also know that we are all in this together and we should have worked together. I was just too upset learning that she might not make it, and then I went and almost got us killed by Lorimar when we were coming back."

Nova nearly fell over on his chair. "You what?"

"Lorimar was at Flora inspecting it," Sara explained. "He caught us just as we were about to leave."

"If it wasn't for Sara, we wouldn't be here right now. So it's for all those reasons that I'm sorry."

The room was quiet. I could see both Nova and Sara gazing at me, yet I couldn't tell what they were thinking.

"Are you done?" Nova finally asked.

"What?"

"Good. Now let us say something. Each of us has a personal reason for being here, but there are two common things that bind all of us. We are here to help you not only to get your memory back but to make it out of this alive."

Looking at Tansu for a moment, Nova then concluded, "We also have a duty to look out for each other. If one of us gets sick, we all wait till that person is well. We never leave anyone behind."

"Nova's right," Sara added. "We don't care if you're a jerk sometimes or even too nice. It's just the way you are and we like you even when you are like that. Now are you going to let this matter drop, or do we need to explain anything else to you?"

I couldn't help but smile, "Thank you, guys."

"Now that that's over, I could sure go for something to eat." Nova got off his chair and headed out the door in a hurry.

"It sure doesn't take long for him to change subjects," Sara chuckled.

"That's the way *he* is."

"But he has the right idea. Let's go."

I *did* want to get something to eat, but I was still worried about Tansu. "If it's okay with you guys, I'll stay here and keep an eye on Tansu."

"Sure. I'll see if I can bring you anything." Sara started to head for the door. It was then I remembered something else I wanted to say.

"Sara, wait."

She stopped and turned her head. "What is it?"

"I wanted to ask you something, but what with everything that has happened, I never got a chance to ask. Even though I can now use dragon magic, I can't seem to grasp the concept of how to truly use it. You think you could teach me how to handle it while we wait?"

She told me, smiling, to be outside and ready in an hour. The way she smiled made me think about what I would be in store for.

Time passed as we waited for Tansu to recover. During that time, Sara tutored me on how to properly handle my new power. Her training was so grueling that it made my time training with Lorimar look tame. She made sure I knew how to control the energies that went into making the magic come out, or else I might lose control and hurt myself.

"No! No! You keep losing focus too easily! Clear your mind of unnecessary thoughts!"

This was the fifth time Sara had told me this, or rather yelled it. The reason for this latest outburst was I had accidentally lost control of some rocks I had managed to conjure. They went flying toward some students that were leaving the school. Luckily, Sara was able to keep the rocks from hitting them.

"I'm sorry! I just lost control for a second!"

"It's that split second that could make a big difference! Now watch again!"

And this was one of the better days! But with her help, I quickly picked up the basics and things began to fall in place. However, the one element I still couldn't bring out was fire, but I knew I had a way to use that easily.

At one point during our wait, Zen came to me, practically begging to let him takes notes on my transformed body. My first response was no, but since he was the one who had helped save Tansu, I reluctantly gave in.

The rest of the time I was at Tansu's side. Her welfare was on my mind so much, I didn't spend much time getting any sleep. At one point, I didn't even know I was asleep until I woke to find my head resting on Tansu's bed. As I raised my head, I was surprised to see a familiar smile.

"If you're that tired, maybe you should take this bed."

"Tansu!" I cried out. "You're finally awake! Are you feeling any better? Do you need anything?"

"I'm fine, Shirai, I'm fine! You don't need to be this worked up," she replied.

"I'm just so glad to see you are okay. You had all of us worried. They said you might not make it."

"I know. I could hear what was going on despite the fact that I was in such pain. I want to thank everyone for doing so much for me, but I want to thank you the most, Shirai."

I scratched my head nervously, "It... It was nothing. Just repaying you for the time you helped me."

"I don't think that's really it. I heard from the people working here you not only crossed a four-day distance from here to Flora and back in only four hours, risked getting caught by Grant's knights, almost getting killed by Lorimar, but you were the one who stayed by my side the most. You went through so much just for my sake. Why?"

My first reaction was to change the subject, but then I remembered Sara's words. If I was going to tell her why I did everything, this might be the only chance I got.

"It's because I was truly worried about you. You mean a lot to me. I... I..."

I couldn't finish. The words didn't want to come out. I was going to go back with my original plan and tell her something else when I felt her hand close over my own.

"If you don't want to tell me, it's fine. I'm just happy you took such good care of me."

I saw her blue eyes looking at me with such happiness that it made me feel even more afraid to say what I wanted. I knew, though, that it had to come out sooner or later. So I did the only thing I could think of at that moment.

"Tansu, it's because I love you!" I shouted.

I couldn't believe I went off like that. I was so embarrassed and upset that I left the room without looking back. Finding the nearest open window, I jumped outside, landing on a nearby roof, and then jumped to a terrace that was on top of the school.

No one was there, which was good because I didn't feel like talking to anyone. It was nighttime, and the moon Urula was in its crescent phase while Nege was entering its new moon phase. I sat there for thinking how I could have been so stupid.

"Ugh! Idiot! Idiot! What was I thinking? I can't believe I followed Sara's advice like that! I should never have said anything! There's no way anyone could love something like me!"

Needing to vent some of the anger I felt, I took the Sword of the Wyvern and repeatedly cut into the stone railing that overlooked a nearby garden filled with all kinds of flowers. Finally exhausted, I fell on the ground bottom first. As I caught my breath, I stared at my hands—at the way they now looked.

Neither human nor dragon, but stuck in between.

"I'm nothing but an abomination, something that could never be truly accepted!" Turning my gaze away from my hands, I looked up at the moons. "Tansu must be thinking that I'm a fool."

"How can you say that when I couldn't even give you a response before you ran out like that?"

Tansu was standing in the doorway that led back inside. Seeing her made me feel even more depressed and more ashamed of myself.

"Please just forget what I said before. I wasn't thinking."

"Shirai, do you truly think you are all those things you said you were?" She sounded as if she was close to crying, "You really believe that no one would …"

I cut her off before she could finish. "It's just mindless drivel. I need to go somewhere to think."

I was going to take off again when I felt Tansu suddenly grab my tail and grip it tightly. She pulled me back with such force that once again I landed on my bottom. Then, using both her hands, she made sure to get a good hold on my head. Finally she did something that still shocks me to this day.

She kissed me square on where my lips would have been. She kissed me for ten whole seconds before letting me go.

"Wha… what?"

"Don't say anymore. This is the only response I can give you until I am truly sure how I can answer you." Looking forlorn, she added, "Just don't think so low about yourself. It hurts me when I hear you say such things."

"I…"

"*Promise* me, okay?"

Quickly nodding my head, she smiled as she helped me up "That's good, because if you ever think such things again, I'll make you regret it, okay?"

The way she glared at me when she said that scared me. What frightened me even more was the thought of how she would go about making me regret it.

But that was one of the things about her that I liked.

"Now I'm going to make sure you go straight to bed, mister. And I don't want to hear any argument, okay? I already had to come up with an excuse to Nova and Sara as to what happened before."

With that she literally dragged me inside and hauled me toward a nearby bed.

The next day, we were all standing outside the school preparing to leave. Luwina was there to see us off.

"I'm so glad you are all right, miss," she said to Tansu.

"Thank you for all your help and hospitality. I'm sorry if we were any trouble." Tansu bowed.

"Trouble? Thanks to Shirai's help and Miss Sara's knowledge, we can begin cultivating the flowers brought back from Flora, and our healing arts will eventually become more powerful. If anything, I should be thanking Asteron that you came along."

I was starting to feel embarrassed hearing such praise. It looked like Sara was feeling the same way as she nervously tried not to look Luwina in the eye.

"Better watch what you say, miss," Nova warned, "We don't need these two to get swelled heads."

His remark quickly earned him an elbow jab in the gut from Sara.

"We better be off before there are any more interruptions," I said. We started off, waving goodbye to Luwina.

When we reached the main gate, we found Zen standing in front of it.

"Oh, Zen. Come to see us off?" I asked.

"No. I came to ask for one more favor."

"Another?" I moaned. "I already allowed you to write notes about me. What else do you need?"

He fished out a small old book from his pocket and handed it to me. Not knowing what he wanted, I decided to humor him. I nearly dropped the book when I saw what was in it.

"These… These are dragon runes! Where in Lu' Cel did you get this?"

"A while back, some of us students headed to Kunti to study some of the ruins there. There, barely sticking out of the sand was this book.

I hid it so the others didn't see it. Seeing as you are Ska's chosen, I was hoping you could help translate the text for me."

I was going to say I didn't have the time when I noticed that Nova was peering at the book as though the writing fascinated him.

"Is there something wrong, Nova?"

"I thought this looked familiar! I've seen a place literally covered with this text!" he replied.

"You have? Where?" Sara asked.

"The very same place I found the Tao Spear. The walls were covered with dragon runes."

When I learned that, I began to think about changing our next destination. On one hand, we needed to head toward Hariel to save Ska and meet with Lorimar for our battle. On the other, there could be something written there that could help us.

"Nova, do you think you could find that place again?"

"I think so. Why?"

I faced everyone else. "Listen, guys. I know we are on a mission and all, but in light of this development, I think we should head to Kunti and take a look at that tomb. There could be something there that could shed some light on what is going on."

"But what about Ska and Lorimar?" Tansu asked.

"I haven't forgotten them, Tansu, but we need every edge we can get. However, I want all of us to agree on this. If we don't all agree, we'll head straight to Hariel."

Nova quickly came in. "I'm all for it."

Sara spoke next, "I think we should get this over with, but I, too, am interested in finding out more about the dragon race."

"I agree with them," Tansu responded.

"It's unanimous then." I turned to Zen. "I only have time to translate the most common words in this book. Will that be enough?"

"That'll be more than enough!" he replied happily. "If I can crack the rest of the text on my own, I'll be the first human to be able to read dragon runes."

"You mean second, don't you?"

We all had a good laugh.

*****

"How is this possible?" the unknown voice said in a worried tone.

"Is something wrong?" Grant asked.

"Someone who was ready to fall from my negative energy has fully recovered."

"That's impossible! Even in your current state, people are already feeling the effects of your arrival. How could someone be healed like that?"

"There can only be one answer: it must be because of Ska's chosen."

The king banged his armrest. "Shirai! He has been a thorn in my side ever since he took the Sword of the Wyvern! But it won't matter anymore. He'll meet his end when he comes here."

"It would seem that Shirai and his companions aren't heading toward us just yet," the unknown voice told Grant.

"What? Where are they heading?"

"It appears they are now heading south."

"What for? The Kunti Kingdom is destroyed, and all that's left is ruins. What could they be looking for?"

"Even I can't see that far. Those ruins still reek of dragon magic, hampering my sight."

Getting up from his throne, Grant took two steps forward. "Well, whatever the reason, they must still be dealt with. Ska is almost drained, and we can't have any interference."

"I think now is a good time to send our sentry."

"I believe so. Are you ready, our protector?" Grant asked the knight in dark green armor.

"I am, my lord. I've been waiting for so long."

18 - Final Wall

Our trek through the Kunti Desert wasn't what you would call easy. In fact, it was downright treacherous. Not only did we have to deal with scorching heat and freezing nights, there were sandstorms that appeared out of nowhere. We also had to deal with desert creatures that wanted to make meals out of all of us.

If it wasn't for Tansu's hunting skills, Sara's ability to draw out water from the ground when we needed it, and my new dragon magic, the desert would have claimed us. Despite the good luck we had so far, I couldn't shake this strange feeling I had been having ever since we entered the desert.

Something inside me was extremely anxious and was trying its best to warn me of something. What was even weirder was it wasn't me really feeling this, but as if I was feeling someone else's fear.

"Shirai, what is it? You've looked preoccupied ever since we started through the desert," Tansu asked.

"I… I don't know. For some reason, it's like my body is crying out in distress. I can't shake this feeling."

"Maybe you're getting worked up because you are excited to see what the dragon runes say," Sara suggested.

"I hope so, Sara. I really hope so." I tried hard to ignore the feeling.

"Well, we'll be there soon, so we won't have to stay any longer than we need to," Nova said.

He was in the lead holding the map, since he had been in Kunti before, but as we continued walking, I heard him say to himself, "This is really strange. The way to Kunti wasn't this bad. Did something happen?"

I didn't understand what Nova meant, so I didn't bring it up with him. Just like he had said, it didn't take us long to reach Kunti Kingdom.

But none of us were prepared for what was waiting for us.

In only a few short years, the so-called "desert oasis" was in complete ruins. The once great walls that surrounded the kingdom had crumbled. Dead trees now cast their shadows on the ground, and time and wind had begun to bury the castle. The large fountain that lay near the entrance, which continually sprouted precious water, had stopped flowing, and only sand now filled it.

I didn't want to think what Grant could have done to bring such a place like this down. "What happened here?"

"I knew it was hit hard by Grant, but to end up like this?" Nova commented.

"Something isn't right." Sara got down on the ground and touched the sand. "I can hardly feel any energy in the area. It's as though this place is dying."

"How could something like this have happened?" Tansu asked.

"That's why we're here, Tansu, to see if we can find out why this happened." Hoping to get an answer for that, I turned to Nova, "Can you still find the tomb, Nova?"

"I hope so, Shirai."

He then led us around the castle perimeter. The other parts of the castle were worse off than what we first saw. Sections of the wall looked like they were literally blown away by some unknown force.

Something incredibly powerful.

I hoped we didn't have to face what ever caused this yet. We needed more time to prepare. I began to think about how it must have been horrible for the people living here to watch as their homes were being destroyed.

However, my thoughts were cut short when Nova suddenly shouted, "Aha! It's over there!"

He was pointing to something sticking out of the ground about a half a mile away. As we got closer, I saw that it was the ruins of an ancient temple.

Most of the walls had fallen victim to the passing of time. Columns of very hard stone stood where they were planted long ago. I knew even with my increased strength, I couldn't hope to lift one of them.

They were carved so smoothly, you couldn't find any evidence of a chisel ever used on them. No human tool could've possibly been able to do that. The roof was long gone, and what remained was lying on the ground in a huge pile of rubble.

Nova had stopped over a section of the temple that was bare except for sand. He then asked both Sara and myself, "You two think you could clear away some of this sand?"

The two of us quickly got to work. After a few minutes of clearing away sand, we were rewarded by finding a large slab that was half crumbled away, revealing a large staircase leading into an underground tunnel.

"Watch your step, ladies and gentlemen," Nova cracked as he went inside. Sara followed him while I helped Tansu go down.

To our surprise, the tunnel was lit by the same strange crystals that were in the dragon's tunnels. In the darkness of the underground tunnel, they were like mini-suns. As we walked, I was half expecting one of us to accidentally trip some hidden trigger setting off an ancient trap. But we made it to our destination without that happening.

Nova was not been kidding. The chamber was completely covered with dragon runes from top to bottom. In the center was a pedestal that looked as though something was once held there. The entire room was filled with the presence of powerful magic.

"Feels really weird being back here. Like I'm back to see if it was okay to take the Tao Spear," Nova commented.

"Seeing as how you just took it without asking permission, it's more like you are returning to the scene of the crime." Ignoring the look Nova gave me, I began to look at the dragon runes. "I can feel the magic of the dragons seeping from the very walls. They must have constructed this temple. There's no way a human could have done this alone."

I looked for the beginning of the text. I soon found it and began to translate.

"I, Ska, Lord of All Dragons, as I am called by the people of this world, leave this message for future generations to read so they may learn from the past. Since my chosen and I were the only ones to go against the evil that once held Lu' Cel in its cruel grasp, it must be known that this desert was once a beautiful area of green, but as it was also the area where our battle took place, it was quickly reduced to a barren wasteland by our fighting."

"This place was once alive with plant life?" Tansu asked.

"What kind of power did these two have that could have done such damage?" Sara wondered.

I continued reading, "Despite our best effort, the one who helped me was killed by the evil while trying to seal it away. In his honor, his body and soul have been laid to rest here in a sacred tomb that only we of the dragon race can find so he may find rest."

"You mean *this* is that warrior's resting place?" Nova asked in shock.

"I don't think so, Nova, if you found it."

Nova quickly let out a sigh of relief. "Thank goodness. For a second, I thought I was a grave-robber."

I wanted to make a joke about that, but I resisted and went on. "Even though this place was barren, somehow life still tried to cling to their once-beautiful home. In order to see that it could continue, I asked the wisest wizards at that time to create the Tao Spear and lay it here so it could serve two purposes. One was to make sure what energy was left in the land would continue to circulate throughout the area. In this way, the life still living could try to grow back one day."

"The spear had another purpose?" Tansu gave a quick glance at the Tao Spear. "If it had that kind of power why is this place dying?"

"I think that when Grant attacked, the power he used took so much energy that, with the spear gone, the land couldn't take it," Sara suggested.

"Are you saying it's my fault that Kunti became what it is now?" Nova argued.

"You didn't know. And even if you did I doubt it would have made any difference."

She's right, I thought to myself, *That would also explain why Nova thought the way to Kunti was now so dangerous. The land's life is literally nearing its end.*

Of course we weren't here to discuss such matters. I was nearing the end of the text. "Its second purpose is the most critical: it is to neutralize any kind of magic used for evil intent to harm this land. In turn, using that same power, it keeps hidden the location of two very important objects, which lay at the very bottom depth of Orem Lake. They are the Sword of the Wyvern, used to seal away the evil one, and its dark counterpart, wielded by my foe, in which he was sealed, the Bloodbringer."

I stopped reading while taking a step back away from the wall. I'm sure my friends were in shock too.

"A second sword... there was a second sword... a second...!"

My head suddenly began hurting again. Unlike the other times, however, the pain was so excruciating that I felt like I was dying. I let out a bloodcurdling scream as I collapsed onto the floor unable to move, violently thrashing around.

"Shirai!" Tansu was at my side as soon as the scream left my mouth.

"The pain... I can't stand it!"

"It must be big!" Nova tried to get me to stop squirming violently around on the floor. "He must be trying to bring back all of his memories!"

"That's not good! If remembering a few things causes him discomfort, this could kill him," Sara said fearfully.

"What can we do for him?" Tansu asked. "We can't leave him like this!"

"I... I must continue..." I struggled and tried to get up. "Need to find out... who Ska... fought!"

"No, don't, Shirai! We need to get you out of here!"

"Let me...do this...one last thing!"

The pain I was feeling was so great that my vision was getting blurry. Tansu wanted to say something else when Nova stopped her. I scanned the wall for any name, but unfortunately Ska intended to keep the evil's identity known only to him.

"Help me... out of here..."

Both Nova and Sara helped me up and carried me out of the place with Tansu right behind me. As we where on our way out, the same voice that I heard back on Russ's ship came once again.

No! I will not let you! I will not let you remember! Never!

Whatever triggered this must be the final key I needed to unlock all of my memories, and I wasn't going to back down. But when we finally came back into the sunlight, a new feeling came over me.

Fear.

Fear filled not only my body, but I could sense it coming from the Sword of the Wyvern.

"Wait! Something … something is here," I warned everyone.

The air suddenly filled with familiar evil laughter. Then, from out of the very sand itself, someone rose from the ground.

It was a knight in dark green armor with a black cape. The knight wore a full face helmet. In his hand was a blood red sword with a gold hilt.

"It would appear that I caught you at an opportune time, Shirai," the knight chuckled in a voice all of us knew.

"Ignotus! So you still live!" Sara angrily replied.

"I see the elf girl is with you too! You may have caught me off guard last time, but never again. Lord Grant has given me more power and a gift. Behold!"

Ignotus raised the sword he had for all of us to clearly see. It was an almost exact replica of my sword, except for the fact it looked more sinister, and the runes carved at the bottom of the blade were not known to this world. I could sense that the Sword of the Wyvern was absolutely terrified of Ignotus's sword, and I knew why.

"So Grant found Bloodbringer."

"What?" Nova asked.

"So you know about your sword's evil twin?" Ignotus cackled. "Then you might as well know that its power is greater than your own sword. You can take that knowledge with you to the afterlife!"

I suddenly felt dark energy coming from Bloodbringer. If Ignotus used that here, I knew something bad might happen. Using what strength I could bring out, I pushed everyone down to the ground and brought out the Sword of the Wyvern.

Holding it was difficult, for the fear coming from the sword made it hard to control, but I wasn't planning on using it for long. I just needed for Ignotus to block my attack. While he did, I used my magic to blow tons of sand at Ignotus with extreme speed. It hit him directly in the chest, making numerous dents in his armor.

"What was… you can use dragon magic?"

"I will… I will not let you… or Bloodbringer… scare me… I will defend my friends against… both of you!" Even though I *was* ready to do so, I couldn't take the pain I was feeling much longer.

"How could he have sent me here without telling me about this? This calls for a change of plans. It looks like your luck continues."

He then began to slowly sink into the sand.

"Wait! Who are you talking about? Is it Grant?"

"The world will soon find out! The end is drawing near for you and Ska! However, I will be the one who will kill you!"

He finally disappeared. Even if I had wanted to stop him, I couldn't. I had reached my limit and fell to the ground, blacking out the second I felt sand.

I opened my eyes to find myself standing in the middle of a vast, open, rocky place. It was completely empty, devoid of any life or sound. I couldn't even see anything past the horizon. The sense of pure sadness and despair hung in the air.

"What is this place?" I was hoping for someone to answer, but no one did. "Hello? Is anyone here?"

As before, no one answered.

"This place. It feels like a dungeon. I've got to find a way out."

I began to walk forward. As I walked through this desolate place, I still couldn't find any sign of life. The further I went, the more I felt sadness surrounding me. I slowly began to think I would be stuck here forever.

"Please! Anyone! Where am I? Please tell me!"

I was getting frantic. I wanted to leave and never come back here.

A voice suddenly called out to me.

Shirai.

"Who's there?"

Shirai, go forward. You must go forward…

"That voice… it's the one who talked to me back at the Dante Mountains! Who are you?"

The voice didn't respond. With no idea of what else to do, I followed the voice's directions, and I continued onward. As I did, I could literally feel sadness on my skin.

When I thought I couldn't take it anymore, I finally came upon something. It was a giant wall that stretched all the way past the horizon on both sides of me.

"What is this?"

I reached out to touch the wall when several spikes suddenly erupted from it and nearly impaled my hand.

"What the hell?"

Go away... Don't see... Go away... Don't see... This time it was the voice that spoke to me on Russ's boat that I heard. It kept repeating the same thing over and over again in a quiet tone.

"What is going on here?!"

You are at the wall your own mind has created, the second voice spoke to me. Only this time, I could hear it coming from behind.

I turned around and was faced with the largest dragon I'd ever seen.

Twice as big as any of the other dragons back at the Dante Mountains, its gold-colored scales glistened, even though there wasn't any sunlight reflecting down on them.

Two pairs of magnificent wings grew out of its back, made of the purest white feathers ever. It had dark brown talons and sturdy-looking legs, sky blue hair ran down the top of its head all to the way to the tip of its long tail. A large diamond shaped crystal imbedded in its chest emitted a peaceful glow.

The most noticeable feature was its face. Instead of the typical stern dragon faces we had seen before, this dragon's face actually showed kindness.

"Are you Ska, Lord of All Dragons?"

Yes, Shirai. I am glad to see you are still alive. I hoped to all of Lu' Cel that my power saved you when you were attacked by Ignotus back then.

"Back then? You mean we met before?"

Ska nodded his head. *In a way we did, but what I truly hoped for was to get a chance to apologize for any inconvenience by doing what I did to you.*

"What are you talking about?"

The dragon lord

Since you carry a part of my power, I have been able to sense what has been happening to you using the Sword of the Wyvern which was made with my scales as a medium. He became a little worried and said, *Had I known how much you would have been affected by how others would think of you, I would have tried something else to save you.*

He was obviously talking about the incident back at Tsura when I confessed my love to Tansu. I was a little mad at him at first for spying on me at such a time, but I was more surprised by him asking *me* to forgive him for something *he* did. If someone as powerful as Ska is able to ask something like that, then he must really care about the people of Lu' Cel.

"I'll admit I've had a few problems with the way I look now, but honestly, I thank you for your help. In fact, if it wasn't for your actions, I wouldn't be here or have met all the friends I made on my journey."

Ska actually smiled.

It is gratifying to hear you say that. His smile disappeared as he now stared at the wall behind us with serious eyes. *But despite all my power, even I couldn't have predicted that your own mind would close itself after your transformation.*

I also looked back at the wall, especially at the spikes that almost took my hand. "Why is it doing this?"

Ska shook his head. *I'm afraid only you can answer that yourself.*

"But I need to remember! Is there anything you can do?"

Unfortunately, in my current state I can't do anything to help you. The only thing I can do is give you advice.

"And what is that?"

You must have faith in yourself and those who care about you. Realize that even when things look bleak, no one should face them alone. If you believe that with all your soul, you can overcome this hurdle and anything else. I know you can do it. That is why I chose you to help me. I knew that you would soon bring a change for the better for Lu' Cel.

Before I could ask him any more questions, he began to fade away.

"Ska! Wait!"

Please hurry. Everyone needs you.

Then he was gone, leaving me alone in front of the wall. I looked back at it, seeing the spikes still there. I knew if I tried to get closer, I'd be skewered, and if I attacked the wall, I'd only hurt myself.

Standing there, I tried to think of something to do when I heard a faint voice speaking over my mind's voice. *I'm alone... I want someone to talk to... but I don't have anyone anymore... I want to go home... but I can never go back... I have nothing... I have no one...*

Even though my memories were still sealed behind the wall, I instantly knew who that was. I could feel it in my heart.

"That's right... I once felt like that... not so long ago," I said to myself. "I can now feel the pain and loneliness coming from behind that wall. Ska's words finally make sense. I understand why you locked away our memories, but you must realize that things have changed. I'm not alone anymore. Tansu and Sara are with me. Even our old friend Nova is with me too."

At first there was no response. I thought I had failed, and then I heard something snap. It was coming from the wall as a tiny crack appeared on its surface.

"If there is something I remember that's so horrible, I would normally tell someone close about it... I had no one at the time. That's not the case anymore. I know so many people now that I can tell them when something makes us sad, angry, or happy."

More cracks began to appear on the wall and the one that first appeared began to spread.

"But how can I tell anybody anything about what happened to me if I can't even remember? I can't remember any of the good times or grow stronger from the bad times. I want to remember all of this. I want to remember so I can tell my story to my friends. Let me remember!"

Finally, in a deafening crash, the wall fell. I was quickly overcome by light that was coming from the other side, and I passed out.

I slowly awoke to find myself laying on my side with a blanket underneath me. Sitting up, I saw I was now inside the ruins of Kunti. It was nighttime and a small fire was blazing nearby with my friends sitting by it.

Tansu saw me sitting up and dropped the piece of food she was about to eat. "Shirai! You're all right!"

I didn't say anything in response. I just nodded my head.

"You need to stop making us worry so much about you. I don't think my heart can take anymore excitement," Nova joked.

I still didn't say anything. I just stared at them.

Staring and remembering.

"What's the matter, Shirai? Why are you just looking at us like that?" Sara asked.

I could feel tears starting to form in my eyes.

"I… I…"

"Are you okay, pal?" Nova asked in a worried voice. "You look like someone who lost something important."

I shook my head.

Tansu sat next to me. "Did you remember something? Do you want to talk about it?"

When she said that, I started to cry very hard.

"Yes… I remember. I finally remember. I've wanted to talk to someone for a long time, but I was alone… I don't want to be alone again."

Tansu gently took me in her arms as she stroked my hair to try to comfort me. Nova and Sara got up to sit next to me, so I knew that they were there also nearby.

In that moment, I knew in my heart I wasn't alone anymore.

19 - Tragedy of Life

"**S**o you finally got it all out?" Nova asked.

It was the day after I regained all my memories. I was finally able to let go of all the anguish and despair I had before but had forgotten about when I had lost my memory. Now I felt like I could truly enjoy life again.

"I did. Thank you all for being there for me. I know I may have acted like a baby the way I was going on."

"I think you really needed to cry. You seem so much happier than I ever saw you," Tansu pointed out.

"If you needed to have a good cry, you should have done so long ago," Sara commented.

"I didn't even know I needed to until last night."

"The way you were crying, you must have remembered something terrible," Tansu said.

I nodded slightly. "I'm afraid so. I hope you are all ready for a long tale."

"Hey, it's not like we have some important engagement we have to get to," Nova half-argued, half-joked.

Sara gave Nova an evil look, but I was too happy to have my memories back to care what he said. And so I began to tell everyone everything I remembered.

My original home was Hariel. I had been abandoned by my real parents when I was a baby. Fortunately, I was found by a nice couple. Since they were childless, they decided to raise me as their own.

I had a happy childhood, despite the fact I never knew who my real parents were. Most of the time, I helped my foster parents with their work. Their job was to make special-ordered clothing for people in the town and even the people in the castle.

One day, when I was eight, I saw a bunch of the townspeople watching someone important go up to the castle. It was a giant of a man, wearing silver armor with our kingdom's emblem on the chest plate.

"Dad, who is that?"

"That's General Lorimar, our kingdom's greatest knight. They say no one has ever beaten him in battle."

"What's a knight?"

He smiled like he always did. "A knight is a person who defends those who need help."

"Wow. I want to be a knight!"

From that day forth, I dreamed of being a knight so strong I could protect my parents from everything. I was constantly reminded by them that it was not easy becoming one, but I didn't care.

When I was twelve, I decided to go and see how knights were trained. Ignoring my parent's warning not to do so, I snuck into the area just outside the castle and found the training grounds the knights used. I was so amazed by how they trained that I didn't see one come up from behind me and grab my shirt collar.

"What are you doing here, lad?" he demanded. "This place is off limits to civilians!"

"Hey! I just wanted to see how you become knights! I didn't do anything wrong!"

He, of course, didn't believe me. "Then explain why you are here without our knowing? If you can't, I know a place where you can tell us."

At the rate things were going, I thought for sure I was going to end up in a dungeon, but at that moment, a proud voice spoke out, "What is going on here?"

It was Lorimar. He had just entered the training grounds and seeing the scene between me and the knight immediately came over. I couldn't believe I was actually with the Great Lorimar.

"I'm sorry sir." The knight saluted. "I caught this ruffian spying on our troops. I was about to remedy the situation."

"I told you I didn't do anything wrong!"

Lorimar looked at me, and for a split second, I could see he was shocked about something. "Let that boy go. I will personally deal with him."

The knight quickly did so and left the two of us alone. At first I was afraid that Lorimar would also think I was spying, but instead he asked me, "Young man, what is your name?"

I was too terrified to answer at first. "I… I'm Shirai. I live with my parents in town. I didn't mean to sneak in here. I just—"

"So you are called Shirai," he said with his eyes closed.

"Is something wrong?"

He opened his eyes "No. I was thinking. So why did you come here?"

I told him how I was hoping to find out how I could become a knight just like him. Afterward, Lorimar chuckled a little. "I see. Well, you seem set on this idea of yours, so how about I personally train you?"

I nearly fell over. I couldn't believe I would be training with *the* Lorimar. I quickly said yes. He led me to a nearby shack where some of the knights slept. Inside Lorimar began to write a letter to my parents. He instructed me *not* to look at it and to only show it to my parents. Not wanting to disappoint him, I did exactly that.

When my parents read the letter, they too had the same look that Lorimar had when he saw me.

"Is something wrong?"

"No, son. It's nothing," my mother replied.

"We're just surprised is all. Who would have thought our son would be chosen by Lorimar himself to be a knight," my father added.

With that, I began my life living with the other knights. Just like Lorimar promised, he taught me everything from basic knowledge of the world to using a sword. At first I found that training was a lot harder than it seemed. I couldn't even do most of the sword skills I needed to practice correctly at the time.

"You need to relax your muscles. You're too stiff when you swing the sword," Lorimar once told me while I was practicing.

"I'm trying! I really am! But this sword won't do what I want it to do!"

Lorimar grinned slightly. "I think you need to have someone show you how it's done first. Luckily for you, there is someone here who can."

He brought over a boy a few years older than me. That was the first time I met Russ. Back then, I didn't know that he was Lorimar's nephew.

"Russ, could you show Shirai how to do that maneuver?"

"Yes, sir," he replied.

He did show me, and he was better at it than I was. I was a little jealous that he could handle a sword and I couldn't. This developed into a bit of a rivalry between us.

Over time, Lorimar became like a second father to me. When I injured myself, he would personally fix me up. When it was meal time, he would sit at the table I was using and talk with me.

Of course, I didn't always have a good day. One day, I was so depressed over a mistake I had made during training that I snuck away to find a place to try and cheer up. My search led me to the nearby village of Ranu. I had never been there before, and I was lost and afraid.

At that moment a boy my age came up to me. "Hey, kid, you look like you could use a hand. What's the matter, you lost?"

"No. I mean yes. It's just I've never been here before, and I don't know my way around."

"Well I can fix that! I would be happy to show you around! What's your name?"

"I'm Shirai."

"Nice to meet you. The name is Nova."

And that's how I first met Nova. Over the next five years life was good. I got better with the sword, and I managed to sneak away and constantly meet up with Nova and have a good time with him.

Things were going great, but during one year, I just couldn't get away from my training to go see Nova. I didn't mind at first… until I heard the news that Ranu had been burned down. I wanted to see if Nova was okay, but I couldn't tell Lorimar where I had been going all these years. Then another thought entered my mind.

What if Lorimar himself was a part of it?

When I asked him this question, he said nothing. I wanted to go ask the king why Ranu was burned, but Lorimar told me never to let the king himself or the prince see me. When I asked why, again he said nothing. I soon got over my grief, and life went on, but since the day Ranu was destroyed, I began to sense something strange.

"What is wrong, Shirai? You are off today," Lorimar asked one day.

"I… I don't know. For a while now something has been bothering me."

"What is it?"

"I feel as though there is someone nearby I know very well, yet I have never met this person."

He told me it must have been my overworked mind. I decided that must have been the case, but the feeling still continued.

A few days after that incident, Lorimar suddenly came up to me and asked, "There is something that I have been wondering about for a while. What is the main reason you wanted to become a knight?"

"Well a knight's duty is to protect, right? I want to be strong enough to protect the people I care about, especially my parents for all they did for me."

He laughed a little before replying. "It's true that a knight protects that which he holds dear, but it takes more than determination to accomplish that. You also need the resolve to push yourself further than you think you can. Remember that."

During the next three years, our king continued to take over much of Lu' Cel. I begged Lorimar to ask his king if I could help him in the war, but each time, Lorimar refused.

"I don't want you to get involved with such bloodshed. You are my prized pupil. I need you here for now," he would say.

I finally got tired of waiting, so I decided to go see the king myself. When I opened the door to the throne room, I wished to all the gods that I hadn't. Inside with the king were my parents, along with the one I now know as Ignotus.

"So you are the ones who have been hiding that brat from us!" Grant yelled.

"But, sire…"

"Silence! Now that I know this, I need to take care of him soon, but as for you two, you have no reason to be here!"

With that, he picked up a red sword, which I now realize was Bloodbringer, and with one swing, struck down both of my parents.

Witnessing this I wanted to scream, but I couldn't let them know I was there. At first, I was planning to quickly run away, but at that moment I saw one of the castle workers coming my way, carrying a green sword, the Sword of the Wyvern, on top of a big cushion.

Filled with anger, I quickly ambushed the worker and took the sword, planning on killing Grant for what he had done to my parents. Before I could, some of the knights discovered me. I ran for my life, and as I made it to the gate leading outside the castle, Lorimar appeared in front of me.

"Shirai! What are you doing here? And why are you holding *that* sword?"

My face was full of tears as I told him what happened.

"By Asteron, what has happened to him? I need you to listen to me, Shirai! Go away from here! Hide yourself, and protect that sword with your life! I'll make sure they don't know where you went!"

"But—"

"*Go!*"

I fled the castle, never to return to Hariel. For the next three years, I went from one place to another, making sure that the Sword of the Wyvern and I were never discovered. During that time, I wasn't able to make direct contact with other people for fear they might find out about the sword. I didn't have anyone to talk to or to share my grief during those painful years.

It soon became too much for me to take. I eventually made my way to Arian Ravine. I planned to throw the sword in there and find a place to try to get on with my life. As I was prepared to throw the sword away, someone discovered me.

"So we finally found you, Shirai!"

It was Ignotus and a few of Grant's knights.

"You! You were with Grant when he killed my parents!"

"I don't think you should be worrying about that right now. Besides, if you want to be mad at someone, why not be mad at yourself? You, who trained with Lorimar and couldn't even protect those pathetic peasants."

As he laughed at my parents' death, I made up my mind. If I was to die here, I at least wanted to have the satisfaction of knowing that I took him with me. I fought through the knights, trying to get at Ignotus while he watched as though he was amused by my situation. It was during this struggle that I got the scar on my left eye.

I finally defeated all of the knights and went after Ignotus, but he used his powers on me, tearing up my body in the process. It was then I accidentally fell off the edge and into the ravine.

I... I'm not strong at all... I guess I never had the resolve needed... I failed you... Mother... Father...

I waited for death to claim me, having lost the will to live. As I fell, I sensed someone was with me. It was then I noticed that my falling had, for some unexplained reason, slowed down.

Do not give up, Shirai! You are strong! a voice suddenly spoke in my mind.

"Who... who are you?"

I am Ska, Lord of All Dragons. I am talking to you through the Sword of the Wyvern you hold tightly in your hand.

"What... how is that possible?"

There is no time. The day you first touched this sword, I was able to sense what's in your heart. I know you really don't want to die. You want to live.

I shed a couple of tears. "I do. I want to avenge my parents, but now..."

That is why I am here. I can save you, but I need your help in return.

"Help?"

The world of Lu' Cel is facing its greatest crisis ever. I need someone courageous, caring, and strong to help. I know it might be too much to ask, but I sense you can do it.

"I... I'm not strong... I... never... was..."

I could begin to feel myself getting weaker from all the blood I was losing. I knew it would only be a matter of time until I was dead.

You are stronger than you think. I believe your parents thought that too. However, if you just accept death like this, you're not only hurting yourself, but those who once cared about you. I care too. Believe in yourself. I cannot force you to make a choice. Only you can do that.

"I... I want... I want to live..."

In that instant, I was surrounded by a golden light that somehow transported me somewhere else: the outskirts of Kenga Village.

Using what little strength I had left, I slowly staggered to the village. I didn't get far as my energy was exhausted and I collapsed where I stood. Ska must have given me part of his power before I was discovered. He transformed me into the dragon man I was today in order to save my life.

But just as he said before, he didn't know that my mind would shut away all my memories because of all the shock and suffering I lived through over the years.

"And the rest is as you know it," I concluded.

"Wow. I never knew you had it so rough," Nova said. "And after I made that crack earlier."

"I'll let it go if you will."

"There's something I don't get," Sara said outloud.

"What is it?" Tansu asked.

"How did Grant get both swords in the first place?"

"I think we'll get all our questions answered when we confront Grant," I replied. "But first I have to see Lorimar and have a talk with him."

With renewed spirits, we began the long walk toward my confrontation with destiny.

*****

"Why didn't you tell me he learned to use dragon magic?" Ignotus argued with Grant.

"You let something like that scare you back here?" the unknown voice asked.

"No, but I think you deliberately sent me there without telling me that information."

"Is that what you really think?" Grant asked.

"Whether it's true or not, I don't like being left out like this! You would do well to remember that. I have to prepare for Shirai's homecoming."

Ignotus disappeared afterward.

"He is getting too confident in his ability," Grant said.

"Does it really matter? As long as he and Bloodbringer do their job, he can be replaced. The final act is coming soon. Ska will learn that he shouldn't have helped this world."

Grant added, "And I will soon be all powerful. It's all thanks to Ignotus."

20 - Battle for Truth

It was a long journey to get to Ranu Village, but I had to get there and finally get the truth out of Lorimar. However, I was also taking time now to truly enjoy our trip. I never had a chance to take in the sights around me when I had been hiding all those years. I never knew how beautiful Lu' Cel was before now, and I knew I had to do what I could to protect it and all the people I met—especially my friends.

"Slow down, Shirai! You know we're not all gifted with incredible speed like you!" I heard Nova call out to me as I was running ahead of everyone.

"No chance, Nova! I'm going to make up for all those years I was hiding and enjoy myself!"

"Let him have his fun, Nova," Sara commented. "He's been through a lot. I know I would love a chance to relax myself."

"I would like to relax too, Sara, but I think you all are forgetting why we are on this journey."

"We all know how you would like to relax," I taunted. "You drink yourself so far into the ground, we'd need a ladder just to get you to sober."

I saw Nova's face grow red from anger. "Oh, you want to make something out of it? Come here!"

He started to chase me all over the place, but he couldn't keep up with me. Tansu and Sara watched from the sidelines, unable to stop laughing.

"I can't believe how much Shirai has changed since I first met him," Tansu remarked.

"No kidding. I thought he was too uptight most of the time, but now, he's like a completely different person." A sly smirk crept up on Sara's face. "I can imagine any girl would love to be his girlfriend."

When I saw a down look form on Tansu's face, I broke away from my skillful dodging of Nova and ran over to her. "Is something wrong, Tansu? Are you feeling ill again? We can take a moment to rest if you want."

She shook her head. "No, no, I'm fine, really."

Tansu didn't say much afterward. I wanted to know what was bothering her, but she kept saying nothing was wrong.

Eventually I stopped asking, but every once in a while, I would see her staring at me as though she wanted to say something.

*****

The night before the group reached Ranu, Tansu stayed awake staring at the fire still burning as Shirai and Sara were asleep. As she continued to watch the flames, Nova came up behind her after coming back from patrolling the area.

"I thought you'd be asleep by now," he said.

"I… I have a lot of things on my mind. I couldn't get to sleep."

Sitting down next to her, Nova too stared at the flames. "It's probably none of my business, but you wouldn't be thinking about Shirai, would you?"

Tansu was completely caught off guard by Nova's question, "Wha… What makes you think I…"

"You may be to able fool him, but I have a keen sense for these kinds of things. In fact, I bet you're trying to figure out your real feelings that you probably have for him, right?"

Tansu was speechless.

"Is it that obvious?"

"I suspected back at Tsura when me and about ten other people heard Shirai shouting that he loved you. On a similar note, you need to work on coming up with better lies," Nova chuckled.

Tansu was blushing wildly by now. "It's not funny, Nova! I don't know what to do."

He looked confused. "Is there something wrong with him, I mean aside from him being part dragon?"

She shook her head. "No, he's a great guy. Kind, caring, and brave, but I…"

Nova cut in, "Before you continue on, let me tell you something Shirai failed to tell us back at Kunti. You said that he is brave, but back when I first met him, he was anything but that. Even over the years, I could tell he still wasn't completely sure about himself."

Tansu stared at Nova in disbelief. "Is that true?"

Nova nodded. "But when I met him again back near Gale, I could instantly tell that he wasn't the same Shirai I had known. In fact, I could tell that he had finally started to learn how to be brave."

"I knew he was already brave when I first met him."

"I don't think it was the same thing. You have to remember he lost his memory at that point, so he had no idea what he originally was like before."

Tansu turned her attention from the flickering fire to where Shirai was asleep, "Then… where did he learn to be brave?"

Nova stood up slowly. "If I had to guess, he must have learned it from meeting you. I believe he became brave to protect you. In fact, the two of you meeting was probably the best thing that could have happened to him."

With that, Nova went over to where the others were and was soon asleep, leaving Tansu still sitting next to the fire. She glanced down at the bracelet from Shirai. It shone as the light from the fire hit its surface. Before she went to sleep, she glanced up at the sky, seeing all the stars that had appeared.

"Brother, I wonder what you would have said about Shirai if you had met him. Probably the same thing I'm thinking right now."

*****

We finally reached our destination, but when I saw what had become of Ranu, I nearly started to cry. The busy village I once knew was completely decimated. There was burnt lumber lying on the ground, broken stones all over the place, and the only occupants of the village were now weeds that had started to consume the area.

"*This* is Ranu Village?" I asked in disbelief.

"Unfortunately, it is, pal," Nova replied with a small growl. "This is all that was left when Ignotus was done."

"This is terrible." Tansu turned away for a moment. "How can humans be so cruel?"

"It was no human who did this, lass," a familiar voice replied.

From behind some of the wreckage, Lorimar stepped out.

"Lorimar…"

"I see you all made it." He looked at Tansu, and a relieved smile appeared on his face. "I am especially glad to see you are well."

"I wouldn't have been if you had done your job back at Flora."

"I'm not as coldhearted as my brother has become."

"Maybe so, but I didn't come here to talk about such matters," I told him.

"Indeed, you didn't." He noticed the way I was glaring at him. "From that look of yours, I take it you finally remember everything?"

I nodded. "I came here to get the truth, not from the famous General Lorimar, but from the man I once looked up to. If you truly didn't want to have any part of this madness, why did you follow Grant's every order?"

"It's the same reason I didn't send you into battle when you were young. I would've forgotten it if I didn't find that you were still alive back at Gale. It was to protect you."

"Protect me!" My tail flicked the ground hard, sending up bits of stone in the air. "Like you could have protected my parents?"

"I swear to Ska, I didn't know about that."

"So why did you even take me in anyway if you had no intention of sending me into battle? And if you knew who I was, why did you try to kill me each time we met?"

"I'm afraid I can only answer that when you finally surpass me in battle."

Lorimar slowly drew out his sword as I did the same.

"If that is the only way, then so be it!"

"We'll help you," Nova added.

"Please, everyone. Let me do this on my own. I alone must lay the past to rest. I must show him I have the resolve to overcome him!"

"But—"

Tansu stopped Nova. "We understand. Just be careful, okay?"

I stared down Lorimar, waiting for a chance to go in. When I found one, I charged at him. Lorimar quickly jumped backward to dodge a sword stroke. He then brought down his sword on me, but I jumped high in the air to dodge it. While I was in the air, I brought forth a small windstorm to try to keep Lorimar busy. As I came down, I managed to leave a small cut on his cheek.

"I see you learned a few new maneuvers," he commented.

"You haven't seen anything yet!"

Lorimar came at me with a wide sweep of his sword, barely missing my legs. During that split second when Lorimar was wide open, I laid into him with a powerful kick at his chest, leaving a huge dent in his armor. However, he quickly recovered, and before I could move out of the way, he left a large gash on my left arm.

"Shirai!" Tansu cried out.

"Stay where you are!"

Ignoring the pain, I magically brought up a large rock from the ground. Using all my strength, I punched into it, sending all the rubble toward Lorimar. He was pelted by hundreds of rocks and didn't see me come up from behind him as I backflipped him into a nearby broken house.

"Not bad for someone who couldn't handle a sword their first time, huh?" I called out to him.

He rose up from the wreckage, a small bruise now on his forehead. "Indeed you have grown stronger in strength and skill, but it'll take more than that to bring me down."

I prepared for another attack. "Is that what you normally say to those you killed during the war?"

What Lorimar said next came as a shock to all of us: "I never killed anyone in my life."

"What?" I lowered my sword.

"Have you ever wondered why I am called the Greatest Knight in Hariel? It's because I have always managed to win without having to bring down anyone."

"But… then what about Tansu's brother, Dai?"

Lorimar closed his eyes as if he was remembering the event in his mind. "I *did* best him in combat, but when I learned he had a sister, I tried to make sure he escaped. Unfortunately, one of my overzealous men brought him down with an arrow. I still curse the fact I couldn't have saved him."

I could hear Tansu crying softly in the background. I wondered if they were tears of joy knowing that she didn't have anymore reason for revenge; or perhaps they were tears of despair because she knew that her brother was forever gone.

"Well, don't think this changes anything between us."

"I knew it wouldn't. Now watch and see how strong my resolve is!"

With great strength, Lorimar brought down his sword on the ground, which caused a small fissure to open toward me. I was so occupied trying to not get caught in it that I almost didn't see Lorimar throwing his sword at me. I had little time to bring up my sword just to try and deflect it away. With great speed, Lorimar retrieved his sword and did the same thing over and over. I knew if this kept up, I would eventually get tired and ultimately lose. That's when I came up with an idea.

The next time I deflected his sword away, I quickly froze the ground under Lorimar, and he slipped on the ice. Using this opportunity, I quickly formed a ball of lightning with my free hand and infused the Sword of the Wyvern with it. Small bolts of lightning escaped from the sword as I went after Lorimar, who at that moment escaped the frozen field I had created. Seeing me come at him, he quickly brought up his sword to block my attack, barely avoiding electrocution.

"Using the elements to give your sword its powers. A very shrewd maneuver," he said, actually sounding impressed with my idea.

I didn't say anything in return because it took a lot of concentration to keep the lightning from escaping. I began swinging my sword at him forcing him to move backward. He finally had his back against a broken wall. The moment an opening was shown, I let loose what lightning was left and used it to make Lorimar drop his sword.

"Looks like you are bested."

"Have you forgotten the most important lesson I gave you? Use whatever you can as a weapon!"

Using all of his strength, he lifted a small section of the wall behind him and quickly swung it my way. It felt like I was hit with a large boulder as I fell to the ground. I was lucky that the blow didn't break any bones, but I was in a lot of pain nonetheless. As Lorimar picked up his sword and walked toward me, I had a plan ready.

That's it... just a little closer...

Lorimar stopped two feet away from me. "You have improved a lot, but one must also have years of experience to know how to effectively attack an enemy."

"Well, I did learn something important just now."

"And what's that?" he asked.

"Use whatever you can as a weapon!"

I made the ground shake underneath Lorimar's feet. As he tried to keep his balance, I did a somersault over him. As I flew through the air, I swung my tail hard, striking him hard in the face and back, the force of which managed to crack his armor. When I landed, I used a small portion of Ska's power to send Lorimar flying to the ground. As he got up, he was looking at the tip of my sword, which was just an inch away from his throat.

"It's over, Lorimar. I win."

"It looks like you found your resolve. You have indeed surpassed me."

My friends began to cheer for me.

"Amazing, Shirai! You really let him have it!" Sara said excitedly.

"Well, Nova told me that I should be original, so I did just that." I then looked toward Lorimar. "I believe you said if I bested you, you would finally tell why you decided to train me in the first place."

"If Grant knew about you, he would have had you expelled from Hariel, or even worse, killed. He already had my now-dead wife expelled long ago. I had to keep you safe from his eyes so I decided to train you myself."

"Your... wife?"

"Yes. Even though he said it was for the good of our kingdom, I was devastated when she left. I didn't want to feel that again. That is also the reason I can never kill you." He said that last part like he truly meant it.

I was going to ask him why he cared so much about me when a nearby explosion caught all of us unguarded. The blast sent us flying everywhere. When I regained my senses, I saw Ignotus was standing over me, holding Bloodbringer in his hand.

"Ignotus?"

"I thought I was going to lose my chance to kill you myself, but it would seem that Lorimar has gotten senile."

I tried to move any part of my body, but I was still worn out with my battle wit Lorimar.

"You won't get the better of us this time!" Nova shouted.

He was coming toward Ignotus with the Tao Spear ready, but he was met with some kind of invisible wall that kept my friends separate from where I was.

"This time, I won't have anymore interference! Not even the Tao Spear can break through that barrier!"

"Why are you here?" Lorimar demanded.

"I'm here on orders by Grant, to end the life of Ska's chosen!" Ignotus then looked at me. "For so long I've been waiting for this exact moment, Shirai, where I can personally make that head of yours leave your neck. Now fade away!"

He started to bring Bloodbringer down on me. I didn't have enough time to protect myself. My friends tried to break through the barrier, but they couldn't. I was sure he would finally succeed, when out of nowhere, Lorimar got between me and Ignotus. The sword went through the cracked part of the armor and sliced deeply into his back.

"What?" Ignotus cried out in surprise.

"I know now. You are too far gone… to be saved… but I will not let you harm Shirai."

I was still trying to understand what just happened, but when I heard Lorimar groan, I finally snapped out of my daze. Seeing how severely wounded he was, I quickly brought out a fully charged blast of Ska's power. I flung it at Ignotous, who went flying headfirst into his own barrier, which disappeared when he struck it. Even though *that* didn't kill him, I didn't care, as I wanted him far away from Lorimar.

"Lorimar! Why did you do that?" As I checked on him, my friends stayed where they were and left us alone.

"It's like I said… I couldn't stand to lose… anyone else important… to me," he said softly as his breathing began to grow slower.

"No! I will not let this happen! I'll have Sara help you!"

Lorimar shook his head. "No… It's time for this old soldier… to finally be able… to stop fighting."

Huge streams of tears started going down my face. "You can't go! Not after all the time you took care of me! You still have so much to teach me!"

Lorimar slowly moved his hand so he could grasp my own, "You've learned all that you need… from this fool of a man… I want you to go on living… to have the life you deserved… before fate intervened."

"Lorimar…"

"Before I go… you need to know the truth."

He whispered something to me. What he said shook me so much that I wasn't prepared when Ignotus impaled Lorimar with Bloodbringer right in front of me.

"Loathsome relic! You were just as foolish back then as you are now!"

"You monster! How could you?" Tansu shouted. She already got her bow out and had an arrow ready to implant itself in Ignotus.

"Don't worry, girl. Everyone will soon be joining him. All I have to do is decide how to go about it!"

Ignotus was so busy being full of himself that he didn't realize that I was already in front of him. He didn't even realize that I had death grips on his hands with my tail, his neck with my left hand, and the talons of my right hand ready to plunge through his armor and cut his stomach away.

The only thing he managed to see before he realized what was going on was the look of death in my eyes. I wanted him to see the twin trails of blood where my tears were before.

"How…"

Do… not… talk!

I was growling viciously while displaying my fangs so he understood the situation he was in.

"Shirai! What are you doing?" Tansu asked.

"Tell us, Ignotus. Before I crush the bones in your hands, tell us why you are doing Grant's dirty work!"

I started to slowly coil my tail around his hands. His screams of pain could be heard loud and clear.

"That's enough, Shirai!" Nova demanded.

"And before I cut off the air entering your body, tell us why you hate me so much!"

I tightened my left hand around his neck, slowly choking him.

"Stop it already, Shirai!" Sara cried out.

"And before my talons pierce into your body, severing any vital organs…"

This, however, I didn't follow up with. Instead, in an angry rage, I threw him with all my strength headfirst past everyone and right into a pile of rubble nearby.

"Tell us, Aynor! Tell us why you brutally killed our father!"

21 - Lost Control

"What did you just say?" Nova asked, trying to fully take in what I just said.

"Did you say Aynor?" Tansu was next. "As in the supposed missing prince Aynor?"

Again, I didn't answer any of them. Stomping by my friends, I picked up Ignotus by the collar of his armor, my fingers tightly grasping on the metal so hard that it actually bent.

"He's no prince. He never was."

"So that's what that old fool told you before," Ignotus said with resentment in his voice.

"Be quiet! Show them! Show everyone your face!"

He chuckled dryly. "Gladly. I want them to see what you never told them back at Elruan."

He took off his helmet and finally revealed his face. It was just as I thought I had seen. He was a young man the same age as me with short dirty blonde hair, gray eyes, and the beginnings of a beard. His eyes glared at me with extreme hatred, and his face was scowling.

"Damn that Grant! It's like Lorimar told me!"

"That's right!" Ignotus replied. "Lorimar was our true father … and I am your twin brother, Aynor!"

"Twin brother?" Sara gasped. "That… that can't be true, can it?"

"I wish it wasn't," Nova replied downheartedly, "but that's exactly what Shirai looked like when he was human!"

"Shirai, what in Lu' Cel is going on?" Tansu asked.

"Go on!" I shook Aynor hard. "Tell us before I end your life!"

"I'll tell you," he replied, "only to see you suffer more. At the time we were born, our Uncle Grant's wife died of an illness before she could bear him any heirs. He wanted to give his younger brother Lorimar the throne since he had children. However, Father long ago abandoned any claim to the throne to be a knight protecting Hariel."

"So he took you as his own so he would have an heir," I said, half-guessing.

"Correct. He had our mother expelled from Hariel and then made Father abandon you in hopes that you would die so no one would ever know about his deception. I wasn't told any of this until I was ten."

"How can anyone be so cruel?" Sara gasped.

Aynor stared to sneer. "Oh, it gets better. Since I thought my dear brother was dead, I began to want our true father to notice me. However, Uncle kept me hidden until it was time to pass the throne over to me. I would have been happy with that…"

I didn't care when Aynor started to glare at me and continue, "But then… then you suddenly came out of nowhere, wanting to be a knight! You already had parents, but that wasn't enough for you! You began to take up our father's attention!"

"But he didn't know Lorimar was his real father or that you existed!" Nova argued.

"It doesn't matter! I grew so jealous of my brother that I was willing to do anything to make Father forget him! When I learned about the strange crate that was brought to Uncle, I let my curiosity get the better of me and managed to open it!"

"The same crate in which the Sword of the Wyvern and Bloodbringer were sealed in, and hidden in Lake Orem?" Tansu asked.

"Yes. It was at that moment that Uncle came in. By then, the evil that Ska had sealed so long ago had started to awaken. It took him over, then promised me that it would give me the means to make Father love me over you, and I jumped at once at the chance!"

My brother was grinning evilly the whole time.

"I was the one who lured Ska into a trap! I was the one who did all of Grant's dirty work! Yet … even after all I done, Father wouldn't even give me a second glance!" Again Aynor glared at me, only this time there was a glint of madness in his eyes. "So I decided to try something a bit more drastic!"

"What do you mean?!" I demanded.

"Who do you think tipped Uncle about the fact that you were still alive?"

"*You?*" Sara growled, "You were responsible for Shirai's parents' death?"

Aynor began to cackle. "I wish I could have seen his face when he watched them go down like that! To see the very reason for his 'resolve' dashed like that."

He soon stopped laughing when he felt my talons rip into his face.

"Shirai! What are you doing?!" Tansu shouted.

"It was you… you killed our father… you got my foster parents murdered… you ruined my life… so you must die. You must be slashed and torn apart slowly. You must beg me to send you to hell!"

I was going to strike Aynor again when I felt someone hold back the hand that I was going to use.

"No, Shirai! Don't stoop to his level!" Tansu cried out.

My rage. My anger. The devastation of losing my real father. I was so filled with these emotions that even though I was aware my body was moving, I didn't remember what happened afterward. It was only later when I was told what occurred.

*****

Shirai pushed Tansu back with his arm so hard that she fell to the ground.

"Tansu! Are you all right?" Sara asked, coming to her side.

"I'm fine."

"Shirai! What's got into—" Nova stopped mid-sentence for a moment. "What is happening to him?"

Everyone looked toward Shirai, who bared his fangs at Aynor. As he did, his talons slowly started to grow longer. At the same time, his four canine fangs started growing longer too. Seeing this made Aynor so worried that he quickly used a lightning spell to make Shirai let go of him.

"No!" Aynor shuddered at the way Shirai was glaring at him, his eyes having the look of a demon in them. "Keep him away!"

Aynor started running. To everyone's shock, Shirai got on all fours and started to chase Aynor like a wild animal.

"No," Tansu whimpered "It's happening again."

Nova started to go after Shirai when Sara stopped him. "Nova, don't!"

"Are you nuts, Sara? He's going berserk again! We have to stop him!"

"I know, but something is wrong! I can feel dark energy coming from his direction! It's even stronger than Aynor!"

"What are you talking about?" Nova asked.

"Shirai's dark side has begun to feed on his emotions," a voice suddenly spoke.

"Who's there?" Tansu asked.

The image of a giant, golden dragon suddenly appeared in front of them.

"I am Ska."

"Ska? What are you doing here?!" Sara asked.

"We don't have time for such questions. You must bring Shirai back to his senses before it's too late."

"What do you mean?" Nova asked.

"The portion of my power I gave Shirai is controlled by his emotions, but just as it can be used for good, it can also destroy the user. If one lets hatred control the power, their dark side will grow strong and slowly transform them into a monstrosity of their former selves."

"That's horrible! Isn't there anything you can do?" Tansu asked.

Ska shook his head. "Unfortunately I can't. My body is still being held captive by the Chains of Deist. I can only manage to do this much."

"The Chains of Deist?" Sara remarked, "The chains made by the ancient Kunti's to subdue any creature?"

"Indeed, young elf. I can't do anything for Shirai, but there is something you can do."

"What's that?" Nova demanded.

"You must make him remember that he has a good side, by any means needed. Time is running out for all. Please stop him, not just for my sake, but his too."

With that, Ska slowly faded away and was gone.

"Well, you heard the dragon! By any means!" Nova went after Shirai and Aynor, followed closely by the girls.

Meanwhile, Shirai had been chasing Aynor all over the ruins of Ranu. During this time, the feathers on his wings began to fall off, revealing tattered-looking wings underneath them. This slow change started to really scare Aynor.

"Let's see how you handle this!"

He launched a barrage of spells at Shirai in an attempt to stop him, but he was shocked to see his spells had no effect. Shirai then jumped at Aynor, trying to plunge his talons into his face, but Aynor managed to evade them. It was at that moment that Aynor looked at Shirai's eyes again and saw that they were now completely white.

"So you brought your own doom on yourself, huh? However, I will not let you take me with you, dear brother!"

Summoning Bloodbringer to his hand, he sliced at Shirai, who easily dodged and countered the strike with a blast of fire from his mouth. This time, the blast was twice as powerful as any Shirai had brought out before. The heat from the fire alone instantly made Aynor's cape catch on fire. While Aynor tried to lose it, Shirai came in, ready to pounce on him, but was met with the Tao Spear hitting him in the chest.

"Calm down, pal! Don't let yourself go like this!" Nova yelled trying to get through to Shirai.

As Aynor used that moment to try to escape, Shirai looked at Nova angrily, howled like a wolf, and then leaped on him. As he had Nova pinned, spikes slowly began to come out of Shirai's back and went all the way down to his tail.

"That new look isn't doing much for you! Snap out of it!"

Nova used both his legs and pushed Shirai away with one powerful thrust. As Shirai met the ground, the earth wrapped itself around his feet, locking him into place.

"You heard Nova! We're only trying to help you! You must regain control of yourself!" Sara told him.

Shirai started acting like a ferocious animal trying to escape from a trap.

"Please snap out of it, Shirai!" Tansu pleaded. "Come back to us!"

But he didn't listen.

"Let's see if this works!" Nova said as he whacked Shirai hard on the head with his spear.

"What was *that?*" Sara asked.

"I said I would give him a good whack to the head if he went wild again."

Instead of helping, though, that action just made Shirai more enraged. He began madly punching away at the rocks holding him. When that didn't work, he brought forth a huge orb filled with Ska's power.

"Everyone get back!" Tansu yelled.

Everyone managed to get far away as Shirai flung the orb to the ground, causing a large explosion. Once free again, Shirai went after Aynor.

"That was close," Sara commented, "but that power... he must be in a deep rage."

"If we don't do something soon, we'll lose him!" Nova said. "There must be something that can snap him out of this state!"

Tansu suddenly looked like she knew of a way, and without saying anything, she went after Shirai without the others.

"Tansu! What are you doing?" Sara called out as she and Nova went after her.

Aynor and Shirai were still battling. Aynor tried every spell he knew, but they still didn't have any affect on Shirai. All the while, Shirai kept changing. His horns changed color to pitch black, and his upper body became more muscular.

"How is this possible? He's becoming a mindless beast, and yet his power seems to keep on growing as he changes!" Aynor argued with himself.

Aynor was so busy watching out for Shirai that he didn't see a plank that was in his way. Tripping over it, he fell backward to the ground. When he looked up, he saw Shirai staring at him. He began slashing at Aynor, ripping off all his armor, and when that was gone, Shirai started punching him repeatedly. By the end, Aynor was a bloody mess. With incredible strength, Shirai hurled Aynor into a nearby stone pile.

On the brink of no return

"It can't be. I, who was given incredible power… beaten like this!"

Aynor tried to get up, but he couldn't move any part of his body from the beating he had taken. All he could do was watch in horror as he saw Shirai coming at him at top speed, ready to finish him off. But at the last second, Tansu got in front of Aynor, holding out her arms to block Shirai from getting at him.

"Shirai! Stop it now!" she shouted at the top of her lungs with tears in her eyes.

"Tansu! Get out of the way!" Sara cried out as she and Nova came onto the scene.

It was too late for anyone to stop Shirai. He had his arm out, his hand ready to go right through Tansu to get to Aynor. Then, at the last possible second, he halted his attack—his talons a fraction away from Tansu's heart.

"Please Shirai. No more. You can't go on like this. You'll only destroy yourself," she calmly said.

Shirai stared at her, his talons still where they were. No one dared move from where they were standing. Only when he saw Tansu's bracelet did Shirai lower his arm. He began to growl curiously.

Tansu saw that Shirai was looking at the bracelet, so she held out the arm it was on. "You remember my bracelet, don't you? It's the one you gave me back at Gale."

Shirai slowly reached for it.

"Tansu, look out!" Sara tried to get to her, only to be held back by Nova.

"No! Let her do this! This may be the only chance we have! She knows what she's doing!"

While the two talked, Shirai was slowly running his fingers over the surface of the bracelet, all the while growling softly.

"I cherish this because you wanted to show how much you care about me. Now think about all the people who care for you, the people you helped, and the great things you have done. I know you can still remember them!"

Tansu slowly tried to take the hand that Shirai was using to feel her bracelet. When she came near him, Shirai began to slowly back away, whimpering like a frightened animal.

"Remember you asked me to make sure you never became a monster? I'm trying to help you, so please don't back away."

She kept trying to get closer. In an attempt to stop her, Shirai tried to slice at her with his talons. This time they did make contact, but they only grazed her arm. Pulling back his hand, he prepared to try again. Instead of trying to take his hand again, Tansu took off the rose pendant she had around her neck.

"This pendant was given to me by my brother the day he left for Gale. It means a lot to me, but now that I have the bracelet, I want you to have it."

She gently put it in Shirai's open hand as he looked at it curiously. The color in his eyes began to slowly return.

"Remember that night back at Tsura? I said I wanted to wait before I gave my answer about how I really feel about you? The truth was... I didn't know what to do when you said you loved me. I was unsure about how things would have been between us. But that isn't the case anymore. I can finally give you my answer."

She put her arms around Shirai's neck.

"I do love you. I've loved you for a long time."

As she held onto Shirai, a single tear ran down his face as he slowly put his arms around her. The second he did, a brilliant flash of light engulfed the two. When the light faded, Shirai was back to his previous form.

*****

"Love? Tansu, what are you doing?" I moaned as I looked at Tansu, who was holding me for some reason.

"I'm just glad you are okay."

"What do you mean? Did something happen?" I suddenly felt that my head was hurting slightly. "Ow! And where did this bump come from?"

She pulled away from me. "You... don't remember?"

I shook my head. It was then I noticed I was holding her pendant in my hand.

"How did I get your pendant?" I also saw the remains of a tear trail on her face and the cuts on her arm. "What happened to your arm? Is that why you were crying?"

"It doesn't matter, I'm fine," she said happily. "So you don't remember anything?"

I was going to answer her when I looked over her shoulder and saw Aynor lying on the ground, looking like he was attacked by a pack of wild animals.

"What happened to him?"

"I will tell you everything later, Shirai. What do you remember?"

"The only thing I remember is… I was about to strike Aynor again… then everything went blank. I thought I heard you say you love me. Was I dreaming that?"

She shook her head. "It was no dream."

"I… I don't know what to say."

Tansu was blushing lightly. "You could tell me again how you feel about me."

I smiled, "Okay. I…"

"Tansu! Shirai!" Nova's voice surprised us both as he and Sara came over.

"Are you two okay?" Sara asked.

"Yes. We're fine." Tansu sounded annoyed with the interruption.

"Well, that was quite a risk you took there, Tansu," Nova commented.

I had no idea at the time what he meant. "What is he talking about?"

He was about to tell me something when Tansu stomped on his foot, very hard. "Like I said. I'll tell you later."

As much as I wanted to know what was going on between everyone, it was fun seeing Tansu give it to Nova like that. I then looked at the pendant I had in my hand.

"I don't know why I have this, but here's your pendant back, Tansu."

She refused to take it. "I want you to hold onto it."

"What? But why?"

"Because I want you to, that's why."

That was all she would tell me at that point. Knowing her, she wouldn't tell me until she was ready, so I took it. It was then I noticed that Aynor was slowly getting up.

"Don't go celebrating… just yet," he groaned.

"I have nothing to say to someone who looks like that."

"Say what you will, but I'm not beaten yet. I still need to get rid of you … the only one remaining of my old family."

He tried his best to keep himself up as I got ready for a battle with him again. However, what he said about family a moment ago made me realize something. So instead, I just looked at him with pity.

"No, I won't fight you anymore. As of now the only family I have are these guys. You are no brother of mine."

"What? How dare you… you can't just do this…"

"Oh yeah? Watch me. Come on, guys. We have a date with Grant."

I started to walk away from Aynor with my friends. Before we even got as far as five feet, I began to sense incredible evil coming from behind us. Quickly turning around, I saw Bloodbringer was hovering in the air right behind Aynor. A split second later, it hurled itself at him.

"Aynor! Look out!"

But it was too late. The sword pierced my brother's body.

"Why… what is going on?" Aynor cried out, blood coming out of his mouth.

You have failed miserably, Aynor! a loud booming voice from out of nowhere replied. *Even with the power I gave you, you couldn't take down Ska's chosen, who happened to be your own brother. What is worse, you failed to kill him with Bloodbringer, the very task you were sent here to do. So now I'll just have to use someone else.*

Once again moving on its own, Bloodbringer pulled itself out of Aynor's body and then re-entered him, this time going through his heart. The sword took itself out of Aynor before he collapsed on the ground dead.

"Who are you? How could you do that to my brother?" I could feel the Sword of the Wyvern was as scared as it was the first time we encountered Bloodbringer.

As I recall, you claimed to have no brother. As for who I am, I'm the one Ska sealed away long ago. Of course, to break the seal, I needed

Bloodbringer to soak up the blood of one more person, mainly one with incredible power. Of course, strong negative feelings in a person will also do, and since Aynor failed to kill you, his hatred for you will be the key!

The evil sword plunged into the pool of blood that had formed around my brother's body. As his blood touched the blade, several flashes of black light came out of Bloodbringer. As the flashes appeared, I thought I heard the sword moaning. Finally, the flashes stopped, and Bloodbringer once again floated in the air.

The seal now dissolves! All that's left is to drain off the last of that miserable Ska's power! I will be free to get revenge on this world! I think I will start on the pathetic Hariel Kingdom! Come. Come and join them in their fate!

The voice stopped speaking as Bloodbringer flew out of sight into the air. When it did, I suddenly felt a chill run down my body. The air was beginning to fill with something diabolical.

"What is this energy?"

"I can feel it too," Tansu said, sounding scared.

"It feels like it's coming from everywhere," Nova remarked.

"This is not good! This kind of energy can have a negative effect on Lu' Cel!" Sara pointed out

"We need to hurry to Hariel! This isn't just about stopping a war anymore! If we don't save Ska now, the entire world will be doomed!"

With that, everyone was on their way to Hariel. I stayed behind for a moment and looked at the dead bodies of my father and brother. Despite what had happened, I was glad to know I met my real family. Taking that knowledge in my heart, I quickly caught up everyone.

22 - The Ancient Evil

"So my brother is dead," Grant said grimly.

"As is that annoyance, Aynor. Both played out their roles quite well however," the evil voice added.

"Indeed they did. The seal is now breaking apart, and Ska is nearly drained. Lu' Cel will finally be ours."

Something slowly came out from the darkness, "Before that can happen, Grant, there is one last detail to finish…,"

*****

As we got closer to Hariel, the feeling of maliciousness we all felt became stronger. Something else worried me more, though. Ever since Ska had made contact with me, I was able to sense his presence even from all the way in Kunti.

But now, I couldn't sense him anymore.

"Something is wrong," I told everyone, "I can't sense any sign of Ska."

"Do you think we're too late?" Tansu asked.

"I don't think so," Sara remarked. "If the seal holding whatever Ska put away is still dissolving, we still have time."

"Well, we better hurry up then!" Nova replied as he sped up his running.

It didn't take long to get to Hariel. It was just as Nova once said; it *did* feel weird coming back home after all these years. I wanted to see my old house, but I knew that would have to wait.

When we made it to the town outside the castle, I knew we were going to have a hard time. The sky above Hariel was slowly becoming pitch black, and one didn't need to have good senses to know that something was wrong. My suspicions were quickly confirmed when the screams of people began to fill the air.

"What was that?" Tansu asked.

She quickly got her answer as several townspeople fled past us, being chased by hundreds of monsters.

"Looks like the welcome wagon has been sent to greet Lu' Cel!" Quickly drawing out the Sword of the Wyvern, I immediately destroyed one monster that looked like a demonic dog. Unfortunately, another took its place.

"We don't have time to deal with these things!" Sara argued. Because all the monsters seemed to be coming out of everywhere, she was having trouble getting any magic ready.

"Well, unless you have some kind of plan to get by them, I see no other option!" Nova impaled a huge monster version of a huge falcon with blood red feathers and two-inch talons with the Tao Spear.

Just as another wave of monsters charged us, I heard several sounds coming from behind us. In an instant, a rain of arrows came falling from the sky and brought down hundreds of monsters.

"This is why you're going to need our help!" a familiar voice called out to us.

Up on the rooftops of some of the houses nearby were hundreds of elves being lead by Tybal.

"Tybal? What are you doing here?" Sara asked.

"Eri sensed that the end was coming and had us come here to help!" he shouted while shooting more monsters.

"But how did you get here so fast?" I asked.

Suddenly, big shadows coming from something in the sky flew past us. Looking up, we got our answer. Several dragons were high above us, carrying in loads of people; while those who couldn't fly came in on foot. I was extremely surprised to see the members of Ska's Council here too.

"The Council of Ska contacted us and said they would send some of their people to gather those who would fight!"

"So they came through in the end," I thought out loud.

"If there are no more questions, get going! We'll do what we can here! Go and save Ska!"

Tybal then commanded his men to move in.

"You heard him, guys!" I led the way to the castle.

On our way we had no choice but to fight off a few monsters. Luckily, because all of us have gotten stronger during our long trip, they were no challenge.

In one part of town, some monsters surprised us by crashing through some houses. One, a monster made entirely of a jelly-like substance, was about to engulf Tansu when it suddenly burst into flames. From behind a nearby corner, a teenager and an adult appeared.

"Zen! Luwina! What are you doing here?" I asked.

"Thanks to your help, I was able to translate that book. It was a warning left by Ska himself. It told that the world would be in danger one day," Zen explained.

"At first I didn't believe him," Luwina explained, "but the second everyone at the school felt the negative energy filling Lu' Cel, a dragon landed in our courtyard and told us that you would need help."

As we talked, a monster came up from behind her. Spinning around, she cast a powerful lightning spell that fried the thing instantly. I was starting to see how she became headmaster.

"Leave the rest to us, okay?" Zen said, winking.

"We will!"

"And thank you for that save!" Tansu added.

We were quickly off again.

"First Tybal, then Zen and Luwina. Who's next to come and help?" Sara asked as though she wasn't expecting an answer.

No sooner had she said that when we were surrounded by a group of creatures that looked as though someone took a snake and a cat and just flung different parts together. We were preparing to fend them off when an axe imbedded itself in the head of the lead monster. The axe came from a large man behind the monster.

"Looks like you youngsters could use a hand."

"Chent! You're here too?" Nova said in surprise.

Instead of answering, Chent went to work on the other monsters. He must have been stronger than I originally thought, for he made short work of them.

"What, a guy can't return the favor and help the ones who saved his home?" he complained after he finished with the last monster.

"Right now, I would argue that someone your age shouldn't be here, but now is not the time!" Nova passed by him.

"Thanks again!" I said as I too passed Chent.

Tansu and Sara said their thanks to Chent and followed behind. I couldn't believe that everyone we met during our journey had come here just to help us. Even the dragons had finally taken action.

I was wondering who else was here, when a small explosion blew up a large section of a roof above us. The piece was falling straight toward me when someone jumped up and knocked it away with just an ordinary cane. The one the cane belonged to was the *last* person I would expect.

"Giram! You're here too?" Tansu said in shock when we saw him land on the ground.

"I'm glad to see the two of you are safe," he spoke as though nothing happened.

"But how did—"

"Who do you think taught Lorimar how to fight in the first place?" he grinned toward me.

"You knew my father?"

"Shirai! We don't have time!" Nova reminded me.

"That's right. Don't you die on me, Giram! I want to hear everything you have to say!"

We left him behind and finally reached the castle gates. However, much like what had happened so far, two hulking monsters with huge tusks coming out of their mouths and two large curled horns on their heads blocked our way.

Also there, trying to fight them, was Russ.

"Get out of my way!" Russ shouted while attacking one of the monsters.

He didn't even know we were there until he saw me landing on the shoulders of the monster he was fighting and thrust my sword into its skull. I pulled it out before the thing collapsed face first on the ground. Everyone else made short work of the other one.

"I thought you were recovering from that severe burn!" I argued.

"I was, but one of my men stationed near Ranu came back, telling me Lorimar was dead. I was on my way to see Grant when this horde of monsters started coming from the throne room."

"That's exactly where we're heading right now," Nova said.

"Then get going! This is your fight, not mine."

"We will. Just go and help out in the town!"

We entered the castle, where I led everyone through the interior, going down the very path I took to get to the throne the last time I was here. As we hurried, I felt Ska's presence, but it was slowly fading. When we reached the door leading to Grant, I didn't waste time trying to open it, but blasted it with Ska's power.

Nothing could have prepared us for what was waiting for us inside the throne room.

The throne itself was gone, and the entire wall behind where it would have been looked as though it had been blasted away, revealing a very large chamber. There, tied down by huge chains, was Ska himself.

Standing next to him, draining what energy was left inside Ska, was the deformed figure of a man, wearing the tattered remains of what looked like a royal robe. His left arm was crooked, and his skin blackened as if severely burned. The other arm draining Ska was in slightly better condition, but still ugly.

The body looked like it had begun to melt and then stopped. He stood on legs that were completely different sizes—one skinny and old-looking, and the other from a young man, but dark gray in color. When he turned around and showed us his face, I felt like my heart was going to jump out of my throat.

"Grant?"

"I'm afraid that Grant is no longer here, Shirai," the thing cackled. "I needed to have a temporary body while the seal was being destroyed, and I was finished using him."

"That voice," Tansu remarked fearfully. "It's the same one that spoke to us from Bloodbringer."

"Who are you really?"

"I am the one you people praised as creating this world. I am Asteron."

"Asteron!" Sara gasped.

"Yes, the very same name you pathetic mortals once called me when I had hold over Lu' Cel. It was so easy to take over at the time. My power was so immense, direct exposure to my energy could kill anyone instantly. Just like what nearly happened to you," he pointed to Tansu.

"So it was you who made Tansu sick!" I slowly reached for the Sword of the Wyvern.

"You can also thank my partner, Bloodbringer." Asteron held his unused hand out. In response, Bloodbringer appeared in midair next to his hand. He grabbed hold of it. "Like that damned Sword of the Wyvern, mine too was forged with metal from my original world. Not only did it take from Aynor what I needed to undo the seal, it also amplifies my powers."

I growled softly at the way he talked about my brother, waiting for an opening to attack. "So that's why Ska never said who he fought. So no one would remember the demon that once ruled them."

"And I would still be lord of all Lu' Cel had that interfering Ska and his chosen not come and ruined it all. But in the end, I *did* manage to strike a blow at Ska. That pathetic excuse of a warrior he chose was such an easy adversary… just like you."

Trying not to let his comment distract me, I took this moment to try to attack. Asteron saw me coming, but instead of preparing a counterattack, he let Bloodbringer drop from his hand, where it fell straight through the floor. Then, to my horror, from the ground, the body of my brother Aynor rose up and blocked my attack with Bloodbringer.

"What the…?"

"Did you really think I would be unprepared for your arrival? It was because of Aynor that I was awakened from my long sleep. So I thought he should be the one to keep you busy while I finished what I started all those years ago."

Asteron faced Ska as he continued to steal his energy.

"I won't let you!" I shouted

I tried to get to Asteron, but Aynor quickly blocked my path and began attacking me with Bloodbringer.

"Aynor! Don't do this! Snap out of it!" I pleaded while dodging his attacks.

"It won't work. Bloodbringer is infused with my power and has taken complete control of your brother's dead body."

"You sick—"

"Shirai! Watch out!" Tansu cried.

Aynor had cast a powerful fire spell while I wasn't looking. Even with my scales, I would've burned to death in the flames if it wasn't for Sara's quick thinking. She brought forth a column of water and put the flames out.

"Thanks, Sara."

"No problem," Sara replied.

"We have to stop Asteron from breaking the seal completely!" Nova said.

"But what about…?"

"That isn't Aynor," Tansu told me. "He is dead. Asteron is trying to intimidate you."

"I know, but…"

"Heads up!" Nova called out.

Aynor unleashed a wave of dark energy from Bloodbringer, and it was quickly closing in on us. Even after all that had happened, I couldn't bring down my brother, but if I didn't stop Aynor, we would be killed.

It was at that moment that Nova stepped in front of us holding out the Tao Spear.

"What are you doing?"

"Seeing to it that you all survive!"

He then brought out the power of the spear hoping to neutralize the incoming attack. I knew that it wouldn't work, yet he was willing to do this to save us. Realizing we didn't have much time, I made my choice.

"I'm sorry, Aynor."

I let loose a blast of Ska's power and flung it at the dark wave. The two attacks collided and exploded.

"I was hoping that would light the fire under you. But you cut it a little close didn't you?"

"Leave him to me. I must be the one to do this."

I went at Aynor with everything I had. Aynor matched my every attack, whether it was using the sword, using magic, or even unleashing powers that were given to us. At the rate we were going, there wouldn't be any time left; so I decided to do something drastic.

I left myself wide open, and just like I hoped, Aynor charged at me with Bloodbringer. The moment they were in reach, I quickly grabbed the blade of Aynor's sword with my left hand. The blade cut into my hand, but I didn't care.

"Forgive me, brother."

I thrust the Sword of the Wyvern into where my brother's heart was as I transferred some of Ska's power into Aynor's body, hoping to break the hold Bloodbringer had on him. Bloodbringer vanished, and my brother's body went limp before it crumbled to dust.

"Even in death, that boy was a failure," Asteron snickered.

"You monster!" I came at him, ready to end this battle.

"You are too late! The seal is finally gone!"

I was pushed backward by a powerful pulse of dark energy that was emanating from Asteron. Black smoke rose from the ground and soon engulfed him. A moment later, a giant arm suddenly appeared from the black smoke and fired a blast of dark energy at us.

"Look out everyone!" I cried.

If that dark energy hit my friends, they would be instantly killed. I did the only thing I could think of.

I leaped in front of them, spread out my wings, and, summoning Ska's power, infused them with the power needed to protect my friends. In the end, I took the full brunt of the attack. I was lucky the attack didn't kill me.

The arm went back into the smoke as it began to rise from the ground before crashing through the castle roof.

When it was high in the air, the smoke began to take shape, changing into a human form. The smoke transformed into living flesh.

There, floating in the air, was a demonic-looking man the same size as Ska, with a large, curled horn coming from the back of his head. Covering his body was an elegant, yet morbid-looking robe. His eyes were red in color, and his hair was violet. In one clawed hand was Bloodbringer, now bigger than before. His mouth was in a sinister smile as he looked down at Hariel.

Asteron had completely awakened.

The dark god emerges

23 - Defender of All

"At last!" Asteron cried out, "I'm free! I will once again make this miserable world mine! But first I will deal with those who still oppose me!"

Completely ignoring me and my friends, Asteron slowly floated toward the direction of the town.

"Is… is everyone okay?" I asked.

"Forget about us, Shirai!" Tansu cried out, "What possessed you to do such a thing? Look what happened to you!"

I knew full well what had happened. Since I used my body as a shield, Asteron's attack had completely wrecked it. The armor I was wearing had been shattered, replaced by numerous gashes that covered my chest, arms, and legs. My wings looked worse off. Each one was torn apart, and nearly all of the feathers that covered them were gone. I looked and felt like I had just come out of a massacre.

"It was the only way… I could think of to protect all of you," I fell to my knees at that point and would have fallen onto the pool of my own blood coming from my legs had Tansu not rushed forward and held me up.

"A fat lot of good that did us," Nova sounded downhearted. "We failed miserably."

"How can anyone stand against such power? Is this the end of everything?" Sara was near tears.

She was right. Even with the power I was given, I couldn't do a damn thing to stop Asteron. In the end, I had lost not only my father and brother, but now Lu' Cel was doomed. I didn't even have the strength to get up. Everyone had started to lose their faith, and I also began to think it might be better to just quit.

Shirai, the fight is far from over! Do not give yourself to fate!

"Ska?"

Looking over at the still trapped Ska lying across the room, I was surprised to see that his body was glowing slightly in a pulsing rhythm.

Do you know the true reason I chose to have a human fight at my side? From the moment I first saw your ancestors, I could tell that you had something unique that we dragons never needed. You have the power to combine your strength with others to do the impossible. Asteron might not be here right now if only they had banded together back then. But it's not too late. You can show him what it means to be human.

Combine our strength?

It was then I realized that it was true. During our journey, we'd been spreading something more than just hope. We'd brought people of different nations together. The dragons, the humans, even the elves were here right now risking their own lives to make sure we succeeded.

Don't let your will be broken. Together, even the weakest person can overcome any obstacle!

The glow that was coming from Ska's body slowly pulsed faster.

"Don't give up!" I shouted to everyone.

Reaching for the Sword of the Wyvern that lay nearby on the ground, I slowly got to my feet and limped toward Ska.

"What are you doing?" Nova asked.

Placing my free hand on Ska's body, I began to concentrate. I could feel a little bit of his power still inside him, which he had managed to keep hidden from Asteron when he was draining him. With this, I thought, maybe we had a chance.

Without facing everyone, I told them, "There is still a way! But I need all of you to trust me!"

"We do trust you, but what can we do against Asteron now that he's revived?" Sara asked.

"On our own, nothing, but if we combine our strengths, we are able to do things we normally can't do by ourselves. And that's what I need you to do." I finally faced everyone, and in a resolved tone, I concluded,

"Please lend me your strength, and together with Ska, we'll overcome Asteron."

"You're going to try and borrow power from us *and* from Ska?" Sara argued. "You're already a wreck after taking that attack for us! What if your body can't handle it? You could die before you …"

"Sara, I think he's right. We need to help him," Tansu said as she came over and placed her hand on Ska.

"But, Tansu…"

"Come on, Sara. After all that we've been through, do you really think Shirai would get himself killed if it wasn't a good idea?" Nova asked as he too came over and put his hand on Ska.

Sara stayed where she was, and then, in a huff, replied, "I can't believe I'm doing this, but I did say a moment ago that we did trust you, and I don't want to make a liar out of myself."

She came over and placed her hand together with the rest of us.

"Now focus your thoughts and will and give them to me."

They all closed their eyes and began to concentrate. I could slowly feel their presence enter my body. Their warmth and kindness filled my soul as I continued to take in their strength.

Ska, please lend me what power you have left! I thought to myself. *We need your help too!*

At first he didn't respond to my call, but then I quickly felt a rush of power enter my body. This one was different than the others. Not only was there warmth and kindness, but I could also feel his resolve resonate with my own. I didn't think my body would be able to handle the strain, but my will allowed me to handle the extra power.

I knew I made the right choice, Ska said. *You are so much like the last one who helped me. Do not end up like him. You must come back.*

I will, Ska. I have to return! I replied with my thoughts.

As soon as I finished receiving everyone's strength, my body was surrounded by a golden light. The light also started to heal my body and wings. Knowing what I had to do next, I spread open my newly healed wings and found myself finally knowing how to fly. I started flying into the air through the hole that Asteron had made.

As I went after him, I heard a whisper, "Please come back to us."

It didn't take long to find Asteron fighting off the dragons that made up the Counsel of Ska.

"Foolish creatures! You want to throw away your lives so badly? Your leader is gone!" He fired one attack after another.

"No, he's not, you bastard!"

I took the Sword of the Wyvern and sliced deeply into the arm Asteron was using to launch his attacks. His screams of pain were heard by everyone in Hariel. I hovered in front of him, looking triumphant.

"You? Where did you get all this new power?"

"You severely underestimated the people of Lu' Cel, Asteron! You once used fear and the threat of death to keep everyone in line, but that isn't the case anymore! We've learned how to come together and work as one!"

As I spoke, the sapphire dragon flew close to me. "Shirai? That aura … that's Lord Ska's! Is he well?"

"He is. His soul is with me, but his body is still trapped. Go and help get him free." I then instructed the others, "The rest of you help me end this fighting once and for all!"

The sapphire dragon left us to go help its leader.

"Do you really think I will let you go that easily?"

Asteron launched a huge wave of fire toward the dragon. I was quick to act, and I brought forth a massive waterspout from the ground far below and easily doused Asteron's flames.

"So you learned some new tricks." Asteron sounded as though he was amused. "You really want to try and go up against me?"

"I do! I will show you the true power of people coming together!"

Using all my willpower, I drew on all I had. In a bright flash of light, I underwent another transformation.

My scales now shone with brilliance, and a second pair of dragon wings were now coming out of my back just below my old ones. I was wearing a silver cuirass with small, rectangular plates acting as faulds. Underneath the armor I had a long, regal, blue-silk robe. On my head was a mask-like helmet made of pure gold with large eye holes and five white feathers attached to each side of the helmet.

Even the Sword of the Wyvern was changed, with the blade now a foot longer and the hilt handles changed to look like the tail and the head of a dragon.

"Your power… it can't be… it's…" Asteron was clearly scared.

A true defender

"Now you'll see firsthand the strength of my resolve to protect everyone I love!" I turned to each of the dragons around me and shouted to them, "Let's go!"

The dragons took the first turn, each using their individual power against Asteron. One blew lightning out of its mouth, and another threw huge boulders that magically appeared out of the air. While they did that, I used every kind of magic I knew, coupled with several blasts of energy I received from my friends and Ska, plus a couple of direct attacks with the Sword of the Wyvern.

Asteron tried his best to hit us with his own attacks. He used all kinds of spells, from throwing numerous spheres of lightning at us to trying to cage us in prisons of extremely sharp icicles. However, because of my constant instructions to the dragons on what to do, he missed each time. All the while, his body kept taking damage from us. He was soon covered in his own blood.

"I will not be beaten! Let's see you deal with *this*!"

Asteron used Bloodbringer to increase his own power. When I saw this, I told the dragons to back away. I flew straight at him, all the while dodging the spells Asteron used.

"So you're trying to kill yourself? Allow me to help!"

Asteron opened his mouth and fired a huge beam of energy toward me, but with a sharp turn upward, I dodged it. Afterward, I made sure to fly out of Asteron's sight.

"Hiding out, are we? Go ahead and do that! I'll just kill everyone one by one for every second you hide from me!"

"Hide from *this*!" I divebombed toward Asteron. Using the Sword of the Wyvern and all my strength and speed, I went for Bloodbringer and hit the blade of the sword so hard, it shattered in millions of pieces.

"Bloodbringer? Impossible!"

"Now you have no means of boosting your power. You are on equal terms with me!"

Blinded by rage, Asteron recklessly fired at me with every attack he knew. Slowly I made my way up to him without his knowledge.

I was practically at his face when I shouted, "Let's see how you like having someone leave you with a scar on your face!"

Using the Sword of the Wyvern, I sliced down Asteron's right eye—only this time, I made sure that he could never use that eye again. With a loud cry of pain, Asteron covered his face.

"You lost your sword and the use of your eye. I could kill you now, but I'm not going to stoop to your level and be a ruthless murderer like you. Leave this world while you still can."

The fake god looked at me with his remaining eye, extreme hatred burning in it. At that moment I could feel his evil power rising quickly out of control.

"If I'm to lose, then I will have the last laugh!"

With his free hand, Asteron gathered huge streams of black energy. As the energy accumulated, I could literally hear the earth below cry out in horror. If he let that dark energy loose, it would not only destroy us, but all of Lu' Cel!

I shouted to all the dragons, "Everyone! Gather your powers together quickly! We can't let him win!"

While they did so, I opened my mind to reach everyone all over Lu' Cel. *My friends! Send me your strength, your will, your hope! This so-called god is trying to destroy us, but we must show him we will not take such an act lying down!*

Instantly, I could feel the hearts of everyone I knew. Zen, Luwina, Tybal, Eri, Chent, Giram, the people of Kenga Village, Gale City, Elruan Village, those I met at the Institution of Magic, and what strength my friends had left. I could even feel power coming from Russ. They were all here with me. I gathered every last ounce of power I could muster and prepared to fire one last blast.

"*Die!*" Asteron shouted at the top of his lungs as he fired off all the energy he had gathered at me.

"Now! Attack!" I yelled at the dragons.

They let loose all of their power. Both attacks made contact, and each was trying to push back the other. It was now or never. I fired off my own blast of energy to combine with the dragons'. It was now a battle to see whose inner strength would give out first.

"You don't have the strength to defy me!" Asteron put more force on his side.

Damn it! He's right! I thought. *Even with everyone helping, it's not enough!*

It wasn't just that, my body was slowly starting to give out on me, just like Sara had said. Soon it would give out completely, and we'd all be killed. Just then, I felt as though there was someone else with me.

Son… take my strength and resolve. Win so you can see a better tomorrow! It was the voice of Lorimar.

"Father?"

Another voice came. *Take mine too. If one of us has to live, I want it to be you.*

"Aynor too?"

A third voice came in, but this one was one I never heard before. *So you're Shirai?*

"Who are you?"

I'm Dai. I'm sure you heard about me from my sister? I'm here to lend you my strength also. I can't let my sister lose the one she loves so much.

Nodding, I called upon their souls. I could feel their energy enter me. With this extra strength, I shouted at Asteron, "Feel the true power of Lu' Cel as you enter oblivion!"

I added the energy I had received to our side. That extra boost did the trick as our energy destroyed Asteron's dark energy and struck him full-on in a loud explosion that shook all of Lu' Cel.

"No! I am all powerful… I can't…" Those were his last words as his entire body shattered into a swirling vortex of blackness.

As soon as he was gone, the monsters below disappeared, and the blue sky returned. Loud and mighty cheers rose from the people below.

I wanted to join them, but that last attack had taken a toll on me. Not only did I revert back to my former dragon-man body from before taking Asteron's earlier attack, but now I was falling to the ground. I didn't even have the strength to open my wings to try to stop my fall.

I would have been a stain on the ground if someone hadn't come in on time and catch me.

You have done well, Shirai, a familiar voice told me.

I found myself riding on the back of Ska.

"I see… you are awake… Ska… I'm glad…" I was so tired I couldn't stay awake. The last thing I saw before I passed out was Ska landing in the castle courtyard and all of my friends running toward us.

I awoke to find myself in an extravagant bed. From what I could see, I was probably in Grant's bedroom. Sitting in a chair next to me, her head lying on the covers, was Tansu.

"I'm having a strange case of déjà vu here." I recalled the incident back at Tsura.

Gently I woke Tansu up, and when she saw I was awake, she quickly locked her arms around me and cried softly, "Thank Ska you're okay! I thought I truly lost you this time!"

"I had to make sure that I returned to everyone—especially you, Tansu," I said as I held her close to me.

I felt like never letting go of her. In fact, I even maneuvered my wings to wrap themselves around her just so I would know she would stay close to me.

She stopped crying and looked at me. "I don't want you to leave me yet."

"You'll never get rid of me. My love for you will keep me coming back."

Tansu smiled and slowly brought her head closer to me. I leaned in too, and we kissed. However, it didn't last long, as someone burst the doors open.

"Just thought I'd come and… whoa!" Nova nearly tripped when he saw us. We both quickly glared at him, annoyed with the interruption.

"I hope I didn't come at a bad time."

We responded by throwing pillows at his face *very hard*. He fell on his back, completely stunned.

About this time, Sara came in, followed by Russ. "I see by the mess on the floor that Shirai is finally up?"

"Yes, guys," I said, "and not to be rude or anything, but the two of us would like some privacy."

"Of course," Russ replied. "You should know, though, that you need to make a public appearance before all of the people you helped save as soon as possible."

"I'll make a note of that."

"Oh, before I forget, that old man Giram asked me to give you this letter." He handed me a folded piece of paper.

"Have fun, you two!" Sara said, dragging Nova away by the legs. Russ left with them, leaving Tansu and me alone again to continue with what we were doing before.

Days later, the big moment came, and I stood with Tansu, Nova, Sara, and Russ on a large balcony off the castle overlooking all of Hariel. We wore formal clothing for this event, even Nova. Of course my clothes were made by Tansu. Thousands of people from all over had come to see their savior, including Eri and her people. Even Ska and his dragons were there.

"People of Lu' Cel!" Russ shouted loudly so everyone could hear him. "We have all lost someone important to us during these last six years, but it was nothing compared to what almost happened here. Because of the false god, Asteron, we almost joined those killed in the war. But we were saved, thanks to Hariel's next king."

Because Grant, my father, and my brother were no longer among us, I was next in line for the throne. Of course I'd never say out loud that I wasn't cut out to be royalty.

"Through troubling times and perils to himself and his companions, he has not only helped save our world, but also brought different people from different races together."

Russ was embarrassing me with all this praise. He finally wrapped things up. "So let's give thanks to Lu' Cel's savior; the next king of Hariel: Shirai!"

A loud chorus filled the air as the people cheered, and the dragons bellowed. We all began waving to everyone. As I looked down, I could have sworn I saw my father and brother in the crowd, but they quickly disappeared before I could really tell.

I then remembered that I hadn't read the letter I got from Russ. Unfolding it, I began to read.

To Shirai

I am sorry to hear about your father's passing. He was a good man. Back when I trained him, he often told me that, because of his unusual size and strength at the time, he felt like he was a freak. And every time I told him that what others think of you shouldn't matter, as long as you are okay with yourself. One day he asked that, if he ever had a family, and if his children turned out to be like him or thought the way he once did, that I should try and help them make it through like I did for him. The day after you stopped him in Gale, he came to our village, wanting to see me. When I told him how you came to be here, his resolve changed. Instead of following Grant's orders, he waited for the next time you two would meet. Since his other son, Aynor, was no longer himself, he wanted to make sure you could take care of yourself so he didn't have to worry about you. Please don't think ill of your brother. He too had a hard life. Lorimar also told me he wished he hadn't gotten your foster parents involved when he told them about the situation in that letter you brought them. And so I end with this final thought. If your family is now together in the afterlife, I'm sure they would be very proud of you right now. Never lose sight of that resolve of yours.

Giram, Retired General of Hariel

P.S. I hope you are treating Tansu well, or else I will make sure you regret it.

When I finished reading the letter, I didn't know whether to laugh at the fact that I had been acting just like my father back when he was my age, or cry knowing that maybe now they *were* watching me at this moment. I was also starting to see where Tansu learned to make her points known.

"Well, Shirai, looks like our trip is over," I heard Nova say to me.

"You're going already?"

He nodded. "Have to. I have things to do, places to see."

"Things to steal," I quickly came in.

Everyone except Nova laughed.

"I have to go too," Sara sighed. "Mother wants me to come back home for a while."

"Well, it was great having you on this journey."

She smiled. "Just don't try to act like me when you're busy ruling this place."

Again we all laughed.

I then turned to Tansu, who looked downhearted.

"I'm sorry I can't go back with you to Kenga like I wanted, but I've got to help rebuild this kingdom after what my uncle did."

"I know. I just wish you didn't have to."

I gave her a small kiss. "I'll come back one day. I promise."

"I'll be waiting for that day," she replied with a smile.

Shirai. I hope I'm not interrupting anything important. Ska's voice suddenly came in loud and clear, but it looked like only the five of us could hear him.

"What is it, Ska?"

I once again thank you for all you done for me and my people, not to mention all of Lu' Cel. However, what I really have to say involves you.

"Me?"

Back then when I transformed your body, it was because it was the only way to save you at the time. But since Asteron is gone and Lu' Cel is no longer in danger, I can change you back to your human form, if you want.

I hesitated before speaking. "Really?"

"What's wrong?" Russ asked, "I thought you would be happy to be a normal person again."

I again replied hesitantly. "I should, but I've gotten so used to being like this."

As I said when we first talked, it is your choice and yours alone. If you wish to stay the way you are, you may. I only wish to see you happy.

I looked at everyone to see what they were thinking. Each one had the same expression: like they were saying that it's not their place to tell me what to choose. I thought long and hard about what to do. I'd had so many good times while I was a dragon man. But I also had an equal amount of good times when I was human. It was a tough decision, but in the end I made up my mind.

I chose…

24 - Epilogue

After a proper coronation, Shirai officially became the king of Hariel, with his cousin, Russ, as his adviser. Over the next month, however, everyone noticed he was becoming restless. It didn't come as a surprise when he suddenly left one day, claiming he wanted to find his own path. He then made Russ the next king.

Sara became the ambassador for the region, and with the help of the dragons, reestablished links with other settlements and kingdoms not heard from for centuries. She passed down the story of her friend's journey and victory over the false god. Tybal accompanied her for protection.

After returning the Tao Spear to its tomb, Nova, now the new leader of Ranu, along with his girlfriend Sara and the dragons, helped revitalize his home and the Kunti Kingdom.

Zen returned to Flora with his parents to help rebuild it. He was made overseer of the flower that saved Tansu's life, which he named Shiraium.

Luwina returned to running the Institution of Magic.

Chent continued on his smith work, with his new wife and the child they were expecting soon.

Ska left Lu' Cel to return to the dragons' original home, hoping to finally end the war. He promised to return to his second home one day.

Tansu and Giram returned to Kenga Village and settled back into their old life, where she waited for Shirai to return.

*****

Two years later, Nova, Sara, Chent, Zen, and Russ arrived at Kenga Village for their annual visit with Shirai and Tansu. The village, now bigger, still kept its old charm.

"I can't believe how big this place keeps getting each time we come here," Sara commented, brushing her now waist-length hair off her shoulders.

"What do you expect? It is home of Lu' Cel's greatest swordsmanship school," Nova replied. *Over the years, he lost the braids in his now shoulder-length hair. Even with his new choice in clothing, he never lost his bandana. "Everyone who wants to learn how to handle a sword comes here."*

"And thanks to that school, my business has increased. I can hardly keep up with the orders," Chent laughed. *His beard and hair were now kept trimmed and clean.*

"I'd thought that wife of yours would make you get a real job after your kid was born," Nova said with a sly grin.

"Which is more than I can say about you, my lad!"

Nova confronted Chent. "Excuse me? I've been busy rebuilding Ranu and Kunti! They need me!"

"What do you know about construction? You were hardly any help when I made that armor of yours two years ago."

"Must you two go into this routine every time?" Russ rubbed his temples. "It's bad enough I have to keep an entire kingdom well-treated, but I don't want to have to deal with this."

"Well, they wouldn't be Nova and Chent if they didn't," Sara pointed out.

"Hey, now that I am older, you think Shirai will take me in as a pupil?" Zen asked. Thanks to a combination of elfin healing and a single Shiraium, he no longer needed glasses.

"Why don't you ask him?" Russ pointed ahead.

Shirai had just exited the recently constructed School of Swordsmanship after finishing another session with his students, wearing the clothes he always wore when he taught. It consisted of a gray, long-sleeved shirt he left unbuttoned and black pants with a huge hole in the left pant leg. Mounted above the door he walked out of was the Sword of the Wyvern.

"Hey, Shirai!" Zen ran over toward him.

Looking up, Shirai smiled and shook Zen's hand. "Hello Zen. I see you've gotten bigger since you were here last."

Nova laughed, "Look who's talking about getting bigger. You look like a small version of your father."

During the last two years, Shirai had indeed grown bigger, with more muscles and an added inch to his height.

"Well, when one continuously works on teaching others how to use a sword, not to mention practicing his own sword skills and helping his wife with her planting, you'd begin to develop some muscles."

"Well, it looks great on you," Sara commented, "but you might want to shorten that ponytail of yours. You're going to trip over it one day."

Shirai's hair was now so long, it almost touched the ground.

"I've told him numerous times to do that, but he's as hardheaded as ever," a voice from behind Shirai spoke.

Tansu exited the school, carrying something delicate in her arms. She wore the same green dress Shirai saw her in the first time they met.

"So nice of you to finally join us." Shirai kissed his wife. "Did he finally calm down?"

"Just now. I never saw so much energy in a child before."

"By Ska, you still look as lovely as ever," Chent commented.

"Well, considering she just recently gave birth to our son, you caught her on a good day," Shirai joked.

"Be careful, darling, or I'll make sure you plow the fields with your hands."

"So this is my new cousin?" Russ asked. "May we see him?"

Tansu moved a small part of the cover she held and revealed a baby happily sleeping in his mother's arms.

"He's beautiful," Sara said happily.

"Looks just like his dad," Nova added.

Shirai took the baby in his arms. "Well he does have his mother's eyes."

"Nova's right, dear." Tansu said. "I know one day he'll grow up to be just like his father, a fine dragon man."

222

A new start